Choose your Lane to love!

Readers love the Winter Ball series by AMY LANE

Winter Ball

"Everything about this story is perfect—from the rec league to Skip's job, from the bumpy road to the amazing cast of characters. I love it."

—Joyfully Jay

"This is a sweet, touching story with plenty of humor, sex that spans from tender to dirty, and a range of emotion that should satisfy anyone looking for a good character driven romance, especially friends-to-lovers fans."

—Sinfully Gay Romance Book Reviews

Summer Lessons

"This series is a delight! If only we were all lucky enough to find such a wonderful group of friends."

—The Novel Approach

"This read was a sweet and snarky romance with a whole lot of funny, dirty and sassy moments thrown in for good measure."

—Gay Book Reviews

More praise for AMY LANE

Freckles

"…with true Amy Lane style, it is packed with amazing characters and the best of happily ever afters."

—Paranormal Romance Guild

"This is just one of those feel good books that Amy Lane has mastered… it's an enjoyable ride that Lane take us on through the joys of owning a pet."

—Love Bytes

"I have major kudos for Ms. Lane in creating relatable, realistic and fun characters and breathing some real life into this story. I absolutely enjoyed it and would strongly recommend it."

—Long and Short Reviews

Warm Heart

"It was meant to be a love story, plain and simple, and the catalyst for future installments in the series and, as such, it hit both notes quite well."

—Joyfully Jay

"I have been a great fan of Lane's writing, I love the writing style and I love the down to earth characters who are quite extraordinary in many ways. *Warm Heart* is no exception for me."

—MM Good Book Reviews

By Amy Lane

An Amy Lane Christmas
Behind the Curtain
Bewitched by Bella's Brother
Bolt-hole
Christmas Kitsch
Christmas with Danny Fit
Clear Water
Do-over
Food for Thought
Freckles
Gambling Men
Going Up
Hammer & Air
Homebird
If I Must
Immortal
It's Not Shakespeare
Left on St. Truth-be-Well
The Locker Room
Mourning Heaven
Phonebook
Puppy, Car, and Snow
Racing for the Sun • Hiding the Moon
Raising the Stakes
Regret Me Not
Shiny!
Shirt
Sidecar
String Boys
A Solid Core of Alpha
Three Fates
Truth in the Dark
Turkey in the Snow
Under the Rushes
Wishing on a Blue Star

BENEATH THE STAIN
Beneath the Stain • Paint It Black

BONFIRES
Bonfires • Crocus

CANDY MAN
Candy Man • Bitter Taffy
Lollipop • Tart and Sweet

DREAMSPUN DESIRES
THE MANNIES
#25 – The Virgin Manny
#37 – Manny Get Your Guy
#57 – Stand by Your Manny
#62 – A Fool and His Manny
SEARCH AND RESCUE
#86 – Warm Heart

FAMILIAR LOVE
Familiar Angel • Familiar Demon

FISH OUT OF WATER
Fish Out of Water
Red Fish, Dead Fish
A Few Good Fish • Hiding the Moon
Fish on a Bicycle

KEEPING PROMISE ROCK
Keeping Promise Rock • Making Promises
Living Promises • Forever Promised

Published by Dreamspinner Press
www.dreamspinnerpress.com

By Amy Lane (cont.)

JOHNNIES
Chase in Shadow • Dex in Blue
Ethan in Gold • Black John
Bobby Green
Super Sock Man

GRANBY KNITTING
The Winter Courtship Rituals of Fur-Bearing Critters
How to Raise an Honest Rabbit
Knitter in His Natural Habitat
Blackbird Knitting in a Bunny's Lair
The Granby Knitting Menagerie Anthology

TALKER
Talker • Talker's Redemption
Talker's Graduation
The Talker Collection Anthology

WINTER BALL
Winter Ball • Summer Lessons
Fall Through Spring

Published by Harmony Ink Press
BITTER MOON SAGA
Triane's Son Rising
Triane's Son Learning
Triane's Son Fighting
Triane's Son Reigning

Published by Dreamspinner Press
www.dreamspinnerpress.com

Fall Through Spring

AMY LANE

DREAMSPINNER PRESS

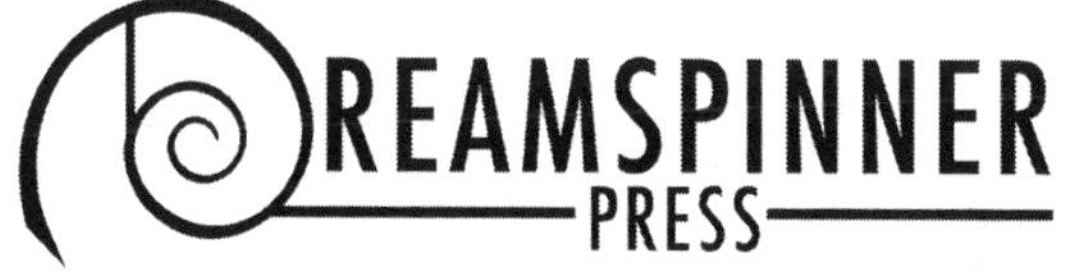

Published by
DREAMSPINNER PRESS

5032 Capital Circle SW, Suite 2, PMB# 279, Tallahassee, FL 32305-7886 USA
www.dreamspinnerpress.com

Trade Paperback ISBN: 978-1-64405-761-2
Digital ISBN: 978-1-64405-760-5
Library of Congress Control Number: 2019946967
Trade Paperback published December 2019
v. 1.0

Printed in the United States of America

This paper meets the requirements of
ANSI/NISO Z39.48-1992 (Permanence of Paper).

So I'm Carpenter and my daughter is Dane, and somehow we make it work and we crack each other up and worry about each other and daily prove that love is the answer. Love you, honey.

Author’s Note

I HADN’T planned on writing Dane and Carpenter at all, but I finished Mason and Terry’s book and somebody DM’d me on FB saying, “Whoever is Dane in your life, I wish you the very best. You obviously understand what that’s like.” And then I realized Dane needed his own book. And other people pinged me on Twitter and FB and said, “Carpenter gives us hope.” And I realized he needed his own book too. And as hard as books like this are to write, I think it’s worth it because we all need our own book, and we all need to know happy is for everybody.

I hope, whoever you are, you find your happy.

Carpenter and Food

At Seven

CLAY ALEXANDER Carpenter was the first to admit it—his first love was a chocolate chip cookie. It was an illicit affair, because he wasn't supposed to eat cookies like that. His mother didn't believe in refined sugar, red meat, gluten, dairy, or saturated fats.

This cookie was four out of five of the things his mother disdained most about the world.

And it wasn't that Carpenter hated his mother. In fact, she was a lovely woman, kind, giving out hugs during appropriate times, very worried about making sure her children grew up to be happy, productive citizens with a closet full of childhood memories that would give them strength as they got older.

It was just that, well, she was a very busy woman—never too busy for her children, mind you—but she had meetings, and she had to give the maid directions to clean the house, and she had a job too, as a lobbyist, and she had to make sure her children were happy and fulfilled and doing extremely well at school.

Carpenter's father was the same way. Kind, civic-minded, spent an allotment of happy, fulfilling time with his children, never yelled.

That was another thing.

There was no yelling in the Carpenter household. Yelling would be the sixth thing his mother hated in her home, but that would have involved hating and bringing the toll up to seven things. And honestly, Carpenter's mother was really a nice person, and she didn't have room in her heart for that much hate.

By the time Carpenter was in second grade, he was beginning to suspect he might.

For one thing, he hated the kids in his school.

He'd shown up on the first day of second grade wearing jeans that fit perfectly and a T-shirt that had a picture of Chewbacca on it. His mother had allowed him to pick his own clothes, and she'd been surprised. "Chewbacca, honey? Do you even know what that is?"

"It's a who, Mother," Clay had answered reasonably. "He's a Wookiee. His species doesn't make a difference in his personhood."

His mother smiled happily. "What a wonderful argument, Clay. Well, with reasoning like that, I'm pleased to buy it for you. But where did you see this movie?"

"I don't remember," Clay lied. Of course he remembered. He'd awakened one night over summer vacation, when they were allowed to sleep until eight in the morning instead of six thirty. He'd been hungry, so he'd made himself an organic peanut butter with sugarless preserves on nut-grain unleavened bread sandwich, and turned the television on in the family room, very quietly. It was after eleven, so he must have found East Coast feed on cable—but he'd never forget that movie.

It had been *perfect.* A revelation. A vision of stars and wars and laser weapons and giant hairy beasts who wore artillery packs on their chests.

When he'd seen the T-shirt in the store, he'd almost cried.

So he was proud of that shirt as he walked into school. And then the kids had hit him with, "But isn't that passé?" "Oh my God, the second series is so dumb. My parents said Jar Jar Binks was a racist stereotype." And, worst of all, "*You're* going to grow up to be a big fat hairy Wookiee just like Chewbacca!"

Carpenter didn't realize that this was the price he had to pay for going to a "good" school, where all the kids had television sets in their own rooms and the parents were rich and trying to send their kids to first-tier colleges, which was why they'd all had flashcards in SAT vocabulary by the second grade. He knew he was smart because he had test scores that proved it—smarter than most of his peers, but he wouldn't know that until middle school when he started to suspect he was the only one who got tutored in algebra by his older sister, Sabrina, and not a college student desperate to make ends meet.

All he knew at that moment was that he would throw himself in traffic for Chewbacca, and while he was not allowed to say "hate" in his home, he *hated* his peer group with the solar viciousness of the suns of Tatooine.

He'd felt that way until Calliope Prescott sat at his table and looked furtively around.

"They're dumb," she said softly. "They're stupid dummy heads and I hate them!"

Carpenter gazed at her with enchantment in his eyes. Calliope Prescott was different from the other kids at school. For one thing, she was not as pale. Without knowing anything about race, Carpenter totally appreciated that Calliope Prescott had slightly darker skin than his other classmates. She also had luxuriously thick and curly hair, often tamed into long asymmetrical braids with bright rubber bands on the end.

Calliope Prescott was *extraordinary*, and she'd said the magic forbidden word.

For a brief moment, Clay thought she was the best thing to ever happen to him.

"I hate them too," he whispered, staring at her with stars in his eyes.

"*Star Wars* is a great movie," she told him staunchly.

"It's the best," he said.

She pursed her lips. "*Empire Strikes Back* is better, I think. And I love the little teddy bear things in *Return of the Jedi.*"

Clay's mouth fell open slightly. "There's more movies than just the one?"

She'd laughed, her mouth open, unafraid to make noise. "Yeah, silly! You should come over to my house and watch them!"

Clay nodded. "Oh yes," he whispered. "I would love that. Do you think your mother would let me?"

She regarded him soberly. "Do you think *your* mother would let you? We're the only black family in the entire school."

"You're not black," Clay said, confused. "You're brown. But my parents have lots of brown friends. They won't care." His parents were lobbyists for a civil liberties organization. Later, he would realize that meant they had money *and* a social justice conscience, but right now he knew she looked a lot like his mother's best friend and her wife. But Calliope wasn't ordinary, like his mother's friends. She was *extraordinary*, because she was *Clay's* friend.

Calliope smiled widely. "Good, then! If you can give me your number, I'll have my mom call your mom. It'll be fun. My brother has friends over all the time—this time it's my turn."

Her brother, Jordyn, was a nice kid—as beautiful as Calliope and just as invested in *Star Wars*. The three of them spent hours watching the trilogy while their mom baked cookies.

Clay was entranced by the smell. To him, the pew-pewing of lasers would forever be linked to permission to relax on a couch with his bare feet up while two friends sprawled over his legs as that scent—perfect and wholesome and sweet and amazing—rolled through a slightly messy house.

After *Empire Strikes Back* spun through the VCR, Mrs. Prescott came into the living room—the *living room*!—with a plate of cookies and three glasses of milk.

Clay stared at that plate of cookies with lust in his eyes.

"Do you have any allergies, Clay?" Mrs. Prescott asked, as if she had just remembered. "Nut allergies, gluten, dairy?"

"No," Clay whispered, because his mother had gotten him and his sister tested, just in case they accidentally ingested a strawberry soaked in cream and deep fried in chocolate frosting. "Are those *cookies*?" They did not look like the applesauce carob cookies he got on special occasions.

"Yes—here. I'll rewind the *Jedi* tape, and you kids can come have cookies. No more than three, okay? Clay has permission to stay for dinner, and I don't want you three wrecking your appetites."

"Three?" Clay loved this house. He loved Calliope, he loved Jordyn, he loved their mother, and he loved the entire Star Wars franchise.

"Is that not enough?"

"It's *perfect*," he breathed.

And oh my God, they really were perfect. He finished the first one and realized that Jordyn and Calliope were staring at him.

"Wha?" he asked, wiping his mouth off with the back of his hand. It came back covered in chocolate and cookie crumbs.

"You were singing!" Calliope laughed that openmouthed laugh. "To your *cookie*!"

For a moment, Clay thought about getting hurt, but Jordyn's eyes were big and excited too. They were looking at Clay like he was *extraordinary.* He smiled at them through his mouthful of chocolate chip cookie and sighed contentedly.

"They're the most wonderful thing on earth," he said, and they laughed like he was the funniest person on the planet.

Maybe he was.

His mother picked him up at seven o'clock, right after dinner, after exchanging pleasantries with Mrs. Prescott. Cheryl Carpenter was nothing if not polite, but in far too short a time, Clay was sitting in the back seat of the family SUV, humming to himself about cookies.

"So, sweetheart, did you have a good time?"

"Yes, Mom."

"What did you have for dinner?"

Clay closed his eyes and tried to remember what Mrs. Prescott had told him. "Broccoli lasagna and salad," he said dutifully. Except Mrs. Prescott had asked him if he was allergic to meat, and he'd said no, and the lasagna had been heavenly, even though hamburger was only an eight on a scale of ten because cookies were an eleven.

"Well, I hope the gluten in the noodles doesn't stop you up or make you gassy," she said worriedly.

Of course he was gassy. He was so gassy that Snoodles, the family dog, ran out of his room whining in the wee dark hours, and Clay's mom and dad spent part of the morning wandering the house, looking for where Snoodles had done his business, because they sure did smell something bad!

But no, Snoodles was the well-behaved rat terrier he'd always been.

Clay was just learning the price of bliss.

At Fifteen

MRS. PRESCOTT took Clay in a *lot* over the next eight years. When he was eleven, he learned how to ride his bike—not because he loved physical exercise, but so he could ride his bike over to the Prescott house and play games with Jordyn and Calliope and watch movies and, yes, have cookies.

One day when he was fifteen, he got there and Mrs. Prescott and Calliope were shopping for a dress. Some douchebag—Clay and Jordyn both believed he was a douchebag—had invited Callie to the school dance.

They sat, alone, a plate of chocolate chip cookies between them, playing video games, until Clay's character died and Jordyn didn't reboot.

"What?" Clay asked, looking at his friend. Jordyn scooted a little closer. He was handsome, with skin a rich gentle bronze and eyes a surprising green. He was about a year and a half older than Calliope. He graduated that year, and had been active all his life. Meat in his lasagna notwithstanding, Jordyn Prescott played football and soccer and worked out almost as much as he played video games. He'd been admitted into several colleges on academics alone, and he'd told nobody—not even his sister—why he hadn't tried to get any sports scholarships.

And he had this kind of charisma, this internal centering, that made everybody love him.

And he was looking at Clay with a sort of yearning in his eyes. A yearning Clay recognized. He *wasn't* athletic. Since his first afternoon in the Prescott living room, he'd tried every sport known to man. Soccer, softball, track. None of it seemed to take. He just didn't see the point—and his opinion of his peers had in no way made him want to run faster or kick the ball better or shoot with any accuracy, just to make them happy.

So his body was a little bit soggy, although his calves were in excellent shape from all the times he rode his bike to see Jordyn and Calliope.

"You're not going to the dance," Jordyn said, from his sudden close distance.

Clay's cheeks heated. "We usually go as friends, but Keith Mancuso asked her for real, so no friends."

"Have you ever kissed a girl?" Jordyn asked, and to this, Clay could give a better answer.

"Yeah, couple times." He smiled winsomely. "Girls like me—I have no idea why."

"Because you're nice to everybody," Jordyn half laughed. "Will you be nice to me?"

Clay was about to ask what he meant by that when Jordyn kissed him.

Clay's eyes widened in surprise. He knew what a kiss was—he knew why you did it. He hadn't had a chance to say it, but he'd gotten to second base a couple of times, and one girl had gone down on him.

And he knew what gay was, and he'd been pretty sure that he wasn't it.

But he liked Jordyn and didn't want to hurt his feelings, so he relaxed and let Jordyn's mouth move over his, and let Jordyn's hands move on his shoulders.

And his body started to do the same things it did when girls kissed him. Pleasant things. Beautiful things. He pulled in a surprised breath and started to kiss Jordyn back.

The car in the driveway pulled them apart, but Jordyn's cheeks showed a flush, and his lips were swollen, and he looked as vulnerable as Clay felt.

"What was that?" Clay whispered as Jordyn straightened his hair and pulled back.

"I'm gay," Jordyn said, sounding panicked.

But Clay liked girls too. "But I'm… not?" But he didn't know for sure. All he knew was that Jordyn's expression turned stricken and sad, and before Clay could explain, Calliope and her mother came in, drunk on talk about A-line skirts and pencil skirts and full skirts.

Clay just watched as Jordyn picked up his remote control and resumed play with a steely-eyed concentration that excluded everything.

Including Clay.

The plate of chocolate chip cookies sat between them, and Clay started to eat them, steadily and without stopping.

He finished off the entire plate of cookies, and Jordyn didn't say a thing.

At Twenty

"OH, HONEY," his mother said worriedly. "You've put on so much weight this semester. Don't they have fresh food options at USC?"

"Of course they do!" Clay practically yelled. Yes, he knew he was becoming a watermelon, but he was actually trying to tell her something. She and his father had come to visit during spring vacation because he'd seemed—in their words—a little erratic.

He was, in fact, miserable.

He'd started out okay. He had a place to lock his bicycle, so he'd managed to keep in decent shape, and he'd done his best in all his classes. Then he'd met a girl—of course, wasn't it always a girl?—and she'd reminded him of Calliope, who hadn't gone away to school but had settled down and attended junior college so she could keep dating Keith and they could plan a life together.

Jordyn had come out in college, and his parents had been supportive and loving—but he never called Clay again. And Clay was forced to be content with playing video games and watching sci-fi with Calliope and Keith, which wasn't bad, but Clay missed Jordyn enough to recognize a crush when it squeezed his heart a little.

He wasn't sure what to do with that information. He still liked girls. But those moments with Jordyn, that surprising kiss, haunted him.

He wanted to kiss another guy, just to see.

But that curiosity hadn't been enough to keep him from going off to school and falling in love with Rebecca Jorgenson, who was serious and earnest and who wrote wickedly funny fan fiction centered in the Star Trek universe. Some of it was Spirk, and Clay enjoyed the hell out of reading that, even if he didn't tell Rebecca.

But kissing another guy was the least of his problems in college.

Rebecca had broken up with him—and she'd taken his entire peer group with her.

Suddenly, there was nobody to play video games with, nobody to talk sci-fi with. He felt bereft, and his grades had slipped. Not horrendously—no. He could have taken some of those tests in his sleep. But if he wanted his MS in biochemistry, he needed a certain GPA, and he didn't think that was going to happen.

He'd tried talking to his parents over Skype, but every time he said *grades*, he got, "Oh, honey, you can just try a little harder. I'm sure it will come out okay. Did we tell you that your sister is doing her residency at John Hopkins, in the oncology ward? And she's met a nice young man—or rather, reunited with him. I understand that she used to go to school with him! Anyway, she sends her love. Now what are you going to do to fix those grades?"

"That's nice for Sabrina, Mom, but I'm not sure I even *like* biochemistry. I mean, I wanted to do something for the environment, but most of the people making really big strides in the field aren't just brilliant—they also have no lives!"

This was, in fact, why Rebecca had broken up with him. Not because she didn't care about him, but because she had landed an internship studying the long-term effects of the bacteria that they were hoping would eat the plastic islands made of trash floating out over the ocean. She was a year ahead of him and going to be spending her entire senior year and the year after that out on the Atlantic Ocean, taking samples and coming up with hypotheses, and she hadn't wanted to string Clay along.

But Clay had become attached, and he'd been upset, and his dormmate had gotten weird because he'd actually *cried* after he'd come back from the breakup dinner. And the entire biochemistry department had sort of labeled him an emo wreck and gotten out the emotional barge poles to give him his space.

So the chocolate chip cookie had become his best friend again, and so had pizza because it was delivered, and he'd officially drunk enough soda in the past three months to make up for all of the years before high school when he hadn't even tried it as an act of rebellion.

Oh yeah.

Some kids went to college to smoke weed, do blow, fuck all the things, and politically shit on their parents' heroes.

Apparently, Clay Carpenter went to school to eat.

Because as sources of comfort went, the chocolate chip cookie had never let him down, and pizza was always ready to give him the "attaboy" if he needed it.

But now his parents could see him up close and personal, and it turned out the sources of fresh food in the campus commissary were the last things Clay wanted to talk about.

"Mom, can we not talk about my weight for a damned minute here?" he begged.

"Well, what *do* you want to talk about, honey?" She said it like there couldn't possibly be anything else wrong.

"Mom, it's my major. I don't think biochemistry is my thing." *Because it's breaking my heart, and I can do the work, but it just doesn't interest me that much, and because I want to work with people more than I want to work with amoebas.*

His mother and father looked stunned. Poleaxed. Because, well, they'd all discussed biochemistry over the dinner table, and they'd been so on board with Clay's decision that they'd carefully engineered since he was fourteen years old.

"Well, Clay," his mother said carefully, "what *do* you want to do?"

"Something people-oriented," Clay said.

"But with science." His mother's eyes never dimmed, and she sounded so proud of herself, as though yes, her son the scientist in whatever capacity was exactly what she wanted.

"Sure," Clay said, shoulders slumping defeatedly. "Science. Maybe the business end, though. So we can use it ethically." There. That sounded socially conscious, right?

"Good, honey. You can stay in science for your bachelor's and move on to an MBA—how's that?"

Clay shrugged and wanted for a moment to just spill the whole thing out on them, the self-doubting, Rebecca, the realization that he seemed somehow defective because he was more attached to people than to his education. Even the bisexuality, because that would be great to have someone to talk with about how his dormmate wasn't a bad guy, sort of dorky-looking with crooked teeth and too much hipster scruff, but after Rebecca had broken up with him, he'd had fantasies about Fergus sort of embracing him and holding him tight. And when he went to sleep with these fantasies, he woke up with wood.

And God, he really wanted to talk with someone about that kiss with Jordyn that he kept tied up next to his heart, because it was starting to dawn on him that if nothing else, bisexuality doubled the dating pool. And at this point, he'd take someone, anyone, who he could bare his soul to and who would still love him in return.

HE ESPECIALLY felt that way after he entered the MBA program.

Because he hated the program. He hated the business world. He hated the homework, and he hated himself because his parents were paying for this and he couldn't think of a way to tell them it was just not his jam.

Right before graduation, he went to a job fair. He was wearing a new wool suit and shiny wing-tip shoes and had shaved and had his hair cut and even buffed his nails.

He had three interviews lined up that day, and he was starving.

His parents had sent him the suit four months earlier, when he'd signed up for the job fair, as "something to shoot for."

Now, Clay had a steady allowance from home—not spectacular, but steady—and had applied for student loans, so he had grant money. He could have bought one that fit, but this one was about two sizes too small, and the hint was obvious.

They loved him, but they would love him so much more comfortably if he was comfortable in that suit.

So he'd dieted.

He'd started eating apples in the morning instead of donuts. He'd stopped eating pizzas and started eating chicken sandwiches. All of the things he'd learned as a child at his mother's dinner table had come back to him, and he'd taken them on in an effort to be the son his wonderful parents had earned with all of their kindness and their attention and their sacrifices to give him an education.

The suit fit great—it really did. The shoes were shiny and pretty, and he looked like a clean-cut all-American boy.

And the nice men in suits all smiled at him and told him his grades were wonderful and his background in science was necessary and important, and then asked him—at each interview—how he would feel if he had to fire mass quantities of employees in the lower tiers of the company in order to continue the company's "main function as a producer in its field."

He figured out later that he'd applied at midsized companies that all had to move so they could afford the overhead, because California's land prices really were outer limits. But in that moment, as the horror of that third request dawned on him….

He snapped.

He didn't know he snapped.

Clay Alexander Carpenter was nothing if not responsible.

He finished his schooling, moved back up to the Sacramento area, using his savings just as his parents taught him, bought a car, rented an apartment in a "startup" suburb, and got a job.

More specifically he got a job at a pizza joint. Where he proceeded to work, pay his rent, dodge his student loan officers, play as much PS4 as he could handle, and put on nearly a hundred pounds.

At Twenty-Four

"CLAY?" HIS mother's voice quavered uncertainly over the phone. Well, his temper had been uncertain since he'd moved back to the area—he could admit it.

"Yeah, Mom," he said, trying to keep his irritation from spiking. He pushed her away. He knew it wasn't fair. His parents truly had been as supportive as possible. Cheryl and Clyde Carpenter loved their baby boy—he knew that.

"Honey, your father got a notice about your student loans. We, uh, know your income isn't what we'd hoped…. Do you need us to pay them off for you?"

Clay wanted to cry. Oh God. It was bad enough that he was a snarly asshole during his whole identity crisis, but did they think he was going to make his parents pay off his student loan debt?

"No, Mom," he said, looking around his dismal apartment.

He had to admit—even for him, the place was looking a bit… well, décor done by takeout was how he'd described it to his last girlfriend.

She'd helped him clean it up, had made them chicken salads. He'd even lost a little weight with her, mostly because he hadn't had to worry about what to feed himself.

But her old boyfriend had popped back into the picture, and even though she hadn't said anything—she probably would have stayed with Clay just because she was that kind of stand-up kid—Clay had let her go.

It had been very emotional and very sappy-movie worthy—very, "But would I really be happy knowing you settled for me instead of reaching for me?" so she didn't have to feel guilty.

But the reality was that she was gone, and he was still there with swollen feet, swollen fingers, and a back that kept bitching at him every time he got off the couch.

And no amount of extra shifts at Meteor Pizza, with the big pepperoni comet in the logo, was going to pay off his college bill.

With a groan he got up and showered, determinedly not looking at himself naked in the mirror, making sure he got all his creases and his other creases and the creases in those creases. He washed his longish brown hair, shaved his longish brown beard, and looked at his tired brown eyes in the mirror.

This was *not* the life he'd looked at in the brochure.

The very least he could do was pay for his own goddamned student loans.

He grabbed his laptop off the coffee table and moved it to the Formica kitchen table and loaded his resume into about six search engines.

And all of them spat out the same jobs he'd turned down the year before.

He scowled. No. God no. But what else was he going to do? What else was he qualified for?

And then he saw it. On one of his search engines, there was a list of related fields, with the number of job openings in parentheses next to it. And there, next to computer science, was the number 3000.

Clay blinked.

Yeah, sure. His degree *wasn't* in computer science, but he'd spent all his spare change putting together his own gaming system ever since he went away to college.

He had a degree in molecular biochemistry, an MBA, and an overwhelming hobby.

He rewrote his resume with an appalling disregard for the facts and started looking up the dress codes for various IT jobs in the local businesses.

When he saw that he could wear jeans and a regulation polo to Tesko Tech, that was the first one on his list.

Skipper

"TESKO TECH, how can I help you?"

Clay winced at the earnestness of the guy sitting in the cubicle across from him. Tall, with fair skin, blue eyes, a fit body, and the smile of a golden retriever, his nameplate said Christopher Keith, but everybody in the office called him Skipper.

Clay had been tempted to hate him on sight. Something about him reminded Clay of every kid who had made fun of his Wookiee shirt in the second grade, and every kid since who had rolled their eyes at him or called him a fat asshole in the pizza parlor or decided his broken heart was too squishy to touch when he'd been in college.

But then he'd seen the inside of Skip's cubicle.

The soccer trophies he could have done without—who keeps soccer trophies out of high school, right?

But there were gaming trophies in there, and lots of squishy, fiddly tchotchkes that Skip liked to play with when he was talking to someone and it was taking a lot of time, and a few team photos of a lot of guys who looked like they'd been rolling around in the mud and were proud of it.

Then Clay got a look at those "Lot of guys" and had a little pop of realization.

There were a lot of different faces in that team of guys looking at Skipper in adoration. This was not the same student population of Clay's grammar school or his high school. There were lots of brown faces in that picture. And Skip loved those guys enough to put them up where he'd see them every day.

The other thing was that Skipper didn't have his BA hanging up in there. Carpenter hid his—people assumed he had a four-year degree, and they thought it was in comp sci. Skip had a trade school certificate, and he came in wearing his green polo shirt and nicely pressed khakis *every day*, like just having this job was an honor.

Skipper didn't slack to get this job. He wasn't "slumming" because he had some sort of political distaste for the corporate world.

Being an IT guy in the basement of this company was Christopher Keith's best thing. And he smiled and came in and did his best job at it, while Carpenter tried not to sneer at people who had never grasped the concept of reboot.

Skipper Keith—who talked genially to Clay every day and called him Carpenter like they were buddies and made special plans for them to go to lunch because he wanted a friend to eat healthy with—was really a rather wonderful creature. Clay gently refused his first couple of sallies to get Clay to play soccer, but he did take him up on gaming nights.

Skipper's house—a tiny fixer-upper in the middle of Citrus Heights—had cracked tile that looked like someone had used baby shit as a palette, and a backyard originally crafted by ogres playing with sticks in the mud. His couch had probably been bought used, his carpet definitely needed to be replaced, and when he had his soccer friends over, including a brightly redheaded hyperactive little goof-in-a-box named Richie, to game together, people had to sit on his bed to play on the TV in the bedroom in order to fit more than ten people in the house total.

And Carpenter—who adopted that name like a badge of honor—couldn't be happier, wedged into that claustrophobic little space. People sat on each other's laps, they shoved a little, they slapped each other's backsides, and they swore like college students at their controllers, at the television screen, at each other.

He wasn't the most emo guy in the science department. He wasn't the political guy getting his MBA. He wasn't the hanger-on-er in someone else's happy family.

He was surrounded by people who did not give three fucks about his weight, his family, his degree, or how badly he'd let down his parents.

Carpenter would have *died* for Skipper Keith.

But oddly enough, he didn't feel the urge to kiss him. Going to work with him, accepting happy little tchotchkes from him for his birthday, gaming with him—these things were the highlight of his life, but Skipper felt like… well, like Calliope, really. Like a wonderful person who was there with unconditional love and acceptance. Clay had never kissed Calliope, and he'd never wanted to. She was too much of a shining star in his sky to want to touch her close enough to make her human. Skipper was the same way for Clay—no helpless yearnings, no dreaming about kissing. Just didn't happen.

In fact, over the span of the next two years, he really didn't have the urge to kiss anybody.

Until he realized that Skipper Keith and the little jackrabbit redheaded kid named Richie on the soccer team had fallen completely and irrevocably in love.

And Clay started to think about how maybe love wasn't what he'd thought it was in the beginning. Maybe love wasn't stolen cookies and forbidden kisses. Maybe love was love when your best friend changed everything that was wrong in his life so he could be the person you needed most.

So that's what Clay was thinking—that's *exactly* what Clay was thinking—when he met Dane Christian Hayes.

Dane and His Brother Go on an Adventure

DANE HAYES'S mother was 95 percent wonderful, 4 percent evil, and 1 percent completely inscrutable. As he walked into his parents' teeny house in Redwood City and checked the mail she'd left for him on the kitchen table, he reflected that today might be a 1 percent day.

"You got something," she said, easing down to the table with a juice. Dane thought it looked suspiciously like Kool-Aid and vodka, which sounded awful, but he suspected it's what got her through his older brother's turbulent, awkward days as an adolescent with no filter between his mouth and his sex-obsessed brain. If Dane hadn't been thoroughly gay himself, he suspected that Mason's obsession with his own penis might have had Dane at least questioning himself. Luckily Mason did all that for the both of them.

Dane hesitated when he saw the letter from UC Davis on the table. *Oh. This.* It was a long-shot—he knew it. His grades were great. Applying to the animal husbandry department at Davis shouldn't have been completely out of the realm of possibility. But his attendance had been… erratic. For his first six years in school, before his bipolar had been diagnosed, he'd been a disaster as a student. He'd managed to finish 90 percent of his classes, but the number of drops, of class changes, of changes in his major—the sheer level of heinous fuckery in his record….

Oy.

Then there was the two-year gap when he'd been wobbling on and off his meds, followed by three years when he'd actually earned a BS. He hadn't cared in what.

In this case, it had been biochemistry, probably because he'd been interested in what was wrong with his own brain and had wanted to see what was doing in there. But he'd always loved animals, even though he'd lived at home and his father was allergic so he'd had to get all his animal contact as a volunteer at shelters. He'd applied to the animal husbandry program in much the same way he'd done most of his life, in fact. A sort of "Hey, what the hell? My grades don't suck now; why not apply for the veterinary school, right?"

It was stupid. It was *insane.*

Veterinary medicine—particularly at the graduate level when the residencies started—was famous for being relentless and unforgiving. It broke up relationships and drove people to the brink of insanity, and Dane had already looked over that precipice and had to remind himself daily that the abyss was wide and deep indeed. He might never live alone. Having someone to remind him to do basic adulting things like taking his meds had turned out to be an absolute imperative. What made him think he could apply to a program that would take him away from his parents, his brother, his entire support system?

And his parents were all out of money from the "Dane's being flaky" years. He'd been waiting tables in a restaurant for the last three years to afford his education, and while he'd been living at home and had tuition saved up, room and board wasn't something he could afford.

Yet another reason he still lived at home, like the big crazy whiny albatross he was.

But… but it was a dream. It was the ability to say he'd done something with his life, even though mental illness had sort of swept his knees out from under him in his twenties. He was hitting the big three-oh in June, and boy, wasn't that embarrassing. Thirty years old and he had nothing to show for it but a pharmacy in his medicine cabinet and parents who still loved him.

Parents who might not be around to take care of him forever, not that he ever wanted to think about that.

"Dane?" his mother inquired delicately. God, she was beautiful. She was in her seventies now, because she'd had Mason and Dane a little later than a lot of moms, but her age was shown in the lines around her eyes and the gentleness of her smile, and in no other place. She was pretty adamant about dyeing her hair chestnut brown every six weeks, so that helped, but mostly, she just laughed a lot, and it kept her young.

"I, uh, applied to the graduate department at Davis," he said. "Veterinary science. It was, you know, just sort of for fun. To see if they'd take me."

She grunted. "Oh, honey—"

"I know. We can't afford it. I don't even know if it says yes."

"Maybe you can ask your brother for help," she said softly. "You know, he doesn't like to brag, but he makes a lot of money."

No, Mason *didn't* like to brag. Which was too bad, because he worked in upper-level administration at a technical firm in Silicon Valley, and he made a smashing amount of money. Mason would probably dump money on Dane's head because Dane had always been his biggest cheerleader—and

Mason seemed to need that. God. Poor brilliant, socially awkward Mason. He could manage a department to make money pretty much in his sleep. He could expand business and get morale thriving and was mostly a walking, talking treatise on economic theory in a bulky, unflattering, American-cut suit.

But opening his mouth on a casual level?

Not Mason's best thing.

"Would Ira even let him do that?" Dane asked caustically. Mason's live-in boyfriend was such a douchecanoe—*such* a douchecanoe. Besides being smarmy and insincere, he made Dane's brother feel like shit.

Nice suit, Mason. You couldn't afford something besides Penny's? Wow, Mason, you managed to put a whole sentence together—in public. Now maybe try not antagonizing your boss. I'd say we can go clubbing, but it would be like asking a pile of bricks to dance. I'll just go out myself, and you can play sudoku or whatever you left-brained people do with your time.

Ira was an artist. A bad one. For the last four years, he and Mason had been putting out Christmas cards with little cartoons on the front that weren't funny, and that made Santa look like a bear on a porn site.

Such a douchecanoe.

"Ira doesn't have a fucking say anymore," Jeanette Hayes said bitterly, and Dane inhaled sharply through his nose and realized he'd been wrong about "maybe." There was *definitely* vodka in whatever she was drinking.

"What happened?" Dane asked. He wasn't dismayed—not exactly. He sort of wanted to do the cha-cha, really. He knew his brother wanted a happily ever after, a husband, a nice house, maybe even kids eventually, the whole nine yards. But for four years, Dane had lived in fear that Ira would be that guy and he'd have to get through Ira's passive-aggressive cruelty to see his brother, who was too sweet to even recognize it for what it was.

But at the same time, watching Mason get his heart trampled was Dane's least favorite thing. Mason was always so… so puzzled. He usually had no idea what had happened, how his marching to a different drum often led to people bailing from his parade.

It was painful to watch, and Dane was already texting someone at work to cover his shift so he could drive out to Walnut Creek to comfort his brother.

"Ira was cheating," his mother said, drinking deeply of whatever fruit punch/vodka abomination had kept her sane during her children's traumatic growing-up years. "Apparently with his boss."

"Oh, the fuck—"

"I told him you were on your way over," she said, looking at him levelly.

He stood and kissed her cheek. "I already texted work."

"I know you did, honey. Because you're a good brother, which is why I bet he'll propose some sort of solution to help you get through school."

"I don't even know what it says yet!" he said, looking at the envelope with a little bit of horrified anticipation.

"I do," she said, giving a ladylike little belch. "Because that's what steam is for."

Dane turned the envelope over and saw the wrinkled edge that indicated it had been opened already.

"So?" he asked.

"Get ready for greatness, honey. You've been admitted for a graduate program. I'm not sure which one—there was a lot of talk about residency and preliminary stuff, and frankly? Your brother called first, and this isn't my first glass of Kool-Aid."

Dane smirked. His mother was pretty much the best on all levels. He opened the letter and saw that she'd been right. He hadn't been admitted into the residency—not the full veterinary science program itself—but he *had* been admitted into the graduate program as a science major. It wasn't going to be a cakewalk—and he'd have to complete it in order to be a resident—but it wasn't bullshit either.

"Congratulations, honey," his mother said, beaming at him softly. Of course she would, because she wouldn't want Mason's tragedy to override Dane's good fortune.

"Thanks, Mom. Let me go comfort Mason."

She saluted him with what was left of her Kool-Aid, and he left.

Mason *was* sad, as it turned out. But mostly he was self-recriminatory, and that was hard to watch. Before he could launch into "How could I be so stupid?" Dane proposed his plan over a glass of super pricey, really awesome Scotch.

For a guy who—like Dane—had spent his entire life in the Bay Area, Mason was surprisingly excited to get the fuck out. And he was super proficient at making big shit happen too. Before Dane could even say "tuition," Mason had paid it, gotten a job up in the Sacramento area at some place called Tesko Tech, and bought a sweet little house with four bedrooms, an office, three-and-a-half baths, and a swimming pool that both of them thought was a stupid waste of money… until they actually moved to Sacramento at the beginning of August.

"Oh dear God," Mason said, getting out of the car as they watched the movers cart their stuff into the house.

"Augh!" Dane took one breath of the incinerator that was August in Sacramento, dove back into the car, and slammed the door.

"What are you doing?" Mason asked, exasperated. "It's a convection oven in there!" He already had a sweat stain between his pecs and shoulder blades, just from *standing up and breathing.*

"Not if you get in here and turn on the car!" Dane snapped. "Do that!"

Mason complied, because he was a nice guy in the body of a gym-rat business-douche, and for a moment, they sat in the air-conditioning and tried to breathe.

"There's a pool," Mason said unnecessarily.

"Can we drive the car into it?" Dane was totally serious. He'd been a creature of comfort since his earliest years, and outside was *not comfortable.*

"No, we can't!" Mason took a deep breath. "But stay here. I'm going to go see how the movers are doing, and we can come back when they're done." Because Mason had marked all his boxes in big black letters, rendering the two of them there for oversight absolutely unnecessary. KITCHEN. UPSTAIRS GRAND SUITE BATHROOM. LIVING ROOM. He'd even included schematics. "If they can follow directions, we should be able to turn on the AC immediately."

"Where are we going in the meantime?" Dane asked, feeling peevish. He hated that sound in his voice—it meant he was stressed, and whatever his meds usually did to keep him balanced, they weren't doing it right now. Things, stupid things, like the temperature or a change of plans could catapult him from being a functioning adult to big whiny baby with his own mood-funk surrounding him like weather.

"We're going to the nearest home and garden," Mason said decisively. "That pool is going to save our lives."

"But you said it would be like swimming in a tub of lukewarm bacteria!" Dane shuddered. He wasn't even a germaphobe, but… ick.

"Well, not when we're done bleaching the shit out of it," Mason said, and he was using his executive voice, which meant discussion was over and they were men of action.

That was actually reassuring. Mason's plans usually worked out. Dane always figured that's why his boss—the one schtupping Mason's boyfriend—hadn't been able to fire him. Mason was just super confident with anything that didn't involve communication with anybody he wanted to impress.

And Mason's plan worked.

Suddenly they were both looking up the most efficient pumps, the best chemicals to put in the water, and were super fixated on how to keep the pool in tip-top shape, because to boys who were used to eighty degrees being warm, one hundred seven was the fiery furnace of hell.

Once they'd bought the best pump in the world and made plans to have it installed, they went back to the house, and Dane got his first look inside—not bad. It had been made up sort of blandly to sell, they both thought, and the walls were white, the carpets beige, and the hardwood covered. Before they'd even moved out, Mason had redone the kitchen as well as pulled out the carpeting in the living room area and replaced it with hardwood and a big, handsome area rug with big blocks of masculine colors. Dane had liked that, and waited to see what Mason would do with his own room.

He'd kept the carpet, but had painted one wall sort of a maroon brown and bought sheets and comforters to match, then added really stunning black-and-white prints. Dane had made vague noises about doing his own room, but then school started, and Dane was getting his ass solidly kicked.

Between the commute—Fair Oaks was a solid hour away from UC Davis, and that was when traffic didn't blow—and the course load, and the medication Dane had switched to when he'd gotten a new shrink in Sacramento, he had his plate full.

And for once, he wasn't getting laid.

He'd been sort of the restaurant slut during his last years of school. His prediagnosis relationships had ended badly—for more reasons than just that Dane could go batshit at any moment, really. But the last one… well. That had ended with an uninterrupted upswing, and the guy hadn't called Dane's parents until Dane had knocked down his walls with a sledgehammer and spray-painted what was left of them black. Not good times, really. Dane didn't remember most of them, because when he got so deep in his head that reality fractured, that's just what fucking happened. He *did* remember his brother hauling him—fireman carry—into the psych ward physically, and then sitting by his bed in the weeks of aftermath. After that, Dane had figured his family would get all his loyalty. Period. Because nobody else was going to have his back.

Let's just say it made him… wary… of any other attachment.

Besides, Dane was, in his own way, as weird as his brother. No, he didn't wear the wrong clothes to work because he mistakenly thought casual

Fridays were a thing when they weren't, and he didn't make dumb jokes about cheese when his boyfriend was hosting a wine-and-cheese party to a bunch of Francophiles. But he *did* make wild movie/game references when they pinballed into his brain, and he *did* take the sarcastic, snarky way out whenever he had the chance, and he just got tired of that, "Oh Jesus, Dane, could you make sense for *once*," look that his hookups eventually gave him, which was why he kept it short.

You kept it to one or two bangs a buck and you didn't have to see that look, right?

He never asked himself, "But what if your crush got you like that from the get-go?" Which was too bad.

Because he wasn't prepared for Clay Alexander Carpenter in the least.

The Meet Cute

WHEN DANE Christian Hayes met Clay Alexander Carpenter, the earth stopped, the sun brightened, the skies turned to turquoise and fairy dust, and all of the angels, the birds, and the kids playing out-of-tune instruments in grade schools achieved a perfect chord.

And then Dane found out Carpenter wasn't gay and the world fell to shit.

It seemed ordinary enough.

Dane had been golfing with Mason, because even though it was November and they'd moved to Sacramento in August, Mason had no social life at that point and was feeling low. And truth be known, Dane was not doing very well and had no friends either.

Well, Mason didn't know that.

Mason still looked at Dane with this baffled adoration in his eyes at all times, and Dane didn't like to disabuse him of that. He'd heard some people say their older brothers were pains in the ass, or control freaks, or complete assholes, or even just distant names on a Christmas card, but in spite of months of adult cohabitation, Dane still didn't feel that way about Mason.

Mason was still the dear, geeky, as graceful as drunken Mercedes—if a drunken Mercedes could grow hands and golf—brother he'd always loved. His split with Ira hadn't destroyed Mason's boundless optimism, which was why his excitement about a round of golf at the beginning of November had seemed like a good idea at the time. Mason just sort of gave it that rosy glow, and Dane went with it, as he always did. Watching Mason's face light up—dark eyes, salt-and-pepper hair, Superman jaw and all—made ditching his homework totally worth it.

Besides, it gave them a chance to talk.

"No, seriously," Mason was saying as he lined up a shot in complete abjection. "I don't understand people at Tesko," he murmured. "You have no idea of the mess I almost made at work."

Dane let out a sigh. *Oh, Mason….* "It couldn't possibly have been that bad," he said staunchly. He took his turn at the tee and eyed his brother, who actually wore golf slacks and white shoes! It was amazing. Of course, it was that bad. Mason's *heart* was in the right place, and workplace harassment had never really been his thing, but his awkward mouth hadn't gotten any better with the change of scenery.

Sometimes people's biggest faults just took over.

But Mason had seen Dane when that had happened to him, and had held his hand and brought him back to the land of the living.

So yes, technically Mason could do wrong. But in the real world inside Dane's head, there was no wrong Mason could do that the rest of the world shouldn't forgive the shit out of him for.

They played on in silence for a few, and Dane looked around the small Fair Oaks golf course and tried not to judge. There were better golf courses on the Bay Area peninsula, and they were greener and the hills were hillier and the sand traps had more sand, he was sure of it. This place was dry. Even when everybody in the world said, "Oh, yes, Sacramento's having a wet year," Dane was pretty sure people were just saying that to fuck with people from the Bay Area or Seattle. He figured there was sort of a joke among locals to keep everybody from acknowledging the perennial drought that seemed to plague the area.

Or at least the golf course, where the grass was only one-quarter green, even in November.

He was just in the middle of a glum contemplation of changing his major yet again and quitting the whole stress-laden graduate program to go into microbrewery instead, when he realized two of the guys from the party behind them were standing nearby, having played through in a relatively few number of strokes.

They were snarky… and *funny.*

"Yeah, Skipper, I don't get where that's fun. I mean, here's guys who profess to *like* girls, but they're going out of their way to be awful to them. I mean, these guys who harass girls in the gaming world need to wear that steel-titted G-string in public and dance the Watusi before they open their mouths, you know?"

Dane turned toward that voice—gruff, deep, hitting all the sweet spots in Dane's stomach—and paused.

The two guys waiting for them to play weren't… weren't like most other golfers.

For one thing, they were in cargo shorts. Mason and Dane's father was a little older than their friends' parents, and he'd given them both sort of an old-world formal sensibility. You didn't wear jeans golfing. You didn't wear cargo shorts. You wore slacks. They didn't have to be white or plaid, but anything was better than cargo shorts.

But these two golfers were in cargo shorts. One of them, a blond guy in a hooded sweatshirt, was making Dane's brother trip over his own tongue as he stood next to an averagely tall, stocky brown-haired guy with scruff and bangs falling in his eyes and glasses, and who appeared to have a liberal streak that Dane approved of.

Mason was doing his suave older-guy thing, extending his hand and introducing himself. When the blond one introduced himself as Skipper Keith, Mason said, surprised, "Schipperke?"

"Are you the guy who keeps calling IT?" Skipper asked, a little dumbstruck.

The brown-haired guy, Clay Carpenter, gave his friend a compassionate, long-suffering look that indicated he would have expected this chance meeting from nobody else but Skipper, which was why Clay obviously loved the guy like a brother. Dane recognized that look.

It was the same look Dane usually had—or at least, what he thought his eyes were doing—when his brother's social awkwardness was out in full force. Sort of like now, as he blushed and stammered and tried to explain to Dane that he and this guy—Schipperke—apparently worked together. Then Dane remembered Mason telling him about the IT guy he'd hit on at work. This must be him.

Dane listened in fascination as his brother welcomed the two newcomers to play with them instead of the group they'd left in the dust, and didn't make a single accidental double-entendre. Skipper Keith *seemed* unassuming enough, but instead of listening to Mason Hayes as he made an ass out of himself, he thanked Mason for sending him Theraflu and a sweater when he was sick at work.

As Skipper and Mason were making conversation, Dane turned to the scruffy guy who gave great voice and said, "How long have you two been together?"

Clay Carpenter snorted. "I'm not the one he's dating, but thank you. Skip would be a catch."

Dane's heart gave a double-flutter. "So *you're* single?" God. Did he sound too predatory? He probably sounded too predatory. He'd gotten a lot of sex by being unapologetically slutty, but he really didn't want to come on too strong. And these guys didn't seem like the fast-and-loose crowd he'd run with as an undergrad or at the restaurant.

"Single, but not gay," Carpenter said with a shrug, and until Dane heard the world crashing around his ears, he hadn't realized how invested he was in the answer. He was so occupied with the sound of his heart's destruction that he almost missed what Carpenter said next.

"But then, Skipper didn't know he was gay until a couple of weeks ago, so, you know, anything could happen."

It was said mostly in jest, Dane knew that. How could he not know? He wasn't stupid. But it was said with the confidence of a man who wouldn't mind if it was true.

Which meant… oh God, it just might… it must might….

"How could he not know he was gay?" Dane asked, fastening on something, anything to talk about so he could hear more of that rusty, self-deprecating voice.

Carpenter paused for a moment, and they both watched Skip swing the club in a perfect arc, and the ball bounce almost to the hole.

Carpenter sent Dane a droll look. "You see that?"

"God, I suck," Dane said in dazed response.

"So do I."

"But not in the same way," Dane said dispiritedly.

"Sure, brag about that now. But my point is, Skipper's never played golf before."

Dane watched his brother take his turn, and stared. Mason had the grace of a giant redwood tree doing the cha-cha. The ball went up too high, fell too soon, and curved to the left in what was probably going to be a six-over-par shot. As far as Dane knew, his brother came out once a month, at the very least.

"First time?" Dane asked, feeling a little adrift. "How does that happen?"

Carpenter shrugged. "I don't know. Skip and Richie have been best friends for six years. Then suddenly, they're banging like beavers. Sometimes you watch and plan and think about what you really want to do; then you score a hole in one."

Carpenter took his turn at the tee, and in spite of a few extra pounds, he moved with a no-bullshit, muscular athleticism that Dane had to admire.

Skipper almost scored a hole in one, but Carpenter was probably going to make a birdie at the very least.

Dane waited until Skip and Mason finished congratulating Carpenter before he stepped up and swung.

Yup. Almost as bad as Mason.

He waited for the fake congratulations from the newcomers, for the pained expressions of pity and condescension.

Carpenter looked at Skipper and shrugged. "Well, he did say he sucked."

All of them burst out laughing, and they trotted joyfully down to the green to finish the hole.

And Carpenter grew no less delightful. His banter with Skip spoke of long familiarity and affection… and loyalty.

"So, Skipper, you gonna add golf to your unholy regime of exercise?" Carpenter asked.

"Nope," Skip said. He was looking for a putting club like a beekeeper looking through spiders. "But that doesn't mean you shouldn't drag me out here the next time you get the urge." Skip pointed at a club wholly unsuitable for the terrain, and Carpenter shook his head and pointed to the one next to it. Skipper nodded and went with the suggestion.

"I get the urge to do lots of stuff, Skipper. I just don't always drag other people along with me."

Skipper snorted and faced the ball. "Well, you can go to the bathroom on your own, but I wouldn't mind holding your hand up here on the green." He adjusted his stance one more time. Dane wanted to tell him he was doing it wrong, because according to every lesson he and Mason had had as kids, he was. But so far, Skip had the best score.

And sure enough, he hit the ball into the cup, when the rest of them still had at least five shots to clear the hole. Mason high-fived Skip and stepped up, and Dane turned to his new friend and said, "What's his regimen like?"

"He's got this sort of church of holy soccer," Carpenter said in an undertone. "I managed to resist for two years, but he's been making me eat chicken sandwiches and walk during lunch at work. Not like parents, mind you, but like, 'Hey, there's this great place to eat about four blocks away. Let's be late getting back!' I mean, he's a fuckin' Boy Scout, right, and he's using being late back as a carrot. Anyway, I lost a little weight, got a little overconfident, and now I'm a part of the church… I mean, team. Go figure."

"Where'd you meet?" Dane asked, impressed in spite of himself. He might as well stare at the blond god too, because apparently everybody worshipped at the altar of Schipperke.

"Same place Skipper and Mason met. Work. But me and Skipper are in the IT department, so we met sort of accidentally."

Dane had to swallow against an unwelcome shaft of snobbery. Mason was VP of mergers and acquisitions. Dane knew the score. IT did *not* talk to VP—it was like some sort of rules of the royal court thing.

But then, Mason wasn't great at rules, and Skipper appeared to be great at people, so maybe Dane could forget his whole…. Oh, who was he kidding.

"What the hell are you doing in the IT department?" he asked, appalled.

Carpenter rolled his eyes. "Not firing people, not being a douchebag, and not hating my coworkers. Fucking sue me. What is it you do again?"

They'd already covered the fact that Dane was a student, so Dane conveniently disregarded that.

"My brother is not a douchebag," he said staunchly.

Carpenter just looked at Dane steadily, and Dane remembered that Carpenter had been there when Skipper should have called HR on Mason.

"I mean, he says dumb shit when he's nervous, but that doesn't make him a douche!"

Carpenter arched one eyebrow. "He asked Skipper if he'd like to come watch porn in his office."

Yikes. "Really?"

"Really."

"But apparently there was the thing with the Theraflu and the making sure he got home when he was sick," Dane pointed out hopefully.

"Porn."

"Often," Dane amended with a sigh. "He's not a douchebag *often.*"

Carpenter grinned at him. "Well, Skipper's giving him a do-over, so I can give him a do-over. Reboot, new lives, let's go kill some bad guys."

Reboot? Dane blinked. "What do you play?" he asked. Oh God, something besides golf.

"PS4," Carpenter said. "RPG, FPS mostly, what's your poison?"

"Anything," Dane said dreamily. He'd lost most of his gaming buddies when he quit the restaurant—they'd been casual acquaintances, really, not friends. "You want to play tonight?"

Carpenter shrugged. "Yeah, why not. Skip's got yard work after this, and I've got to clean my apartment. Log on about eight?"

That easy.

Finding a new friend was that easy.

A new friend with a sexy voice and an adorable scruff and a sense of humor.

Dane could totally deal with losing heinously at golf to a tall blond god if he got Carpenter to boot.

At the end of the game, Skipper and Carpenter joined them for a beer and then departed, leaving Mason—who had spent much of the game talking to Skipper—to swap impressions with Dane.

"So," Dane said, "what do you think?"

Mason let out a depressed breath and rested his chin on his hands. "It doesn't matter what I think. Everything I think is wrong."

"How wrong?"

"Well, I *thought* Carpenter was Skipper's boyfriend, and I got really excited because—"

"Because they wouldn't work at all!" Dane burst out, appalled.

"Right? So if that was the case, I sort of had a chance, but no. He's dating some guy named—"

"Richie," Dane said, remembering Carpenter telling them this. "He's an auto mechanic with red hair."

Mason opened his eyes and closed them again, like he was trying to clear his head. "You got that much out of his friend?"

"Yeah. Carpenter's all right. We're gaming tonight. Should be fun."

Suddenly Mason's sort of doofy, depressed look was replaced by an expression Dane knew well. The "What is the state of Dane?" look, and Dane both dreaded it and welcomed it.

He dreaded it because it implied he wasn't always capable of regulating his own goddamned head.

He welcomed it because he wasn't always capable of regulating his own goddamned head.

"You've made a friend?" Mason asked carefully.

"Yes, Mason. Dane made a friend."

"A gay friend or a straight friend?"

"I thought us gays didn't discriminate," Dane said with a flounce. "Because that's mean."

"Dane—"

"Mason! Look, you're the one who's pining for that thou shalt not have. I'm just playing a video game with a guy who knows an RPG from an FPS from Dungeons and Dragons in Mom's basement."

"Would you play Dungeons and Dragons if we *had* a basement?" Mason asked, as though this was seriously a possibility.

"I did that in high school, and I lost my dice and my big hooded Dungeon Master cape. Or I sold them for food, or for videogames or something."

"Thank God," Mason said with feeling. "Are we ready to go yet? I want to take a nap and pretend I'm being productive."

"That is an amazing idea. I'll help."

In fact, Dane had homework. So. Much. Homework. But Mason knew that, and he wouldn't let it interfere with his nap.

HE WENT home and worked for a couple of hours—and napped for an hour—then logged on to the game unit in his rather plain white room.

Even when he had friends to play with, he tried to choose activities that kept him in the here and now as opposed to cyberspace. Playing golf had been a Mason idea, and it had been a good one. With Dane's medication and his workload, physical activity was sort of a must. It was the whole reason Dane had asked his brother to move out to the Sacramento area with him. Mason's job was to help him stay level, help him remember the things he needed to do to function.

Because forgetting to do those things had led him to some really dark places, and Dane didn't want to go back.

Logging in with a friend to play a game felt like a vacation.

He found Carpenter under the exact handle he'd given—Pizza Physique—and frowned, adjusting his headset so they could talk while they picked out their characters and their challenge.

"Pizza Physique? What the hell does that mean?"

Carpenter's voice on the other end sounded distracted—he was probably trying to find a level they could both play. "Means you don't get this body by eating carrots and beet juice, precious. What did you think it meant?"

"What's wrong with your body?"

"Nothing that a few levels of armor and some new skins won't cure." He chuckled, and Dane rolled his eyes, knowing he was talking about his character in the game and not himself.

"That's hilarious. I'm gonna laugh myself back into the loony bin, that's so damned funny."

"Back? You've already visited?" Carpenter sounded nothing but curious, and Dane had to remind himself that this man didn't know him that well.

"Yeah, about six years ago. We figured out my meds and shit. Don't worry. I'm not going bat-crazy-cuckoo on you."

"That's a shame. I might have followed you there, for kicks."

Dane laughed, recognizing Carpenter's willingness to only go as deep as Dane wanted. "Well, if I go again, be sure to stop and say hi. And bring the euthanasia kit with you, 'cause that place was the suck. Yes. That one—I like that skin."

Carpenter had chosen this sort of all-around-god character—a little like Skipper, Dane could see it—but he'd outfitted him with black armor with a sort of sheen to it. Very… classy. Very superheroish, but not blond-American god.

"Ouch," Carpenter muttered.

"I said I liked it!"

"You also said euthanasia kit! I'm sorry, man, that must have sucked."

Oh shit. Oh shit. Dane had said too much. He needed to keep it light. People backed away from talk about mental illness. He should have known! Too much information! *Jesus, Dane, keep your brains in your ears!*

"Naw, really, it was a trip to the Bahamas."

"You know, people say that like it's a fun thing. Putting this body in a swimsuit and showing it off to the world is a nightmare for me, so you really didn't reassure me at all."

"I'm sorry. You know, I should just log off—"

"Jesus, Dane, chill! I'm not scared by your trip to the looney bin if you're not scared about my extra five thousand pounds."

Dane gaped for a moment. "It doesn't scare you?"

"No." Carpenter took a deep breath. "Mental illness is the suck—it couldn't have been easy for you. I'm, you know, glad you were in a place where we could meet and play golf."

Dane took a few deep breaths and backed up on the death spiral a little. "Are you really? Are you really glad you got to play golf?" He laced his words with a healthy infusion of sarcasm and a giant tablespoon of deadpan.

"No," Carpenter answered, chuckling. "I'm not really that fond of golf. But watching Skipper beat the shit out of the guys we came with? *That* was worth watching."

Dane chuckled back and made the final choice on his character. Ah yes, a thief—lithe, long, a good fighter, with sort of a sassy walk. He'd given her a tight black braid down her back with a strip shaved out of the side for a punk edge.

"Very nice," Carpenter said. "She's got some of the best fighting skills in the roster. I like her. Want to do a test level?"

"Yeah, sure." He waited for Carpenter to set it up. "What's wrong with the guys you played golf with?"

"They're assholes. Entitled fuckers. All they talked about was their GPAs for their MBAs."

"How did you know them anyway?"

"One of them is my brother-in-law's brother—although he's not quite so douchey. I went to school with those pricks. Jesus, they're twenty-six. They should have better shit to discuss, you know?"

"I'm thirty," Dane said, depressed again. "And I'm still in school. How's that for better shit." He hadn't really been able to decide on his major until he'd gotten his whole brain chemistry thing regulated, but he didn't tell people that a lot.

"Man, are you excited about vet school?"

Dane closed his eyes and thought of animals, the way they trusted him, the way he could help them feel better. The way they accepted him without words and without the judgment and emotional complexities of human beings. He yearned for a cat, but he couldn't care for one with his schedule and his commute, and foisting one off on his brother didn't seem fair, no matter how often Mason told him that the house was *theirs*, not his.

"Yes," he said, chest throbbing. "I really love the science, and when I get to volunteer with animals, it makes me really happy. The schoolwork is hard, and God. I'm not even in the program proper and it's still…well, it's intense." Mason had taken to putting his medication in little pill calendars every week, and giving him one to take to school every morning, as well as little plastic jugs of chocolate milk, which helped him regulate sugars and protein when he was too busy to eat.

"Well, good. Because I went to school for… some time, and I didn't like anything I studied. I really hated what people with my degree did, and now I'm the big fat disappointment in my parents' lives because I can barely pay off my student loans. It's a nightmare. So if you had to go back to school six thousand times to take something you loved? That's fuckin' rockin'. You keep doing that, right?"

Dane swallowed and nodded, eyes burning. "Yeah," he said gruffly.

"Awesome. How's that mission?"

Dane looked at the screen, which outlined him and Carpenter shooting their way through bad guys to get to a weapon in the center of the course. "We're gonna get creamed," he said, but this was a good thing. They'd have to take lots of chances in order to get it right.

"'Course we are. You ready to play?"

"Bring it on."

Giving Thanks

CARPENTER CHECKED his phone Thanksgiving morning by habit. Sure enough, Dane's name popped up.

Did you get your casserole cooked?

He grimaced. Yeah. He'd cleaned the kitchen of his tiny apartment, if not the bedroom, after he'd gotten back from golf that day. He'd been able to manage something gluten-, dairy-, and meat-free that his mother might approve of.

I almost wish it was a goose, he texted back, betting Dane would get it. Goose, cooked, right?

Haha. Are you still taking your blond god?

Yeah, because his boyfriend still has weird family drama. Richie was helping his father rebuild his business after it had been vandalized. Unfortunately, Richie's father loathed Skipper, so Skip was on his own.

That's too bad. We're going to see my parents if Mason can get his ass in gear. He seems to think he won't have to stop for coffee.

Carpenter chuckled. *You ALWAYS have to stop for coffee.*

Have a good day, right?

Huh. That sounded like Dane might not. *You too. Text me when you're back online. If I'm home, we can game.*

Of course, gaming was quickly becoming code for *talk*, but Carpenter didn't mind. He loved Skipper—wholly, unabashedly, with all his soul. Skip had been sick a couple of weeks earlier, and Carpenter and Richie had taken turns watching over him because he literally had nobody else in his life who'd do that, and Clay had been proud to be part of that team. He could talk with Skip about anything, and he hoped Skipper was starting to trust him to do the same.

But in a million years, he'd never imagined talking to someone like Dane—someone super quick, and super funny, and super smart—and feeling so very comfortable and at the same time so very alive.

It was almost like he felt a click whenever Dane's name popped up on his phone or his handle—RainbowShorts—popped up on his PS4.

Will do. Don't fall in love with Skipper while I'm gone.

Carpenter chuckled. *Richie would come after me with a shiv—and he LIKES me.*

Does my brother know this? I think he's still crushing a little bit.

Your brother didn't stand a chance, Carpenter texted brutally. *Richie's—* He paused typing and tried to think of how to word this. *—an auto mechanic and fierce. He doesn't look big or scary, but we got into an argument once and I thought he was going to chop me into bits and stuff me in the freezer.*

Holy God.

Well, that did sound a little extreme. *Skip was sick and out of it, and we were both losing our minds. My first thought was DOCTOR. His first thought was FIX IT OURSELVES. Because that's what happens when someone like him and Skip grow up without insurance.*

There was another pause—lots and lots of the little thought bubbles on the phone. *Is this why you're taking Skip to your parents' house for Thanksgiving?*

Carpenter swallowed. *I want him to have more than me and Richie in the world. I mean, as rocky as it's been between me and my folks, at least I knew they were there.*

Why rocky?

Ugh. That was a tangle. *Chat later. Gotta go.* And then, as if to make him not a liar, his phone lit up with Skip's name and it was time to go outside so they could drive up to his parents' place in Rocklin.

SKIPPER WOULDN'T have seen it, but Carpenter knew his mother was nervous. He seriously hadn't brought anybody home since his fifteenth birthday, when he'd invited Calliope and Jordyn to dinner. When they'd left, Jordyn had told him quietly that he was welcome at their place for cookies and video games anytime.

But Skipper had been duly warned about not eating the weird bean dip that his family thought was amazing, and he valiantly smiled when he had to eat Tofurky. And Carpenter's parents took the news about Skipper dating his fellow striker on the team with genuine smiles.

For a brief, shining moment, Carpenter was calling it a win.

Then his mother brought up Clay's older sister—and how her two perfect children were going to spend their Thanksgiving in a children's oncology ward volunteering to help the sick children—and he felt a craving, right in the gut, for cherry pie with the crust made of fat and a half gallon of creamy full-fat ice cream on the side.

And then, while he was fighting that, Skip and Clay's uncle Carter got into the most unexpected dumbass argument.

Skip probably didn't notice it. He probably didn't think of it as an argument at all, because Skip was just that sunshiny sweet summer child, oh yes he was.

But Uncle Carter was sort of an asshole. Lots of, "Oh, so you're finally playing a sport, Clay," and, "They let you on the field as you are?" Which Carpenter was used to by now, but it still wasn't awesome.

And then Skipper started talking about Richie arguing about the offsides penalty—because that's what Richie did, of course—and Uncle Carter spoke up. "Don't you mean the *offside* penalty?"

Skipper stared at him blankly. "Isn't that what I said?"

"No, you said offsides."

"Yeah, the offsides penalty."

"But there's no *s*, Christopher. It's pronounced 'offside.'"

"But that's not how we say it," Skipper said, still completely oblivious. "I mean, you want to say it your way, I'm sure it's fine, but we all say it our way, and that's offsides."

"But that shows poor education about the sport," Carter laughed, and Carpenter wanted to deck him because he sounded like a smug and superior asshole.

"Well, yeah," Skipper said, "on your part. How can you live here your whole life and not know we call it offsides and not offside?"

Carter had gaped and laughed, and the table had followed his example, and Carpenter had felt a little less homicidal.

But not much.

If someone could pick a fight with Skipper—who worked his ass off to be a really great person—what chance did Clay Carpenter stand? Why even try to lose weight, to find a better job, to give to every charity known to man, hell, to pay off his student loans, when his own damned family couldn't look past the difference of one lousy goddamned letter in a word to see that Skipper was trying to drag a scattered bunch of total assholes kicking and screaming into a family unit?

And be proud of Skipper when he mostly succeeded?

Skipper didn't even ask questions when Clay begged him to stop for burgers, pie, and ice cream on the way home.

They had themselves a pity party in Skip's awful kitchen, and Carpenter got to console him for missing Richie, and then Skip did an unexpected thing.

Skip gave him points for being a good friend.

Carpenter had been crying into his cherry pie about how wonderful his sister was. It wasn't like he didn't remember, right? Sabrina helping him with his algebra? The way her husband had tried to make him feel welcome—in spite of the fact that his brother had been the douchebag Clay and Skipper had been ditching at golf.

The fact that he'd gotten to hold her twins first, after she'd given birth right out of medical school? He'd never forget.

His sister was a good person. She was bright and shining and had paid off all *her* student loans, right? And she made the world a better place.

And Carpenter could barely get his fat ass out of bed.

But Skipper told him his good karma was fucking *earned.* He'd taken care of Skip when he was sick. He'd dragged Skip to Thanksgiving. He'd taken him golfing. He'd played soccer because Skip had asked.

He'd been Skip's friend after Skip had told him about Richie, and Clay was still his friend.

To Carpenter, these things felt like the bare minimum. Like he'd been raised to be a superstar and Skip was praising him for using words like *human being*.

But Carpenter was starting to see that to Skip, he had effectively raised the bar on being human. To a guy who had no family, being dragged to a family gathering was a blessing. To a guy who'd just figured out he was gay, having one friend who still treated him right meant he could have a whole lot of faith in the world to come. To Skipper, who had apparently grown up too quickly and too alone, the point wasn't that Carpenter felt happier in his kitchen than he'd ever felt in his life. The point was that Carpenter came into his kitchen at all.

Carpenter had been wondering, this past week, why someone as bright and shiny as Dane would want to hang with a big goober like himself online and play games.

After Skipper said that raw and vulnerable thing about how Carpenter had been the friend he needed when Skip had needed him, Carpenter got the first clue that maybe, *maybe*, the world wasn't quite as dark as he thought it was.

Blessings

DANE WALKED through the parking lot of UC Davis and felt that horrible environmental betrayal for not riding a bicycle almost immediately.

Everybody in Davis rode their bikes. *Everybody.* The fact that he commuted in notwithstanding, he was pretty sure people expected him to have one of those little folding bikes in the back of his Honda so he could make his way around the vast campus and little college town the way society dictated.

And he got it—he did. The entire town was made up of bike lanes and bike racks and students on bikes. It was a giant virtue signal on the edge of the breadbasket that was central California, and Dane was all for the last bastion of liberalosity in all its forms. But he was exhausted, and he would rather take a Lyft to his parking lot than figure out how to pack a tiny bicycle into the trunk of his car.

And as he hefted his backpack over his shoulder, he heard a rattle that started a panic attack in his gut as his general funk and pissiness took on a whole new context.

"Oh shit oh shit oh shit oh shit." He got to his car and unzipped the backpack, almost weeping when he pulled out the full pill calendar.

"Mother*fucker*!"

Two doses. That was his morning dose and the lunch dose, and he had two hours until his evening dose. "Shit shit shit shit shit…." No wonder he was feeling vertigo.

He pulled out one dose and the little chocolate milk jug and guzzled everything down before slamming his head back against the seat rest.

It was the third time he'd done that this week.

Goddammit. No wonder he needed his brother as a babysitter for probably the rest of his life. It was his last day of finals—*thank fuck*—but his meds were out of whack, and he knew better than to let them get wonky. Mason had made sure he had his pill calendar every fucking morning, and this was going to have consequences that Mason didn't deserve. Oh hell, the next few days were going to be a *joy.* Dane squeezed his eyes shut and resisted the beginnings of an all-out anxiety attack in the parking lot.

Breathe in. Breathe out. Come on, man, hold it together. If you can get home, you can do this in your boring bedroom and Mason never needs to know. Dane was such a big whiny baby—it was so embarrassing that he couldn't hold his shit together.

His chest was getting tighter, though, as he thought about how bad it could get. He hadn't been sleeping—was that an upswing or was that just finals? What if it was an upswing? What if he ended up repainting his room purple because suddenly, at two in the morning, magenta seemed like the thing to do?

You'll be up playing games with Carpenter anyway.

Oh yeah. That would be great. Why not let Carpenter see him like this, panicking and fighting tears and getting ready to scream and pound on the ceiling of the car?

It's missed meds, Dane. Oh my God, stop being such a toddler. Mason loves you. He'll help you out. Come on, man. He'd rather have you call him, right?

Dane pulled out his phone, startled a little out of his spiral when it buzzed in his hand.

Carpenter.

Oh God, it was Carpenter, with his raspy voice and his easygoing banter and his way of making Dane feel completely normal.

Congratulations on making it through your trimester! How'd the finals go?

Dane's fingers shook as he texted back.

Fine. I unbalanced my meds, though. Trying to deep breathe through it.

His phone buzzed in his hand. He hit the Accept Call button.

"Unbalanced your meds? Is that like when you put a bunch of them on one end of the scale and a fat bastard on the other and the meds are swinging out of your reach?" Carpenter asked.

Dane let out a cracked laugh. "Yeah, Carpenter, that's what it means. Fucking Jesus."

"Okay, so do I need to get off the scale?"

And Dane realized through his panic that Carpenter was inviting him to play along a little. "No, no, you can stay on the scale. We can just share the drugs, maybe," he said, but his voice was still wobbling, and he wasn't fooling anyone. "Tell me about your day."

"Sure. Richie got a job, and we saw your brother at lunch."

"Got a job? Wasn't he temping?" Carpenter had kept Dane apprised of the Skip and Richie show. They'd both breathed a sigh of relief when they'd moved in together the day after Thanksgiving. Dane had even had a celebratory bag of microwaved popcorn.

"Yeah, but he's now working at an auto parts store instead, and he's ridiculously cute about it. So, your folks are gone for Christmas? That's what Mason said."

Dane let out air through his teeth. "That's because he's a dork that doesn't read Mom's emails. They were *going* to be gone for Christmas, but I think Mason and I are driving down Christmas Day now because Mom's cousin got the plague or a heart attack or is suddenly dead or something."

Carpenter snorted. "That's a very compassionate diagnosis, Dane. How fond are you of this relative anyway?"

"She keeps giving Mom brochures on how Jesus can cure my bipolar disorder *and* my gayness."

"The suddenly dead plague it is," Carpenter endorsed staunchly like the good friend he was. "And good, because that means you guys can still come to Skipper's Christmas party on Christmas Eve. It should be fun. Skipper's getting a firepit for outside, and there's going to be marshmallow toasting and assholes bragging about their feats of prowess in soccer. You didn't hear it from me, but Menendez and Cooper and Thomas are all baking cookies together. I mean, it's not supposed to be sexual, but I can't be held accountable for what these mild-mannered teachers and lawyers and accountants do when covered in sports testosterone and flour."

That did it. A laugh broke through. Some of Dane's tension had begun seeping out at the sound of Carpenter's voice, and with the apparent normalcy of his conversation.

"Do you want to imagine a threesome, or should I?" Dane had been in his share, but he'd found they'd been overrated. Lately, the thought of people he didn't know touching him just felt… awkward. As Carpenter's raspy voice cascaded over his skin, soothing away the rough edges, he felt an attraction based on nothing more than comfort.

"I got no idea. Thomas is this sort of goofy-looking school teacher with a shaggy beard and hair like a blond dandelion. Cooper looks like Jared Padalecki, and like he should be a college professor instead of an accountant. Menendez is small and he's mean. You can imagine these guys having all the sex you want, but I've seen them covered in mud and down five points. I don't think I can."

Dane laughed some more and realized his eyes were closed and he was breathing normally.

"Who do *you* want to imagine in a threesome?" he asked, not really caring who the starlets were. What mattered was that Carpenter kept talking.

"Hm…. John Krasinski—"

"*The Office*?" Dane's voice squeaked.

"Uh, *Jack Ryan*, because *duh.* Anyway, John Krasinski, Joel Kinnaman—"

"Who in the *fuck*—"

"He's in *Hanna*, the series. Super tall, a little gangly, but very Swedish. You'd like him."

"Swedish?"

"Okay, Jay Hernandez—the new *Magnum* reboot. Not as good an actor, but I'd have a beer with him. And… hmm… oh. Aldis Hodge. Easy."

Dane's brain exploded, but in a good way. "Carpenter, aren't you straight?"

"Maybe—I was trying to plan a threesome you'd enjoy. How'd I do?"

"I don't know," Dane said, the descent from his almost-anxiety-attack washing him in melancholy and making him table that "maybe" for later. "I think I need to watch more TV to see some of these guys with their shirts off."

"Well, how about you come home, and I'll meet you there with takeout. You, me, and Mason can leave the games for the night and watch mindless fucking TV and you can chill." Carpenter's voice dropped suddenly, becoming terribly, terribly gentle. "You really need to chill, don't you."

It wasn't a question, and that's when Dane realized he hadn't fooled Carpenter one bit. This whole twenty minutes or so of conversation had been Carpenter trying to distract Dane from his anxiety attack, and it had worked.

"I really do," Dane said, tears of weakness squeezing out from the corners of his eyes. "Don't take this wrong, but can you show up before I get there?"

"Yeah, sure. No worries. What do you want for takeout?"

"Anything," Dane said. "Just… just I'm going to start the car so the phone can start through Bluetooth. Could you, uh, text Mason for me and ask him to buy chocolate milk, then tell him you're coming over tonight?"

"Not a problem. Did you want to call—"

"No." Dane couldn't stop the note of pleading in his voice as he turned the ignition. When Carpenter was linked up with the speaker, he said, "I… just keep talking to me, okay? I just really want to come home."

"Yeah, sure. Have you seen this newest version of Fortnite? I am *digging* the new skins. How about you?"

"I'll be more impressed if we can put some of the big muscular male characters in a dress. Because that would be fun."

"Wow. That's a little kinky for me. But your character might carry it off."

"She's happier in leather," Dane said, closing his eyes for a moment. Yeah. His brain was clear, and his meds were probably kicking in. He had no idea if that was true or not—he knew he needed blood levels of those chemicals to stay even, but he had no clue if just throwing them all down his gullet did any good at all.

But he was going to tell himself it did so he and Carpenter could keep talking.

All the way home.

HE GOT home expecting hell to pay—but there wasn't. Just Mason with two gallons of chocolate milk and Carpenter with something that didn't look like takeout.

"What the hell…?"

"Yeah, well, Skipper's got me on this health food kick," Carpenter explained. "So, chicken on whole wheat with pesto. I caught the sandwich place before they closed, got like six of them, so whatever."

Mason looked up from his corner of the pale leather couch in his spacious living room. His tatty sweats and rumpled cardigan were a signal that his weekend had already started, and he must have seen Skipper and Richie together, so his Skipper Keith pity party had not quite wrapped up.

"How're you doing?" Mason asked. "Here—sit down. I'll get you some dinner."

Dane dropped his backpack in the entryway and then hung up his coat and let Mason take care of him. Mason was good at it, like their parents, which was probably why Skipper wouldn't have been a great idea anyway. Because according to Carpenter's stories, taking care of people was Skipper's main joy in life too.

"Tired," Dane said briefly. Carpenter got up from the recliner and gestured for Dane to take his place, but Dane shook his head. "Let me go put on some sweats," he said instead. "And then, seriously—a sandwich, some TV." He swallowed and felt that terrible vulnerability come back. "Uh, we can sit on the couch." *Please, Carpenter, pretend you're not straight. Please, please, please.*

"Sure. I'll go get you some chocolate milk. Your brother bought enough of it."

Dane nodded and made his way up the stairs. As he changed—and took a quick shower, because he'd had lab practicals that day and he was pretty sure he smelled like cat zombies and horror movies—he had time to wonder what Carpenter and his brother were saying to each other. Did Clay tell Mason about their last conversation? Did he say anything more than "It was a rough day?"

What did Dane *want* him to tell Mason?

God, it would be great if his big brother could nurse his broken heart in peace without having to worry about Dane swinging from the light fixtures and then hibernating like a bear. Dane was so *over* being a burden.

But by the time he got downstairs, they were talking about politics, and given they were both as Marxist as the comfortably well-off could possibly get, they seemed to get along just fine.

But politics, even when he was on board, always bored Dane shitless.

"Yeah, fine, vote Democrat," he muttered as he walked into the kitchen. "But what I want to know is why we haven't seen *Umbrella Academy* yet."

"Because there were too many hot people in *The Magicians*," Clay said happily. "Have you seen the latest season?"

"Yes. Twice." Because Hale Applebaum was one of Dane's not-so-secret "I would hit that with my last breath" people.

"Well then, *Umbrella Academy* it is!" Carpenter's smile was full amperage, and some of the gray around Dane's vision faded.

And then he yawned—the kind of yawn where it probably looked like his mouth was going to open completely, hinge backward, and swallow his own head.

"Maybe stupid Friday night shit instead," Carpenter amended. "C'mon, let's get you fed, watered, and wound down. You can do nothing tomorrow but sleep."

"Can't you?" Dane asked plaintively.

"Are you kidding? I have to drag my carcass onto the soccer field to practice so my fat ass doesn't get solidly creamed when the season starts up again. It's part of joining the cult—it's in the bylaws."

Dane started to giggle. "Oh my God!" And it just got funnier.

"What?" Carpenter demanded, but Mason was covering his eyes, so he'd heard it too.

"You don't say 'ass creamed' to a gay man!" Dane chortled, and then Clay blew his mind.

"Well, look who's a slutty bottom!"

And Mason gasped in horror. "That's my *brother*!"

Dane was laughing so hard he almost couldn't say it. Almost. "It's so true!"

He fell on Carpenter, so undone Carpenter needed to hold him up or Dane would just lose his shit all over the kitchen floor.

But he did. Hold him up, that is. Solid, sturdy, dependable as a granite foundation, Clay Carpenter dragged a giggling, overtired Dane to the living room while Mason brought his food and chocolate milk in and shut off the lights in the kitchen.

The next thing Dane knew, he was sitting in the *V* of Carpenter's legs as he munched doggedly on a chicken-and-avocado sandwich and mindless action-TV Friday was blowing shit up onscreen.

Every now and then, Carpenter would pick up the glass of chocolate milk and set it in his hand, and by the time the first commercial came on, the sandwich was gone, and so was the chocolate milk. And his life was all about leaning on Carpenter's solid, warm, muscular frame, his brain pleasantly fuzzed out and his body getting ready to relax.

Mason was the one who shook him gently awake. "Here—one last swallow of milk." And also the pills from Dane's calendar. Dane met his eyes miserably, because it was obvious he'd been missing meds, but Mason just ruffled his hair.

"Finals are the suck," he said gently.

Dane nodded, too exhausted to even protest.

"I'll refill the calendar. Make sure you take your breakfast dose, okay?"

"Thanks, Mace."

And then Mason was gone, up the stairs. And Dane was alone with the fuzzy, muscular top of his dreams and his entire body was a noodle.

"Don't go," he begged softly. "Wait until I'm asleep."

Carpenter yawned. "How about you go upstairs and I'll sleep on your couch. I can get up early and change for the game."

Dane thought about that for a minute. "If I promise not to molest you or otherwise bother you, do you just want to sleep in my bed? We'll both fit, there's a comforter, and you can plug your phone into the charger."

Carpenter blinked. "Uh… sure?"

Dane had to laugh. "Mason and I grew up sharing a queen-sized bed—houses cost a *fortune* on the peninsula, even small two-bedroom ones with tiny backyards."

"Gotcha," Carpenter said softly. "Then, sure. No gropey, no nopey. It'll be fine."

And it was. Carpenter turned out the lights and stripped off his cargo shorts and hooded sweatshirt, revealing the solid, stocky body beneath.

Yeah, there were some bulges and overlaps. Dane could see that through the T-shirt. But he could also see the muscular calves and the broad shoulder and upper arm definition.

Carpenter's body was a work in progress. Dane approved of works in progress—he'd hate to think his goofy smile and hipster scruff was the finished product of anybody's imagination.

"Not much to grope," Carpenter muttered, embarrassed. "Or, you know, too much to grope."

"Shut up," Dane said thickly, turning his back to the center of the bed. Fat didn't bother him. Cruelty bothered him—because he'd dated cruelty in a pretty package before, which was how Mason had ended up doing the fireman's carry with Dane into the psych ward. But he'd banged all shapes and sizes at the restaurant, and hadn't regretted a single bang. "I'd be all over that shit before you could say cream of ass."

Carpenter's chuckle warmed his toes. "Which, frankly, is something I will never say again."

"Aw, please," Dane begged, still giggling. "For me?"

"No. Only boys who go to bed on time can hear me make a complete asshole of myself. It's a rule."

"Fine," Dane grumbled, snuggling into his pillow. Carpenter's weight depressed the bed, and Dane thought longingly of spooning that big warm body and rubbing his tummy to see if he had a silky happy trail or a fuzzy one. But he'd promised, and frankly, just having that body at his back reminded him of being a kid, when Mason kept the monsters at bay and wouldn't let anything hurt him.

You don't want him to be your brother.

Well, no. But right now, Carpenter was kindness and safety and laughter. Dane would take what he could get.

Freedom

CARPENTER HAD tried to prepare Dane for Skipper's small house and how truly awful the kitchen tile was. Dane was a bit of a snob, and Carpenter got it. His own mother knew the difference between off-white, eggshell, ecru, pale beige, vanilla, and cream—and even the wine in the low-fat gravy was more than fifty dollars a bottle.

But Skipper was his friend—his best friend—and for some reason it was of vital importance that his boss's little brother see Skipper's house and recognize it for the bastion of peace and kindness that it actually was.

Dane didn't seem to notice the kitchen tile.

He was starting to regain his edge and his snark after that seriously shitty day the week before Christmas. Carpenter had never heard anybody that close to losing their shit before. Pulling Dane back from that edge had given Carpenter a greater appreciation for mental health care professionals and sufferers alike.

His heart had been thudding in his chest like a basketball against wooden floorboards in an old gym.

And Mason—well, he had to give it to Dane's older brother.

Carpenter had texted, *Dane's on his way home. He's having a rough day*, and Mason had texted back his address and asked Carpenter if he wanted to bring takeout or should Mason order in.

That simply, Carpenter had been invited into their nice little home. Four bedrooms, three baths, a pool—it was about a third the size of the house Carpenter's parents lived in, but three times the size of Carpenter's apartment.

Mason did okay for himself as a VP at Tesko, but he didn't like to brag.

And Carpenter could respect a guy who would rather have a nice little house and a pool because that's all he needed instead of a mansion and a pool boy because that's what everybody thought he should have.

But that didn't stop him from worrying.

Skip's house had become sort of holy to him. He really hoped Dane would worship in the same church.

Dane didn't seem to be shopping for churches—but he didn't seem ready to piss on Carpenter's either.

He smiled graciously at Skip, brought a giant tin of homemade sugar cookies that made Carpenter hate him a little because he'd brought the store-bought ones and felt inferior, and made himself comfortable on Skip's recently repaired back deck, hanging out by the firepit and shamelessly flirting with anyone who came to talk to Carpenter.

"So," he said, giving a grin made more endearing by his slightly crooked front teeth, "you're the soccer-playing schoolteacher. Do they give you extra credit for that?"

Thomas shook back his curly blond hair and gave a heavy-lidded grin that suggested he was the most laid-back guy at his high school—even as an adult.

"Naw, dude. I just imagine that the ball is my current administrator; then I kick the ever-loving shit out of it. Clears away a lot of bad karma, you know?"

Carpenter chortled. On the field, Thomas was a showboat, and a ruthless midfielder who had actually scored a goal once on a blocking kick to save Carpenter from having to go after the ball as keeper.

The guy could kick a soccer ball into the next state with very little effort.

"Brother, that's a lot of rage," Dane said with respect. "What did that asshole ever do to you?"

Thomas snorted. "Wrote me up for calling him 'Dude.'"

Carpenter and Dane looked at each other in disbelief and then stared at Thomas, waiting for the rest of the story.

"Do tell," Carpenter said, edging away from Mason while keeping his ass toward the firepit for blissful warming. Jefferson was on Mason's other side, and he kept crowding Mason, so it wasn't really Mason's fault that he was almost sitting on Carpenter's lap. He wasn't trying to be rude, but was just trying to maintain a respectful distance from the much younger, super adorable, squirrelly blond-haired, brown-eyed Terry Jefferson.

"Aw man, it was the dumbest fucking thing!" Thomas shoved his hands into the pockets of his jeans and slouched forward, smiling winningly at both of them, and Carpenter appreciated him for a minute. Long hair, surfer scruff, bright green eyes—Elwood Thomas was the perfect high school teacher. Laid-back, smart… and, from what Carpenter had heard him saying to Skipper, extremely organized. He taught history, econ, and American government, and when he was on a roll about how the curriculum needed to change in order to more accurately reflect American diversity, Carpenter found himself wishing for his Trapper Keeper and a pen so he could take notes and learn something.

"Clarify 'dumbest fucking thing,'" Dane urged, his brown eyes lighting up. Carpenter swallowed a little surge of resentment. He rather liked having all of Dane's attention on himself, as it had been for the last week or so, since the super-shitty day. But hey, even *if* Thomas was bi and Dane was his speed, what was Carpenter going to do? All of that pondering about kissing another man was just that. Pondering. If Dane needed someone, what was Carpenter going to do about it?

He tried to scowl at Thomas, but the guy was just so sunshiny bright that Carpenter found himself listening to the story instead, while his stomach did a bunch of confused flip-flops that could have meant anything from "I'm going to lose my anal virginity to a guy named Elwood" to "Jesus, I ate a lot of fuckin' cookies."

Or maybe just "Dane looks really happy tonight, and I'm glad I get to be near him."

"So," Thomas was saying after kicking back a swig of beer, "you ever have one of those shitty days?"

"Don't even ask that," Dane muttered, and Clay shoulder-bumped him gently so he'd know it was okay.

"Yeah, right?" Thomas nodded like that was an entire conversation. "Anyway, so I was having a *day.* Menendez and Wyatt Cooper are sort of my buddy support system, you know?"

"No, I didn't," Carpenter said. "But now I do, and I may forget in the future."

"Heh-heh." Thomas took another chug of his beer. "Anyway, so they'd just helped me move back to my parents' after me and Sonja broke up, and it was… it was bad. It was so bad they got me toasted and I crashed on Wyatt's couch that night and had to, like, borrow his jeans and underwear and shit, because… it was fuckin' bad. And then, to top it off, my car wouldn't start, so I needed him to jumpstart it, and I was really fuckin' late. And, like, I've got tenure and everything, but I'd, like, left my *school keys* at my parents' place, and my name badge and *everything.* So I get there late, and I'm out by the back gate, and my classroom is right *fuckin' there.* And I know somebody has got to be in there with the kids, because that's what they do, right? Security or administration goes in until we get our shit together! So nobody is letting me in the back gate, and I call the front office, and the front office bitch is a piece of work. Hates my ass, hates all the fuckin' women, hates the GSA, the Spanish club—you get the idea. Bitch. And she's like, 'I'm sure you'll find your way in.' So I start throwing shit, right?"

Dane and Carpenter blinked long and slow. Carpenter wasn't sure what was going through *Dane's* mind, but he was imagining a big dandelion-headed baby tantrum right outside the school gates.

"Where?" Dane asked. "Where did you throw shit?"

Thomas burbled a laugh over his next sip of beer. "Like, at the window, man. Like, so the kids could see me and come let me in! The gate opens from their side, not mine, right?"

"Oh my God!" Carpenter sputtered. "You were pulling a Romeo and Juliet in your own goddamned classroom?"

"*Right*?" Thomas jumped up and down on his toes. "Right? I'm, like, so pissed. Anyway, security finally lets me in, and my door is locked, but I can hear a voice inside. The principal opens the door—motherfucker was lecturing my seniors on what dumbasses they are—"

"Wait, what?" Dane frowned. "Does he do that?"

"He stops rallies to tell the kids they're being shitty, when they're just being fucking kids. And this class is sweet. Lazy, but sweet, right? You give them a little rah-rah and they kick it into gear. So this motherfucker is shitting on my kids, and he doesn't say anything to me, just finishes his lecture and turns to leave. Without a fucking word."

"Is that when you called him 'dude'?" Dane clarified.

"Naw, man—not yet. So I talk to the kids. They're my kids, right? And they were like, 'Omigod! Thomas! Man, we're so glad to see you!' and I was like, 'Didn't you hear me throwing shit at the window?'"

"Did they?" Carpenter was fascinated. After that ill-fated interview day, he'd been absolutely convinced douchebaggery was an exclusively rich guy thing. But apparently, it existed in all levels of civilized society.

"Yeah! And the kids were like, 'Johnstone! Johnstone! We've got to get our teacher, man—we like him! We've got a project we gotta do today, and he's outside with our handouts!' I'd paid for the damned photocopies myself, right?"

"Dude." Carpenter abruptly forgave Thomas for being cute and smart and blond and about six inches taller than he was. This story was actually sort of appalling, and poor Thomas hadn't deserved it.

"Right? Anyway, it's exactly what I said, and the kids all nodded back, like, seriously, and I said, 'Look, we've got twenty minutes left. Let's get something done, right?' And just as we were starting, asshole comes back in again. I was like, 'Dude! Can I help you?'"

"What did he say?" Carpenter caught his rather sad look at his empty beer and reached into the cooler that was only a couple of feet away and handed him a new one.

"Thanks, my dude. And the motherfucker didn't say a damned thing. Just turned around and left. And then called me into a meeting the next day. I barely had time to grab my union rep, and she's a witness. That asshole wrote me up for calling him 'Dude.'"

"Dude," Carpenter and Dane both said in tandem, and they didn't even laugh.

"Right?" Thomas gave his bottle cap a vicious twist and took a healthy swallow. "Anyway, union rep said it was bullshit and she'd fight it, but it hits me, right? I'm working for a douchebag. Me and the kids, we got our thing going, and their test scores are good, and I'm loving the job, but that Thursday at soccer, man, I was kicking the shit out of that fucking ball, and that Saturday at the game, I was all hip action, man. That game keeps me from losing my shit, 'cause I can't. The kids need me, right?"

"Absolutely," Carpenter consoled him. At that moment, Wyatt Cooper—brown-haired, hazel-eyed, lanky and wiry like a guy who worked for his dad's lawn service on the weekends should be while working an office job during the week—came to lead Thomas away.

Carpenter was left blessedly alone for the moment with Dane, next to a roaring fire, underneath a sugar-frost scattering of ice-bright stars.

"Huh." Carpenter was sleeping on Skip and Richie's couch that night, because he didn't want to spend Christmas Eve alone and because they'd all gotten each other gifts that they were going to leave under Skipper's little tree. Richie had let it slip that Skipper hadn't had a Christmas tree or presents since his parents split when he was about twelve, and Carpenter had felt super shitty about blowing the holiday off the year before. Celebrating consumerism hadn't meant that much to him back then, and he'd yet to realize how much Skipper *did* mean to him. Carpenter had always had enough, and more than enough.

For some people, the little ceremony with the presents under the tree was to celebrate the things they had on that day that they hadn't had for most of their lives.

Skipper and Richie were those people, and Carpenter wanted to be a part of that this year. Watching them fall in love had given him a little bit of hope.

"Huh what?" Dane asked, leaning against him a little. He seemed to like doing that. Since that night on Mason's couch, Dane had been within touching distance a lot. Carpenter found he didn't mind. It was… pleasant, having a warm male body nearby.

"I just really admire people like that. People who keep jumping back into the classroom or the hospital room or the wherever, in spite of the fact that their administrators are complete dickheads who need to make it about themselves instead of the student or the patient or whatever." He sighed glumly. "I always wanted to make the world a better place, you know?"

Dane wiggled against him, and Carpenter's whole body warmed. Interesting. That was… interesting.

"You do make the world a better place," Dane said, his voice a sort of low rumble. He was maybe an inch or two taller than Carpenter, but that didn't stop him from laying his head on Carpenter's shoulder. "You make it better for me, and I have to say, I'm the six kinds of selfish that thinks that's seriously okay."

Carpenter had to laugh. "Skipper says the same thing. Which is funny, because Skipper has more reason to be selfish than anyone, but you should see him take care of the team like the nanny we all know and love." He pitched the last part of that to Skipper, who was nearby, so Skip would know he wasn't saying anything mean.

Skip looked up from his conversation with Menendez, the firelight making his handsome Nordic features almost poetic in their beauty.

"I know you're trying to give me shit," he said, a thread of pride creeping into his voice, "but I'm already planning next season."

Carpenter chuckled. "I know you are, Skip. Carry on."

Skip went back to being the host of his backyard, and Dane snuggled in a little closer. "He's what Vikings should have been," Dane said softly. "No wonder my brother was so smitten."

Carpenter glanced to his other side, where Mason was awkwardly trying not to crowd him some more and Jefferson was advancing on him with a predatory gleam in his big brown eyes.

"Uh, I think your brother may have a new problem," he murmured, just low enough for Dane to catch. Dane smelled like… cedar wood? Did men wear cedar wood? That wasn't the firepit, Carpenter was positive. He sort of loved it.

Dane stood up straight enough to let his brown eyes flicker to where Mason was looking bemusedly at pretty, squirrely Terry Jefferson, and then he straightened up completely.

"Mm. Yeah?" he said quietly back, his breath tickling Carpenter's ear.

Carpenter nodded. "Money down?"

"I wouldn't take that bet," Dane returned. "You're right."

"Does Mason know it?"

Dane snorted and Carpenter giggled. "Oh my God, you freak, that tickles!"

Dane covered his mouth—and the attractive brown scruff that had started up in the last week or so—and laughed into his hand. "No," he chortled. "The answer to that question is no!"

"No what?" Mason said, looking over at them with wide, guileless eyes.

"No, we're not staying at Mom and Dad's all week," Dane said, in what Carpenter had to admit was the best recovery ever. "He just wanted to know if I'm going to be around to game."

"Yeah," Carpenter said, backing his boy. "My parents usually give me gift certificates to GameStop or Amazon—we should have some of the newer shit to play by the time you guys get back."

Dane met his eyes, his own sparkling in amusement, and offered him a fist bump.

Carpenter took it, feeling not only virtuous but excited and rushed, like a kid with a secret.

"Do your parents always get you gift certificates?" Dane asked casually, and Carpenter tried not to sigh.

"They… they do," he said, feeling some of his ebullience fading. He wasn't particularly looking forward to his dutiful Christmas visit tomorrow. Waking up and having waffles with Skip and Richie? Yes. Going to his parents to have bean-curd-shaped-like-ham? Not so much.

"You got sad," Dane said, his voice assuming tones of wonder and horror. The two of them backed up, almost like a dance, so they resumed their original position next to each other facing the yard, with the firepit warming their backs and backsides. "Why did you get sad?" he asked, and Carpenter looked out into the darkness beyond their happy little gathering of hot chocolate and sugar cookies.

"Richie's getting him a dog," he said wistfully. "That's his Christmas present. They're going to go get a dog together, from the shelter. I might even get to come."

"That's sweet," Dane told him, not asking what this had to do with Carpenter's parents, for which he was grateful. "We could never get pets—my father is deathly allergic. My mother would take me to the shelter to volunteer all the way through high school so I could, you know, get my dog on."

Carpenter laughed slightly. "We had a dog when I was a kid. After Snoodles died, I wanted another dog so bad. A cat. A gerbil. But it was always a test. Were my grades good enough? Was my room clean enough? Did I improve in soccer, science, reading, math, and thaumaturgy?"

Dane didn't laugh at the thaumaturgy joke, which told Carpenter that his voice was too shaky with the underlying hurt. "I just… you know. Close, but no cigar. And maybe it was just a way to not have another animal, because animals are giant colossal pains in the ass that shed and shit and eat and knock over trash and stuff. But…."

"But you didn't care about that," Dane said. And maybe because he'd gotten his dog on, because he saw animals on a daily basis in the veterinary science department, or maybe because he just really got Carpenter and Carpenter's heart was sort of wounded, as if seeing his best friend fall in love had shown him what Carpenter was missing, he nodded, completely honest.

"I would have cleaned up all their shit just to have a creature who loved me, however."

Dane made a hurt sound and leaned on him again. "Maybe you can get a cat," he said encouragingly. "And then I could come over to your place and visit your cat, since Mace and I aren't working pet-friendly hours at the moment."

"If you saw my apartment, I'd kill myself," Carpenter muttered, thinking about how there were clothes everywhere—and not just clothes. A combination of giant clothes and slightly smaller clothes, and dirty clothes and clean clothes, and shoes to fit his feet when they swelled and shoes to fit his feet when they didn't, and Skipper's soccer equipment, and six different gaming systems and—

"Ouch!"

Dane had smacked him on the back of the head.

"That's real." His voice was flinty. "I've said that to my family and meant that. We don't use those words unless we want to be dragged into a shrink's office for six shots of Wellbutrin with a lithium chaser."

"Wouldn't that be lethal?" Carpenter asked, appalled.

"Well, I wouldn't have cared," Dane snapped back. "Now find another way to say that."

Carpenter swallowed back the sarcasm, his heart cracking a little. *I've said that to my family and meant that.* "My apartment is a shithole, and I don't want you to see it because now you like me."

Dane cocked his head, as though he'd been speaking in another language. "How bad could it be?"

"I don't know. I haven't seen the floor in months."

Dane's angry scowl brightened. "So it's like a treasure hunt? I could come see your house like a treasure hunt? Now you've got me super excited to see it! Can I see it now? Can we go today?"

"No!" Carpenter almost backed into the firepit in an effort to get away from that idea. "No! You can't come see it today! Jesus Christ, I just told you it's too ugly to see!"

"No—you told me it was a shithole that needed cleaning. I can clean. I'm great at it. We could spend an entire day cleaning your apartment, and then we could game."

This was not how Carpenter expected this conversation to go. "You're insane," he said decisively. "So insane."

Dane appeared unfazed. "We've covered that. Bipolar depression, anxiety—you've seen it. But that doesn't mean I don't want to help you clean your place."

"I'm a grown man," he said with dignity. "I can clean my own place."

Dane snorted. "Obviously not. Here—I get a month off. You get it to a place where I can come help. And I'll come help."

Carpenter dropped his chin to his chest and rubbed the back of his neck. "Dane, man, not even Skipper has seen my apartment."

"Really?" Dane batted his lashes at Carpenter, and for a moment, between the firelight and the electric lamps hanging from the nearby oak tree, Carpenter got to see Dane's eyes, and the complexity of brown that they were.

"Really what?" he asked, confused.

"The great and almighty Skipper Keith, slayer of hearts, hasn't seen your apartment?"

"No," Carpenter muttered, feeling grumpy. "It's private."

Dane's expression became catlike, and Carpenter just stared at him, mesmerized.

"What?" Dane asked after a moment.

And Carpenter was lost for a manly, strictly heterosexual way to put this. "Your eyes. They're… just, I need to see them in the sunlight."

"They're brown," Dane said, nodding, like he was humoring Carpenter, which was a hoot because he's the one who had just agreed to come over to Carpenter's shitty apartment and play American Maid, like in *The Tick.*

"They're a very impressive brown," Carpenter said, swallowing hard. "I… you know…."

Dane didn't move, and he didn't move, and they were standing super close together, and Carpenter didn't want to put any space between them.

"I know one thing," Dane said smugly.

"What?"

Dane shook his head, that air of cat-and-canary never leaving. "I'll let you know when you're ready," he said. He turned then, so he was sideways and they weren't facing each other anymore.

They were still close, but it was buddy closeness, and part of Carpenter relaxed.

Okay.

Better.

Easier.

So much easier.

Buddies. He liked having buddies.

Buddies who breathed softly in his ear and laid their head on his lap when they were watching television.

Buddies who didn't ask him who in the fuck he thought he was fooling.

"SO, CLAY, how's your friend Skipper?"

Carpenter shook himself and took a baked whole-grain bagel chip and pretended to dip it in the bean curd thing his mother thought he loved.

"He's great, Mom. He and Richie moved in together, and Richie got a new job. They're really happy."

"Is that why you didn't bring them by for Christmas?" she asked, smiling hesitantly and tucking back an invisible strand of her carefully frosted updo. She bit her collagen lip and widened brown eyes that were so much like Carpenter's, he wondered if he'd gotten that gene and that gene only. God. She tried. She tried so hard. And for the last few years, questions like this had usually spurred him to rip her head off, which so wasn't fair.

He took a deep breath and tried to adult. "I actually stayed the night at their place last night on the couch so he could have sort of a nice little Christmas. A friend, a boyfriend, waffles, presents. I…." He looked around his parents' house. Yup, still huge. Every room impeccably decorated in winter white and blue, every surface dusted by a woman paid a fair and living wage with health insurance that covered her entire family.

Skip's mother had been an alcoholic. Richie had paid rent in a tiny room on top of his father's garage.

Carpenter's life was not so goddamned bad.

"You had fun?" She sounded needy, and he tried to give her what she needed.

"They're good people," he said simply. "They had a party last night. The whole soccer team came. Some friends from work too. Mason brought his brother, Dane—you'd like him. Another sweet guy." But Dane had some bite, some edge, maybe because Dane's brain had taken him to some dark places, but Carpenter got dark places. Every chocolate chip cookie and piece of pizza he'd eaten in the last two, three years had taken him deeper into the cave.

"A party?" She brightened. "What did you bring?"

"Sugar cookies and beer," he told her bluntly. "But at least I bought the cookies."

Her entire *demeanor* slumped down, like that artist who drew melting clocks and scissors and things. "Refined sugar?"

"With sprinkles and butter and powdered sugar icing," he confirmed, driving the knife in a little deeper.

"Oh, Clay…."

"People loved them. Thought they were awesome. They sang my praises."

Dane had eaten three of them right off the napkin, practically wriggling in excitement, because apparently he liked store-bought better than the ones he'd made. Carpenter wanted to make him wriggle some more, but that sounded a little dirty, and he wasn't sure what to do with that.

Except… well, wriggling. It was still an important concept.

He turned back to his mother, who looked like she was going to cry, and he felt like shit, but he also felt proud and defiant. It was like when Dane had told him, "Yes, I'm crazy—but that's not what this is about!"

Yes, he was fat, but that's not why he'd bought the extra-good sugar cookies. He'd bought the extra-good sugar cookies because he wanted his friends to be happy, and he'd made them happy. Fuck the world if that wasn't good enough.

"Well," she said slowly, like this next part was going to hurt, "as long as your friends were happy. I'm so glad to hear you've got a social circle."

"I practice soccer on the weekends when we're not playing, Mom," he said in consolation. "Skip is teaching me how to be a better goalie and defender. It's all okay." He didn't tell her about his time in the apartment gym or his efforts at eating a healthy breakfast and lunch, even if his late-night snacking was still a *Game of Thrones* style Olympic event.

She nodded, her eyes wide and shiny. His father—a solid, distinguished-looking man with most of a head of gray hair—had listened to the entire conversation in silence but now put his hand on her shoulder so she could pat it and be brave.

At that moment, his sister walked in, her two kids at her side, and Carpenter had to call it a win.

He thought he was doing okay. Wasn't that important?

"UNCLE CLAY, how come you're so good at Fortnite?" Jason asked as they sat in the game room, side by side.

"'Cause I practice."

"All by yourself? Because that's boring, and I can't get Holly to play with me, and Mom doesn't let me play with anyone over the headset."

Great. Sabrina was a fantastic mom. Just like their own mother.

Carpenter wanted a giant chocolate pie with a dripping beef chaser.

"Well, maybe you and me can play during the week. My friend Dane plays with me, and sometimes my friends Skip and Richie and some of the other guys from the soccer team—"

"You play *soccer*?" Jason said dubiously. "Mom says that for someone your size, running around or exercising wrong can cause injury."

Carpenter's eyes narrowed. "I play keeper," he said. "And sometimes defender. And I'm working on getting smaller." He looked around the room like a comic book spy, and pulled a small box of cherry-flavored chocolates out of the front of his sweater. Skipper had found them on sale and put ribbons around them and given them out as party favors. He'd pressed one on Carpenter as he'd left that morning as a gift to his mother.

Carpenter had taken them but hadn't given them to his mom. He had a feeling they'd be needed somewhere else.

"But not today," he muttered, opening the cellophane with shaking fingers.

"Ooh, is that real chocolate?" Jason asked, lips parted a little. "Mom only lets us have that on our birthdays."

Carpenter gave him three pieces. "Eat up, kid," he said. A part of him was ashamed—*Shame, shame on you, Clay Carpenter, for giving your nephew the same love/hate relationship with food that you have!*

But a part of him was celebrating Jason's three chocolates of freedom. He set aside another three pieces for Holly, Jason's twin, and ate another one himself.

Ah, yes.

Freedom.

Freedom Is Slavery

"GO, UNCLE Clay, go!"

Dane smiled, listening to Clay's nephew cheer him on over the headset. Sometime earlier on in the hour, Holly joined them, but Jason was apparently a really obsessed kid. Or as obsessed as a kid could get, provided he got only two hours of gaming a week. Dane had no problem gaming a little bit with the kids—but he was glad there was a limit.

He settled back into the recliner of his brother's lovely wood-paneled living room and resolved to beat the crap out of Jason so he and Clay could be alone.

Or, alone in cyberspace or whatever. Whatever. Just the intimacy of having Clay to himself, his sexy voice, his kindness. Dane's parents were the sweetest people in the world, but he'd seen firsthand over Christmas that they were getting older. Dane needed his own people, his own support system.

Clay was like patient zero of Dane's happiness virus. Dane needed to catch him.

Clay finished the level, and Jason sighed in disappointment and signed off, while Dane tried not to gloat.

Yeah, kids were fun, but you didn't get to swear in front of them. And since he and Carpenter practiced swearing in a prolific and creative fashion, it was really best saved for after the kids played.

"Nice swath of destruction," he said, watching Clay's character wreak bloody havoc. "Anybody you want to kill?"

"No," Clay muttered. "I mean yes, but I don't want to talk about it. How was decorating your room?"

Dane thought about his newly painted abode and smiled smugly. "Not bad, really. Mason gave me carte blanche, and we both painted and decorated and even laid in hardwood and picked out rugs. It was…." His voice dropped a little, because the gift, his redecorated room, and the gesture, a thing they could do together during Dane's down time that wouldn't stress him out, had meant a lot to him. "You know my brother. Greatest guy in the world."

"Starting to get that, yeah." Clay steered his character into another balletic and bloody campaign, and Dane watched the carnage with a little bit of concern.

"Clay, what's the matter?"

"Dumb shit. I put on weight over Christmas. Me and Skip are gonna work out some this weekend, but…." He made a sound of frustration. "It's all just so fucking irritating. I mean, I cleaned my room two days after Christmas, and you know what? The reason I had so many goddamned clothes was that I had a zillion goddamned sizes. I'm currently two sizes down from my largest, which was right before I started at Tesko, and eight sizes up from my smallest, which was… well, one of those times I bought a suit in college. Don't make me tell you which time; I don't want to talk about it."

Ouch.

There was something… wonky about Carpenter's college degree. Dane had talked earlier about his biological chemistry class, and Clay's questions had been specific and on point, to the level that he actually helped Dane with his homework.

But when Dane had asked him about how a comp sci major had known that shit, Carpenter had shrugged and said he watched a lot of obscure television.

As. If.

Also, a comp sci degree should have seen someone as smart as Clay Carpenter working at Intel, making a shitton of money, or at least more than he was making in the IT department at Tesko.

Dane was intrigued, but he was also not going to pry. Talking about his student loan debt made Carpenter cranky. And while other people got stabby or weepy or even drinky when they had a subject like that, Carpenter got eaty. Dane could give two shits how much he ate or how big his pants were, but when Carpenter got eaty, the bitterness and self-recriminations that followed were… painful.

Just so damned painful.

So no prying about his degree. But maybe he could find out what had made him eaty?

"How's your room look?" Carpenter asked before Dane could settle on a topic.

"I love it. You'll have to come by and see. It's sky blue and cloud white and dark purple."

"Sounds happy," Carpenter said, surprised. "That's probably the greatest thing about owning a house—you can do that shit."

"Yeah. So, I'll come help you clean your room next Friday. Then you come help me make cookies next Saturday."

Carpenter did something complicated with his controller that made Dane totally jealous.

"How in the hell did you do that?"

"Okay, press the *X* button and the right front button and do the thing… you know—yeah, that."

"Damn." Dane did it, and something about his character made the move not nearly as cool. "Okay, so do we have a da—I mean a plan?"

"My apartment needs two days if we're working around my work schedule. And chocolate chip cookies?"

"I figure you'll be so motivated by me coming over to help you that you'll diet all week, even though you don't really need it. And then we'll bake cookies over here so you can see my room and you will be rewarded for all your non-slackitude."

"But when am I going to work out with Skipper?"

"Sunday? Thursday? I don't care! When do you start soccer? Wait, wait—I know the answer to that question."

"Really? How?"

"Because my brother's taking Jefferson golfing Saturday, and the only reason he can do that is because you don't start soccer until the week after that."

Carpenter's character stopped moving, and Carpenter himself made an exasperated sound into the microphone.

"Dammit—you made me do math."

And boom! His character died in an explosion of blood that left Dane unfazed. "You are not bad at math, you big baby. Why'd you stop?"

"Mason and Jefferson are dating?"

"No. They're sporting."

"Heh, heh, heh, heh…."

Dane had to snort. Yeah, when he said it that way…. "No—yes. I have no idea. They're off playing soccer now so Mason doesn't feel too stupid when you guys start in two weeks. And next week—"

"When I'm coming over to make cookies."

"Yeah. They're playing golf. I made the tee time myself." Dane rolled his eyes. Mason woke him up from *his nap in the car* to force Dane to help him with his social agenda, and appeared to show no remorse from it either.

"Okay, fine. I mean it's their life, right? If they want to play games together, that's their gig."

Dane grunted. "Reboot. Yeah, okay, never mind. Let's play *Destiny* instead."

"God you're picky. I need to log off in—"

"Two hours. You promised me until ten." Dane had no compunction about making Carpenter play with him. He didn't find many people he could stand for that long, or who could stand him.

Besides, he'd made a date—or a plan. That was it. He'd made a *plan* to stare into the eyes of the guy whose room he was going to clean.

Wait.

Reverse that.

He was going to clean the room of the guy whose eyes he'd stared into until Carpenter's lips had parted in wonder.

Dane wasn't sure if Carpenter knew this, but he'd *licked* those lips, full and pouty—and Dane had been kissed enough to know what that meant, even if Carpenter was clueless.

So even if no soul-gazing happened during the epic apartment straightening or the chocolate chip cookie feast, Dane had a little faith, some bubbles in his blood, that there *would* be soul-gazing in the future.

"Fine," Carpenter sighed, but without any real reluctance. "Skip and Richie are going to look for their dog at twelve. I can take a walk and shower before I join them."

Dane scowled. "So what you're saying is, you'd totally come over and see my room *today*, but Skip and Richie are more important."

"Yes," Carpenter returned promptly. "Because they wouldn't get pissy and weird over my gross fat ass if I was doing something with you instead."

Dane scowled. "So you prefer not to be chased. This is interesting information, and I need to file it away to use later."

"I'm fat and slow. If you chase me, you'll catch me. I just…." Carpenter's voice dropped, as though he was embarrassed. "Look, Dane, I like you. I'm having loads of fun playing with you, and you want to clean my room, and I've got to tell you, I'm intrigued. But when I started working at Tesko, I was in a really shitty place. And Skipper was… well, Skipper. It took him two years to convince me to play soccer on his team, and he just did it, one chicken sandwich at a time. You've got your brother, and he's great, but part of the reason he's great is that he's a super-big dork and you get to sort of protect him from himself. My sister? She's an oncologist. She took her children to a cancer ward for Thanksgiving so they could volunteer. She thinks I'm the devil because I give them refined sugar, and I'm starting to agree with her. My real family, the family I have to protect from themselves because that's the job I love? That's Skipper for me. Skipper needs friends so bad I had to drive him home from work when he was sick because he got himself stoned on cold medicine. Because besides Richie? He's got nobody else. Nobody. So yeah. I'm pushing my way into their couple time to be the friend who was there when they got their dog. Please don't take that away from me."

Dane sucked in a breath. "Jesus, Carpenter. I was going to be all bitchy and jealous and you had to pull emotional honesty on me. What kind of asshole are you?"

"Apparently I'm the asshole who's going to let you clean my room?"

"Cool. But first, let's start this level again. Seriously, man, you've got to start learning how to give great speeches while your characters are kicking ass." Dane's heart was hammering, and his forehead dripped with sweat. God. This meant a lot to Carpenter, and Dane had almost blown it. He'd almost blown it, and he couldn't remember the last time he'd thrown a fit like that, and Jesus, shouldn't he at least be sleeping with a guy before he let himself get that out of control?

And that brought him up short.

Fuck. Fuck, fuck, fuck, fuck, fuck.

"Clay," he said in a small voice. "Hit Pause. I'll be back in two minutes."

He grabbed the pill calendar from the duffel bag in his room, then went to the cabinet in the kitchen. *Fuck. Fuck, fuck, fuck.* Three days. He had enough extra medication for *three days.* Without even looking at the clock, he took his morning dose, wondering why he'd thought it would be just fine to get back from Mom and Dad's and forget he had to medicate every fucking day.

He ran back to the couch and put on his headset and let out a breath, still shaking.

"What's up?" Clay asked, and his voice wasn't defensive or irritated—it was alert. Like he knew something was wrong.

"Fucking meds," Dane snarled, hands shaking on the remote control. "Goddammit. They don't fucking work if I don't fucking take them. And there I am, screaming like a fucking drama queen at some poor guy who just wanted to play a game. You know what—just, I'll log off now. Just don't worry about it. I'll go flush my head down a toilet until I get my meds leveled out again. Fucking—"

"Stop," Clay said, not so firmly it put Dane's back up, not so gently Dane could ignore him. "You forgot your meds. It happens. Look at my guy. I put a new skin on him just for you."

Dane took a shuddery breath. "Rainbow prom dress," he muttered, half laughing. "Nice. Where'd you find that?"

"I paid a hacker some crypto-currency for a jailbreak," Carpenter said frankly. "That's a highly illegal prom dress you're looking at, and I think it's supposed to get tattered every time I lose life points. Want one?"

Another breath, the pull of the game, the fun, Carpenter's schoolboy illicitness pulling him from the brink of despair.

"Yeah," he rasped. "Send me the deets."

His phone buzzed with a series of directions, and Dane followed them. When he was done, his character sported rainbow-covered body armor, and she looked *fabulous.* In fifteen minutes, he was sucked into the rhythm of the game, the win, the loss, knowing Carpenter's character always had his back.

Mason came in, sweaty and grunty from his time playing soccer with the squirrely little mall rat who had been flirting with him during the Christmas party. He wandered downstairs a few minutes later after showering, and sat, legs gathered under him, on the recliner, more pensive than Dane was used to. Dane signed off to talk to him and to make sure that kid hadn't stolen his wallet or something, and Carpenter waved goodbye on screen and disappeared.

As Dane pulled himself into the real world, he realized it was nearly twelve thirty. Whatever plans Carpenter had with Skip and Richie, he'd canceled them or postponed them until Dane had someone there with him and he could hold his shit together.

Oh Jesus, can I maybe not be so much of a freak to this guy?

"SO," CARPENTER said a week later, face red from either baking cookies or embarrassment. "They're upstairs… now?"

Dane's eyes flickered toward the entrance of the kitchen, which led into the living room, which led to the stairway, which led to Mason's room, where he and Terry Jefferson, oh pretty mall rat of the Harlequin face and squirrel brain, were, oh my God, *having… sex.*

"Well, what was I supposed to do? Tell him no? It's his house! He lives here!"

Carpenter blinked. "No—I mean, you know, roommates gotta deal. I just… we could have gone back to my place, right?"

"Sure," Dane evaded, grabbing the flour from the cupboard. "That was a plan."

"My apartment scared you."

"No, not at all," Dane lied. "But your kitchen's smaller than a gnat's ass." That, at least, was the truth. He'd spent two days helping Carpenter sort the clothes he could fit in now versus the clothes he'd fit into two years ago versus the clothes he was trying to fit into.

The conundrum had been clear.

The clothes he was trying to fit into were from college, and even if Carpenter could get to his goal weight, they'd be out of style and sort of a depressing reminder of college. And Dane wasn't sure that he could wear them even if he *did* reach his goal weight, because he'd seen the musculature of an animal that had lost a great deal of weight, and they were *ripped* because carrying around extra fat was no joke. People were the same. Once Carpenter got enough muscle mass, he would be… well, built. Not tall, but… muscular in the extreme.

So that shit had to go.

And Dane didn't want Carpenter to feel pressured about losing weight or keeping it off. Yes, everybody knew what healthy weight was, but Dane was just so happy to have a *Carpenter* in his life that he didn't want Carpenter to feel shitty about any size that might not make him happy too.

Besides. Everybody backslid and then caught up again. Not being able to fit into your skinny jeans and having no wallowing sweats to fall back on was a bad idea. That sort of thing often just led to entire XL pizzas being delivered to dorm rooms. Dane had been witness.

So, some of that had to stay.

And he didn't have that many clothes in the size he was now.

"We," he'd said on Friday, after Carpenter had gotten off work, "need to go shopping."

Carpenter's dry look in return was not promising. "Let me lose ten more pounds," he said. "That way I'll know it's not a fluke. Besides…." He let out a sigh and flopped onto his bed disconsolately. "I sort of gave away everything I didn't spend on student loans. I'm broke until February."

"You what?" Dane stared at him.

"You know. All those Christmas charities? And I'm like, 'My sister's a cancer doctor, and her kids are little saint children, and my parents are lobbying for a better environment, and I'm a big fat blob of environmental suck, so I should give all my money to charity.' It happens."

Dane gasped at him. "The hell it does!" he managed to say. "Why would you…? How would you even…?" He flailed, the size 4X plaid shirt in his hand flapping like a sail and partially disintegrating because it was one of the old ones. Carpenter was nowhere near this big now. He must have worn this all winter long, three years ago.

"Look, whatever. I just don't have that much money this month."

"But *Carpenter.* Don't you *deserve* anything of your own?"

Carpenter shrugged. "I've got friends. I've got you. It's all good."

Dane's throat worked. "But Clay…." He sat down next to him, hoping Clay's "No boundaries for Dane" rule held. "Clay, how can you not think you deserve more?"

"I've had so much privilege," he said, disheartened. "And I feel like I threw it all away."

Dane swallowed, and his head drifted down to Clay's shoulder. "You didn't throw anything away," he said, his throat sore. "It's not privilege when it makes you feel awful, when it cripples your ability to do good things in the world. Come on, man. Work with me here. You're working like a Trojan on the weight thing. I've only known you two months, and I can see a difference. That much effort at least deserves some clothes, you think?"

"Sure." Carpenter brought his arm up around Dane's shoulder, and Dane wanted to cry. He'd had so many hookups in college. So many boyfriends who'd made him feel somehow lacking. Having Carpenter's arm around his shoulder made him feel so incredibly powerful, so happy that he could help his friend see the best in himself, and yet there was no sex forthcoming.

But that arm, though, weighty and warm and supportive—it meant everything.

That arm around his shoulder was what he was thinking of when Carpenter asked him if the apartment was scary.

Yes, it was scary. The intimacy there had been scary. The potential to fall into the warm embrace of a guy who didn't think he was gay or bi or whatever was scary.

And the fathomless potential for damage Dane could do to their friendship by suggesting or thinking the wrong thing for Clay to do with all those sizes of clothes—that was terrifying.

Dane had never been afraid of roller coasters, but the idea of being locked in a car with a reluctant Carpenter as it hurtled through the ups and downs of both their neuroses was starting to look like the worst idea since someone had come up with those things that dangled you from your seat and whirled upside down.

But that didn't mean that making cookies in Dane's kitchen while his brother was having sex upstairs wasn't a ride completely on its own.

"So, being here and knowing they're having sex up there is *less* frightening than my apartment," Clay said now, as though in clarification.

"Well, I didn't know they would be having sex when I made the date!" Dane argued, because he hadn't even been aware Mason and Terry were anywhere *near* that step in their relationship until Mason had texted him to get the fuck out of the house that morning.

"Yeah," Carpenter agreed, nodding. "It's a little early for that. What is your brother thinking?"

Dane shrugged. "Probably that he's going to get his heart slaughtered. Man, that kid…."

Carpenter sighed and took the flour from him, then measured out six cups of it for the bowl, and at least another cup for flouring the counter… and covering the two of them. The man was definitely not neat! Dane used to think you could just make cookies and that was a thing that would end, but cleaning up this kitchen was going to be an act of divine devotion.

"Jefferson's… he's a good kid," Carpenter said after a moment of coughing as they attempted not to coat the insides of their lungs with glue. "It's… I'm just not sure what a great boyfriend he'll be. He needs training up."

"That's awesome," Dane muttered, getting the eggs. "Because my brother is the *best* at picking them, right?"

"I don't know—how bad was his last boyfriend?"

Dane grunted in disgust. "Well, we came to Sacramento because his last boyfriend was sleeping with his last boss. Because that's just the kind of douchebag who likes to make my brother feel like he's the defective one." God, Dane couldn't get over the losers Mason had dated. At least *Dane's* losers had been of the solid "You don't need a psych eval, baby, if you just smoke another bowl with me!" variety. Drug abusing scumbags were one thing, because they didn't assume they were better than you.

Carpenter snorted. "Poor guy. No wonder he was so nutted up the first time he talked to Skip. All that earnestness just dripping off of Skipper—probably worked like an aphrodisiac."

Dane rolled his eyes. "Yeah, and not just to Mace. You do know half your soccer team has a crush on him, right? It's a wonder *you* don't."

He admitted freely to himself that he was laying out a little bait, seeing if he got a nibble.

He didn't expect Carpenter to swallow the hook.

Clay stopped cracking eggs into the cookie batter and cocked his head, flour-dusted eyelashes moving slowly as he blinked.

They stood close so Dane could hand him ingredients, and as the mixer whirred on the counter between them, Dane could swear he heard Clay's indrawn breath.

"Skipper's not my type," Clay said, a wistful smile on his face. "I was never a sucker for blonds."

Dane couldn't help it—his slowest, flirtiest smile started at his toes. The smile he'd used to seduce his first crush in the tenth grade, the smile he'd used to coax his college boyfriends into threesomes when his manic phases grew into a sexual skin hunger that made him want to scream—*that* was the level of wattage he was aiming at Clay Carpenter. And for the first time in his life, he sweated getting anything back. *Oh God oh please oh God oh please oh please oh please....*

Carpenter arched an eyebrow like he knew *exactly* what Dane was doing, and he reached out to turn off the mixer, which was probably a good idea.

"Do you really think you're the first guy to try to seduce me over chocolate chip cookies?" he asked playfully. "I know what happens next."

Dane's mouth went dry. "What happens next?" he begged.

"We have an amazing kiss," Clay said—and his expression went sad. "And then you never talk to me again, and I'm left alone and confused." He took a step back and turned on the mixer, shrugging. "That would be super depressing. I'd really rather keep seeing you."

"True story?" Dane asked, little chips of his heart flaking into powder.

"True story," Carpenter confirmed. He smiled nostalgically. "The cookies were tremendous, however. I think of kisses with stubble and breathlessness whenever I eat them."

Dane's mouth fell open a little, and he thought of all the time Carpenter talked about chocolate chip cookies. He'd said he wasn't gay—but he hadn't said he wasn't bi.

Which meant he very well could be.

And all this time he'd been craving cookies, what he'd really been craving was a Dane in his life who wouldn't leave him sad and alone.

Dane took in a breath to tell him this, when from upstairs there came a furious pounding sound—like a bed might make as it bounced against the wall as somebody was getting fucked senseless.

The conversation they were having with their eyes changed from yearning to horror in an instant.

Clay took a step backward and looked around. "Vanilla?" he said, although they'd already added it.

"Sugar?" Dane echoed—also in the mix.

"Lemon extract," Carpenter said, blowing Dane's mind, because while it was on the counter, it wasn't in the recipe.

"Sure," Dane told him.

"Almond extract too."

"Why not."

They threw both ingredients into what had been shaping up to be a perfectly normal batch of chocolate chip cookies, as well as what was probably one too many eggs.

And—oh shit!—they'd added the eggs after the flour, and now they needed butter, so that was probably wrong too.

It didn't matter.

They just kept throwing shit into the cookie batter until they got to the chocolate chips, which—thank God—made the mixer louder, as it beat the resulting mixture until it was good and dead. Or blended. Whatever.

When they shut off the mixer to spoon the cookies onto the greased cookie sheets, the sounds overhead were done and the moment was broken. By the time Mason and Terry Jefferson—who looked no less ragged-urchin street-waif than he had the first time Dane had seen him—wandered out, they were bantering like they always did, and that horrifying moment of realizing Dane's brother was getting happily laid was far behind them.

They chatted for about a heartbeat before Jefferson practically bolted out the door and Mason followed to give him a ride to his car. Then it took another fifteen minutes to clean the kitchen.

As they sagged into chairs at the breakfast nook in relief, Clay said the obvious thing.

"You'd think knowing what they were doing would have made me horny," he said. "But it just sort of made me sad. I mean, yeah, part of me's got the chubby going on, but the rest of me is wondering what it must be like to commit to love that fast."

Dane swallowed, not sure whether to apply that sentence to his growing feelings toward Clay or his concern over Mason.

He picked Mason because Clay was too new, too much a hope for the moment.

"You think it's love?" he asked. "Already?"

Clay raised that playful eyebrow, and Dane wanted to smooth it over with his finger. "Did you see the way Mason looked when he handed that kid cookies? And Jefferson's practically feral. I expected him to arch his back and dance sideways when he realized we were both down here. It's like feeding a stray cat. Sometimes that cat comes in and becomes the family pet. Then other times, it bites a chunk out of your thumb and runs off to get hit by a car. I am not sure which way this one's gonna swing, Dane."

Dane groaned. "I can't…. Do you know how much he wants to find Mr. Right? Do you have any idea? He's wanted to be married since he was in eighth grade!" He remembered his mother's fondness for a picture his brother had drawn in middle school. "A husband, a house, and a cat." He grunted. "Why don't we have a cat? I think that's wrong."

Clay tilted his head. "Because in two weeks, you're going to be gone for fourteen hours a day, four days a week, and ten hours a day the other two. You showed me your damned trimester schedule, Dane. You're being responsible here. Don't fuck that up."

Dane buried his face in his hands. Really? He had to be falling for the one guy in the world who saw him as someone who *wouldn't* fuck it up? Where did Clay get that impression? More importantly, did Dane really want him to keep it? Wasn't it easier if he abdicated all responsibility for his actions by playing the Dane's Flaky card until it disintegrated? "Will *you* get a cat?" he begged, and Clay sighed.

"It's a distinct possibility, but I'm waiting for your summer break so you can show me how to deal with it. If I adopted a cat and accidentally killed it by not knowing the secret cat-word, my life would be effectively over."

Dane looked over his hands and rolled his eyes at the dumbass. "There is *no* secret cat-word," he muttered. Great. Carpenter was playing the Carpenter's Stupid card, which apparently canceled out the Dane's Flaky card. Now he knew.

"Yeah, that's what all cat people say. I'm not taking your word for it. It's like these cookies." He took a blissful bite out of the one he'd been waiting to cool down. "Mm. The lemon and almond actually really make this. Anyway, I was good—I ate carrots and chicken and whole grains and protein all week, and this cookie is my reward. You keep your meds steady and take care of yourself all trimester, and I'll get us a cat."

Dane's heart, which had been steadily sinking under Carpenter's solid logic that no sane person would dispute, suddenly perked up.

"Us?" he asked, the memory of that frozen moment in the kitchen resurfacing, Clay's confession that he'd once kissed a boy over chocolate chip cookies and that he'd ended up confused and alone resonating in Dane's heart like a perfect chord in a tuning fork.

"Yes, us," Clay said, taking another bite. "This will be a co-owned cat." He looked at Dane solemnly. "Which means you and I will need to be friends for a good long time."

And Dane got his meaning then.

Friends. They had to be *friends.* Not just lovers—or even lovers. Clay Carpenter valued Dane's *friendship* over Dane's *body.*

And that was sort of a first. Dane had enjoyed having all the sex, as much of the sex as he could possibly manage, plenty of sex and scads of sex. Dane was *the bomb* at putting out.

But between his self-esteem death spirals and his frighteningly manic upswings, *keeping* a lover as a friend hadn't been something he'd done much. He had to admit, part of the reason he wasn't off at this very moment with another student from the veterinary science program was that he didn't want to see what happened to that friendship if they caught Dane having a panic attack in his car like Carpenter had.

It was just so much easier to hook up a few times and then drift apart so that person never got to see you at your worst.

But Carpenter *had* seen him doing that—and he'd *stayed.* Was Dane really ready to risk alienating him as a lover when he was such an *outstanding* friend? But look at him—solid, scruffy, his brown eyes the kindest things Dane had ever seen. Dane wanted to touch all that kindness, thinking it might feed him, soothe his own bitchiness, or at least dilute the solid core of it that existed in Dane's frequently confused heart.

And he also wanted to run his mouth over the back of Clay's car.

"Sure," he said casually, eating half a cookie and leaving the other half for Carpenter to finish off. "We'll be friends forever." He swallowed the cookie and then smiled slyly. "That can mean so very many things."

Clay merely blinked, slowly and—had he known it—catlike.

“It can,” he agreed. “Let’s make sure the things it *does* mean are… healthy.”

“Indulgences can be healthy,” Dane said blithely, taking a swig of milk.

“But they also have to be earned,” Clay responded. He met Dane’s eyes with a steady understanding that told Dane he was fooling nobody.

But that was fine. He didn’t need to fool a soul. He figured it would be good, in this case, if Clay Carpenter knew *exactly* what he was getting himself into.

Breakfast Bar Love

"SURE," CARPENTER said, his hopes for the weekend crashing. "Yeah, Sabrina, I'd love to watch the kids."

"Are you sure?" his sister begged, sounding exhausted. "I know it's a big deal—"

Well, it was, sort of. The week before, Mason had sprained his ankle playing defense, going down like a tall tree in a forest of surprised younger players. Poor guy—his ankle had looked horrible, and the memory of Terry Jefferson running to his rescue in a battered Toyota would stick with the entire team for a long time.

Mason was definitely a Lexus man. Jefferson'd had no idea how outclassed he was, both as a boyfriend and as a knight in shining armor.

But Mason was out for the next few games, which was too bad because he'd actually been visibly improving as the game went on—right up until he'd poked a clump of grass with his toe and rolled his ankle. Anyway, they were short on defenders, which left Clay as a sorely needed relief man, and for the first time in his life, his sister needed help.

She'd driven up from the Bay Area at the beginning of the week because the kids had an inexplicable week off school. She couldn't explain it either. Yeah, she called it President's Week, but it sounded like a scam to Clay. Anyway, she'd been planning to spend the time shopping and doing "very important educational things" with her spawn, but first Clay's mom had gotten sick, and then Sabrina—who swore she had the constitution of an iron-sided ship—had come down with the flu.

The kids had been vaccinated—they seemed to be getting off Scot-free, but Sabrina had nobody to take them that weekend.

Except her baby brother, who had yet to pony up for the family.

"You can get out of work today?" she begged pitifully. "It's not a problem?"

Clay sighed. Unlike Skipper, who would rather die—quite literally—than miss work, Clay didn't mind calling in sick. "No. Not at all. They can crash on the hide-a-bed in my apartment. Do you think they'd mind going to a gamer party? I swear, it's just guys logging into their PS4s and overloading Skipper's internet." Dane was going to be there, and this had been a very big deal for Clay because, well, *Dane* was becoming a very big deal for Clay.

"No smoking, drinking, illicit—" His sister hacked into the phone. "—drug use?"

"Nothing worse than beer," Clay swore.

"Clay—"

"I've promised Skip I'd bring stuff, Brina. It's harmless. Jason and Holly will love it. The guys'll have fun playing with them—I promise. Good people, playing. It'll be great."

He didn't mention soccer the next day because… well, because.

And this way, he could explain to Skipper and Dane personally why he was dodging out when the Holy Church of Soccer seemed to need his pudgy ass on the field.

Skipper's gaming party was, if anything, *better* with the addition of kids and a dog.

Skip and Richie's first choice for a dog, their mutual, oh my God I can't live without him, love-at-first-sight choice of friend and companion for life had been a cross between a wolf and a pony.

Sure, the card had said German Shepherd/American Boxer, but Carpenter had said wolf and pony, and then Richie had remembered that book they'd all read in the eighth grade and said, "We could call him Ponyboy, right, Skip?" And that was it. They were taking the gigantic thing home.

He was barely three months old, and he already looked bigger than Richie. But when Carpenter brought the kids over, Skip had turned on the back-porch lights, and Jason and Holly spent two hours outside in the cold, throwing that puppy the stick, the toy, and the ball while Dane egged them on. Yeah, it wasn't technically gaming at that point, but Skip's house was always super crowded at the beginning, while the people who only stopped by because it was Skip and they loved him ate potato chips. Once those people cleared out, there was room for Holly and Jason in the bedroom, where they excitedly played with the grown-ups in the front room, who were trying desperately to temper their language.

"So, you really can't make the game tomorrow?" Dane asked as they waited their turn on the controller. "I mean, Mason's going to cheer on the troops—"

"How's his ankle?" Carpenter asked. "Seriously, it still looks super painful when we see him at work."

Dane grimaced. "Super painful. Some guys, they roll an ankle and they get back up and play the game. My brother? It takes him out for a *month.*"

"I am aware," Skip said dryly, wandering in from checking on the kids. "You sure you won't come play with us? I was getting used to having subs on the field."

Dane shook his head loftily, but Clay could see the exhaustion bruising his eyes. He'd started school again that week, and had complained of insomnia as well. Clay had poked delicately at the "Are you taking your meds" wound, and the response had been… evasive.

"I shall be watching and evaluating from the corner," Dane said with a yawn. "But you people all enjoy your game."

He said it with that unconscious Bay Area snobbery that seemed to be so deeply ingrained, Carpenter wasn't sure he saw it when it came out. In Dane's case, it was charming, but Carpenter was aware that there were times it wasn't.

Watching Dane freak out over his brother's boyfriend's crappy Toyota was funny. Listening to him talk to Skip about getting a "real" degree so he could teach was not.

"What?" Dane asked when Skip wandered away from the conversation.

"He worked his ass off for that piece of paper on his cubicle," Carpenter said quietly. "I know it's not UC Davis or UCLA, but when you don't grow up with much, having a job that pays health and dental is living the dream."

Dane sucked in a breath. "I'm an idiot," he muttered savagely, surprising Carpenter. "A fucking moron. Jesus, you'd think I could learn to watch my fucking mouth."

And there—right there—was the answer as to whether or not Dane was taking his meds.

"Do you have your meds with you?" Clay asked, a little shocked at the authority in his voice.

Dane winced. "No. No, dammit—they're at home in my backpack. I sort of spaced out and almost didn't get here on time."

Carpenter cocked his head. "There's an on time to a gaming party?"

"I didn't want to be late!" Dane gave a tired smile. "It's a social event. I don't do many of these, and now you see why."

"You're fine," Carpenter soothed. "But you only really crank on yourself when your chemicals are offline. You'll take some when you get home, okay? I'll call you up and remind you."

Dane nodded, his eyes going wide and limpid, and his whole body seemed to sag. He'd been a bundle of energy with the kids, throwing the ball for the dog, making up dumb games to play. Carpenter had needed to sit on one of the creaky patio chairs not made for someone his size and watch them after an hour because his feet hurt and his back hurt and he could only do so much random running before his oversized body asked what the point was.

"I'm sorry," Dane said, sounding tearful now. "I'm sorry. I should just go. I probably fucked everything up with your friend and—"

Carpenter wrapped an arm around Dane's shoulders and squeezed. "Don't go," he begged softly. "Not yet. Come on. We're almost up, and we can kick everyone's ass at this game. Don't you want to issue a righteous ass-kicking? I mean, I'm stuck with the kids tomorrow, so no game for me—"

"And why is that again?" Dane snapped, recrimination in his voice.

Carpenter sighed. "Man, those kids are a year away from competition soccer. Sabrina is going to have to *hire* someone to haul them up and down the state every weekend for half the year so they can play this game. Do you think I want them to see me lugging my fat ass around the goalie box and getting destroyed by Young Accountants in Love?"

"Is that who you're playing tomorrow?" Dane sounded confused.

"No, their name is the Starbursts, but I know this team. There's the art student team, the team that's all nurses, and this one started at an accounting firm. So seventy percent of them are accountants, and they all usually run off after the game to be with their girlfriends."

Dane giggled manically. "Young Accountants in Love—much better than the Starbursts, I get it."

Oh boy. "Yeah, it's hilarious. Anyway, I'd just as soon the kids respect me in the morning. So we'll be doing something like going to the zoo and then maybe a Chuck E. Cheese, because I'm betting good money neither of them has seen fake pizza or fake giant rats before."

Dane snickered, and then Richie called out that they were up, and the conversation was dropped. Dane left about an hour later, after the two of them did, indeed, issue a righteous ass-kicking, and Carpenter thought it was all good. He took the kids to his apartment, so grateful for Dane's help cleaning it, because to his niece and nephew, he looked like a responsible, if boring, adult.

"Why are your walls all blank?" Holly asked, her light body hardly making a creak on the hide-a-bed couch that would have buckled under Carpenter's weight. Carpenter smiled weakly at her and resisted the urge to smooth her mouse-brown hair off her forehead. She was going to grow up to be a stunning woman, with an elegant face and long, lithe body like her mother. But like Sabrina, she was a plain, average child. Jason was the same, but his head was ginormous. It grew more and more proportional the older he got, but

Clay had actually looked at his own childhood pictures to make sure *he* hadn't been wandering around with a noggin like that and nobody had told him.

And he had, sort of. It would be great if that gave Jason hope, but unless Clay could get his shit together, the only hope Jason would have was to be a fat bastard with no cat, no boy—er, girlfriend, and no shit on his wall.

"Maybe we can go out and get something tomorrow," he promised. "I was going to do the zoo—"

"Sacramento's zoo is dumb," Jason said, and it was funny. Clay heard Dane's entitlement in that pronouncement. "San Francisco's is better, San Jose's is better, San Diego's is better…." He yawned. "I'd rather go shopping."

Clay closed his eyes for a second and wondered if his sister would mind just forking over her credit card. "Sure," he said, not sure where pride ended and practicality began. "We've got the Galleria nearby. Let's see what we can do."

He got them settled, then showered and crawled into his own bed, looking around his blank walls with a stunning realization—his apartment sucked.

Not because it was a bad place. It was an average apartment in an average neighborhood in an average Sacramento suburb. Apartments like his were everywhere, and this one changed the carpet with every long-term resident and repainted the walls.

But he'd bought his bedding and his bed right out of school, and his couch had been a secondhand freebie from a friend of his last girlfriend.

And his walls were blank.

It was like he'd gone through college, and postcollege rebellion, and then this weird phase where he worked in the IT department and pretended this was the end of his ambition in life… and had forgotten to establish an identity.

Which was a lie, sort of. He knew who he was now, right?

He was Skip's friend and Dane's friend. He was a guy who tried to do the right thing. He was a guy who hadn't given up on himself or the world. He just failed a lot and kept trying until he succeeded.

He loved video games and he was starting to like soccer, and he had friends and his family didn't suck *too* much, and he would go out of his way to help his sister with her kids. He brought food to all the job functions, and he worked out with Skipper so he didn't let the soccer guys down, and he was really, really worried about his friend Dane, who had amazing brown eyes and sort of a goofy, pure smile.

He was bummed they weren't going to the zoo—he liked seeing animals. He could put animals on the wall. He loved anime; everything from *Mob Psycho 100* to *My Hero Academia* to *Castlevania* could go up on his wall. He even loved Disney/Pixar and DreamWorks movies. He *was* the Kung-Fu Panda, right down to that thing the panda did when he pulled up his pants from the back because his fat ass kept jiggling them down.

He could have this place in wall-to-wall posters, prints, and tchotchkes, things he loved to look at, loved to identify with, in one shopping trip.

Hell, he was paying off his student loans in leaps and bounds. His credit was *pristine.*

He could actually afford to… to treat himself with something besides chocolate chip cookies. He thought wistfully of the game he was missing tomorrow. He could have grabbed Dane right afterward and taken him along. Dane had been so… so happy playing with the kids. Well, happy and a bit manic, as though on an upswing, which worried Carpenter because he understood how mental illness worked. He knew that messing with medication the way Dane had been doing had consequences.

Dane hadn't been worried about whether what he said was right or not today. He hadn't been concerned with status, with what he *should* like or what he *should* be. Dane's world had been narrowed to the ball, the dog, and the two kids running around shouting, "Here, dragon, go get the fair maiden *now*!"

Maybe he'd text Dane in the morning and ask if they could hang out after the game.

His chest actually hurt with the thought of bringing Dane along to help him decorate his place. He *yearned* for Dane's approval and feedback.

How weird was that?

The last thing he expected was Mason's frantic phone call in the morning *begging* him to come play.

"NICE SAVE!" Skipper called from across the field, and Carpenter gave him a wave. Of course, it was a nice save. Carpenter had let three in already, so *any* save was a nice save.

"No, seriously," Menendez said as they took their position—close to the goal box because fucking Jefferson wasn't playing the ball like he should. Goddammit, he had three forwards. Could he not pass the ball to one of them before the other side stole it? "You're getting really good."

Aw, that was sweet. "Thanks," Carpenter grunted. "We really miss Mason today, though."

Mason was sitting, ankle elevated, on a camp chair next to Dane and the kids. Dane's eyes were shadowed, and when they weren't cheering, his face fell into pensive, saturnine lines. Carpenter would have called it resting bitch face, but on Dane, it looked more like he was in pain.

Menendez drew in a deep breath and nodded. There were no defender subs without Mason. Having Carpenter there gave them just enough guys to have Richie sub in for the midfielders and forwards. All the defenders were just flat-out gassed.

"If you could maybe keep the big goombah healthy so he could play with us, I think we might actually start winning. Shit—heads up!"

Oh my God. All the young accountants were charging forward! Hadn't they left *any* players for defense, or were they all convinced that Jefferson would tie up the ball again so they'd have time to set up? *Shit*!

Carpenter dove for the ball and caught it in the chest, then scrambled up in a haze of kicking cleats and shin guards to charge forward and dropkick it. It was a risky move—three months earlier, just getting to his feet without help would have been an adrenaline-fueled feat of strength. But he was pissed, and he was worried about Dane. And his sister's kids were watching him play, and dammit, he'd better not screw this up!

The ball went sailing across the field, past Jefferson, thank God, and straight to Richie, who turned like a rocket and took it in for their second and last goal. The Scorpions all hooted and hollered and the young accountants glared, and for a moment, Carpenter felt like maybe, just maybe, the day wouldn't end as badly as it started.

Because Mason had been *begging* him to come out to the game. He'd called Carpenter Dane's "carrot" to get him out of bed and past his death spiral. And then, in his agitation, and probably because he was Mason and he just couldn't manage a conversation without putting his foot in his mouth, he'd said, "And stop complaining about being fat! He loves you, and it hurts him to hear you beat on yourself!"

And Carpenter had simply frozen.

Because for a moment, he heard, "My brother loves you and wants to be with you, and maybe you could have a relationship with someone who doesn't have somewhere better to be!" And then he remembered that there were all sorts of love, and Mason and Dane seemed to be all about emotional health, so he'd said, "Of course, I love him too."

Because you loved your friends, right?

You loved your friends and wanted to impress your friends and dreamed about your friends and their slightly crooked teeth and their dreamy brown eyes and the way, sometimes, when they stood really close, it felt like their chests were made of magnets and the world had no air.

So yes, Carpenter could say he loved Dane.

Because that covered all manner of sins, didn't it?

But the thing was, however he loved Dane, he really *did* love him. And the idea of him curled up in bed, unable to even get up because he wasn't going to see Carpenter that day, hurt in myriad, unexpected ways.

Dane was the friend and companion Carpenter had always dreamed about. He was like Rebecca or Trisha, but he didn't make secret plans to burn Carpenter's gaming system or wait for Carpenter's lack of décor to dawn on *Carpenter* before making it an issue.

And Dane was fragile. Carpenter had to make sure Dane didn't death spiral in his own head. But he had to do that while he made sure he didn't eat a dozen donuts a day because he was stressing about Dane's internal death spiral, and dammit, he wasn't strong enough to do this and he really wanted some fucking donuts!

He looked over to where Dane was whistling for the team, both index fingers in his mouth like a New Yorker hailing a cab.

"Heads up!" Menendez shouted, and Clay put his head back in the game. Fuck donuts—he'd had a protein bar, and he really did need to get over himself and grow up.

One more goal got through—in what felt like a thousand tries. Carpenter would have been embarrassed by how sore he was, but the entire defense line was out of breath and peevish with the beating they'd just received.

Thank God the Young Accountants all had girlfriends or wives or something to get to, because they didn't even hang around to gloat—or console, as the Young Artists in Angst often did. Their team name was The Picassos, but Young Artists in Angst was such a better summary of that group of assholes.

The best part of the game was the huddling around Mason's car, drinking hot coffee and explaining to Jefferson that he needed to see an actual soccer game so he knew how he was fucking up.

"So what's the plan?" Dane asked quietly, as Holly and Jason took one of Skipper's practice balls and passed it back and forth, remarking in awe at how much heavier a size five was than a size three.

"Well, first I go shower, because dude!"

"Oh yeah. So rank." Dane nodded enthusiastically, and Carpenter stuck out his tongue.

"Anyway, after that, I need to check my phone. I told the kids we'd visit the mall, but my mom's feeling better, and my sister thinks I'm teaching her children how to sacrifice live chickens and small people, so maybe we should hit the Galleria and then go visit my folks. My mom will feed you healthy stuff, my sister will make you feel bad about your life and your career goal just by being so far beyond perfect, it would take a million years for the light from perfection to so much as give her a freckle. It'll be great."

"You're perfect," Dane said passionately. "If they don't like you, they can kiss my scrawny crazy ass!"

Carpenter forced a chuckle. "As much as I'd like to see that, maybe we just concentrate on occupying the rug rats and…." He swallowed and wished for donuts. "Making sure you stay on your meds."

Dane closed his eyes for a moment, raising his face to the sun. "Yeah. Sure," he said. "Do you have any idea how much it sucks to be forced to do something *every day*? Other people don't have to regulate their brain chemistry with an entire fucking pharmacy. But if I stray so much as a centimeter away from the pill bottle, I'm fucked!"

"Yeah, but you don't have to remember *not* to eat donuts by the dozen, Dane, so I think we're gonna call it a draw."

Dane blinked, and Carpenter glared back at him, and someone on the team—Thomas, maybe?—was asking Mason if he could really get them tickets to a Republic game.

Dane let out a breath and apparently decided to call it a truce. "So, should we all go in the spring?" he called out, and Mason nodded happily, the hero of the entire soccer team. And as far as Carpenter was concerned, it couldn't have happened to a nicer guy.

Later they loaded themselves into his old Ford SUV, and Carpenter ignored Holly and Jason's whines about why he couldn't own a car that had an entertainment system and a charging station on every armrest, while Dane asked them who could win the most games of Simon's Cat between the field and Uncle Clay's house.

That did it—the competitive instinct gene that Carpenter could have sworn had skipped his body entirely kicked in, and the kids were silent and locked into their own game, and he and Dane could talk.

"Thanks for coming with me today," he said, meaning it. "You and the kids get along so well. I was going to text you about getting together after the game anyway—" Shit. How much did Dane know?

"But my brother called you first." Dane sighed, tilting his head back with his eyes closed. "It's funny how people think he's so bad socially, but he sure did have *my* number, didn't he?"

"What happened?" Clay asked quietly.

"You were right, you know," Dane murmured. "About Skipper? About telling him that when he went to a 'real' school, he'd see how tough things are. I was being an asshole—"

"A snob," Clay corrected. "And not on purpose."

"A bitchy, whiny, entitled white guy—"

"No, because that guy wouldn't be in my car right now for an exciting day of babysitting and visiting my parents. Look, man, we're all works in progress. It rolled right off Skip's back, and you're obviously thinking about things differently. You have worked on yourself and made progress. Ding! You get some time off the hook. Okay?"

Dane let out a small sound. "You know what? You need to meet my parents. It's frightening how much you're like them. They do that too."

"Do what?"

"Make me feel like… like I was human. Not a freak. Not even a screwup. Just a person who made a mistake."

Carpenter breathed out carefully. "Well, I'm glad," he said, after a moment. "I'm… that's a good talent. That's…. My parents—maybe it's just me. Maybe it's not them. Maybe I just take everything the wrong way, you know? But they mean well. And if I turned out okay enough to make you feel better, then they didn't screw up entirely."

"They did really good," Dane said, and he set his hand on Carpenter's knee and squeezed. Carpenter's breath stopped entirely, and he was lucky he didn't wreck the car.

That hand on his knee was everything. It was lightning and thunder. It was heavy breathing and promises in the dark. It was a dozen donuts and steak and potatoes and that proud feeling that went with knowing you hadn't eaten any bad things and you felt just fine.

It was Dane trusting him to do what was best and his complete fear that what was best for Dane wasn't going to be a whole lot of fun for Clay Alexander Carpenter.

But when Dane shifted to move his hand, Clay put his hand on top of it and squeezed back.

To Touch a Star

"BUT WHY can't I get a new system?" Jason complained, and Dane rolled his eyes.

"Nice try, kid. But I'm pretty sure your mother would throttle your uncle Clay if he sprang for that much green."

Jason and Holly had been fun—kid fun, "Oooh, let's ride the carousel and look at the stuffed animals" fun—but they were tired and hungry, and Clay was up at the front of the store buying them both a giant jigsaw puzzle, of all things, because he'd loved them as a kid and thought it would be fun for them all to put one together.

Dane was looking forward to spending an afternoon at Clay's parents' house, doing just that, but first Clay had to wade through the line with the bored-looking salesgirl who was taking her sweet-ass time, and Dane had to entertain Jason and Holly for just five to ten more minutes without losing his shit.

"Well, Mom says if he'd get off his fat ass and get a real job, he'd have plenty of money," Holly parroted, and Dane had to breathe through the red that filled his vision.

"Holly," Jason whispered, "we're not supposed to say that word."

"Ass?" Holly asked, suddenly sounding seven again and not thirty-five.

"Fat. Mom says it's not nice."

"But why do she and Grandma use it when they're talking about Uncle Clay?" Holly asked, legitimately confused.

"Because they're judgy bitches who do not appreciate your uncle for the awesome guy he is," Dane retorted acidly. He took a deep breath. "And if you tell them I said that, I'll tell them you're listening when you shouldn't be and you're repeating things like 'fat' and 'ass' when you're talking about the man who just took you shopping on his limited budget for stuffed toys and big containers full of jelly beans that he's not going to get to eat."

Jason and Holly both nodded, their faces burning with shame.

"Okay, Dane," Jason said. "We're sorry."

"*I'm* sorry," Holly asserted. "I'm the one who said it. You forget," she said, matter-of-fact.

"Forget what?" Jason asked.

"That grown-ups aren't always right. Mom told me that once when Dad lost his temper. He doesn't do it often, but when he does, we all just hide in our rooms, and then it goes away and it's all good. He just yells, that's all. Mostly at the dishwasher or the garbage disposal or the toilet backing up. Not at people."

Dane found himself smiling and wondered if he could forgive Clay's sister for the "get off his fat ass" remark after all. Maybe.

He would need to meet her first.

Clay finally got to the front of the line and smiled at the salesgirl. Dane watched her expression go from bored exhaustion to pert, "Oh my God, let me help the nice guy with the scruffy chin!" in about two seconds, and he wanted to growl. The really hysterical thing was that Clay thought he wasn't attractive. He had no idea—none—what being accessible and kind could do for someone having a crap day.

It had certainly become the center of *Dane's* world, and Dane hated that, at this moment, he had to play the "Dane's Flaky" card to spend time with him, and not the "Dane is a responsible adult who can pick his friends and develop a decent relationship" card instead.

The girl practically slobbered over herself, and Clay walked away with the big jigsaw puzzle and two smaller ones for no extra cost on some sort of buying plan that he'd sworn he'd never use, but she'd waved that off, right? Because he was *nice* and he'd made her *laugh*, and Dane would *eat her spleen* if she put her hand on his arm one more damned time.

"She was really nice," Carpenter said. "Look, guys, you have your own puzzles to work on, and me and Dane can start that one."

"Why can't you finish it? You can stay the rest of the weekend, can't you?"

"Dane has to be home tonight," Clay said, looking at Dane, who nodded soberly, the dose of meds in his pocket weighing on his soul. Yes. Given what a complete asshole he'd been to his brother that morning—and what he recognized of his mood, now that it had passed—he needed to go to sleep, well medicated, in his own bed, and wake up and take his medicine with breakfast immediately.

And given that Mason was probably engaged in wild animal sex with his squirrely boyfriend, swollen ankle and all, even as they left the Galleria, the odds of Dane wanting to bring Clay home, even to play video games, were less than nil.

Clay's discomfort the last time had put the kibosh on that, and Dane was just so grateful for him right now. Watching him muddle his way through uncledom with minimum cash and maximum good will was so… so *fulfilling*. Like beef stew for his hungry soul.

"Can we get food, Uncle Clay?" Holly begged like the little mind reader she was. "You let us get things like In-N-Out, and Mom never does."

Clay sighed and sent an apologetic look at Dane. Dane took pity on him.

"Yeah," he said brightly. "I think your uncle Clay has worked really hard on being healthy all week. Maybe we'll have to skip the cheese and special sauce, but In-N-Out sounds just fine."

"I really shouldn't," Clay said with a sigh as they cruised toward the In-N-Out near Fairway.

"I'm starving," Dane lied. "And your sister would probably not appreciate it if we brought them home hungry."

"They have the weekend maid there," Clay said absently. "She usually does snacks and lunch for the kids."

Dane squeezed his eyes shut. "The weekend maid?"

Clay pulled into the parking lot and took the end of a seriously long line. "You can't be weird about the house," he said. "Or the money. Skipper almost didn't come in. I had to talk him off the ledge to get him to even get out of the car. The house is big. The folks are rich. It's embarrassing, okay? Especially after you've seen my dinky apartment."

"What does your dinky apartment have to do with your parents' money?" Dane asked, feeling as confused as Holly had been.

Clay just rolled his eyes. "Whatever."

"And your apartment will look much better with the prints we just bought. That store had some great stuff."

Dane had taken the kids to get cookies while Clay had schlepped the posters and frames out to his SUV. That print store had been fun too. Clay had allowed the kids to pick out one each, and they'd gone for Disney/Pixar for the living room. Dane had picked a Japanese-style print of the ocean for the bathroom, and Clay had picked one garden print for the kitchen and a couple of ocean life for his bedroom.

"Still small," he said. "Still working a nowhere job. But I like the job. I have friends through there. I just… I'm plenty happy with my life until I see it through their eyes, you know?"

"How about through my eyes?" Dane demanded, hating the dejection. "I like your life too."

Clay gave him a grin as he pulled up to order. "Yeah, but you and Skip and your big dorky brother are some of the things I like about my life, so I'm not sure if it's fair you get a say."

Dane grinned back and let him order, then asked for his to go without sauce too, just so Clay didn't feel bad. He was fed, watered, pleasantly tired from a busy morning, and in a decent mood when Clay got him to his ginormous fucking castle of a house, and that was probably a wise move.

Because Dane wanted to kill Clay's sister in about two and a half minutes.

THE MAID seemed nice. Sixtyish, as colorless as water, with eyes as bored as the salesgirl's had been, she brightened up a little when she spotted Clay and the kids on the doorstep.

"Come on in," she said, ushering them in. "Kids, have you eaten? I just baked some apple pastries."

"Yes!" Jason pumped his arms. "I mean, no, Bridget, we just ate, and apple pastry would be much appreciated." He smiled winningly, and Holly did the same thing at his side. Bridget laughed.

"Clay? Would you and your friend like some apple pastry?"

"I'd love some," Dane said quickly, knowing Clay would eat to keep him company.

"But first we should go check on Sabrina," Clay said. "We'll be down in a minute."

"Of course. She and your mother are in the upstairs sitting room."

"Watching old TV?" Clay said, his mouth twitching.

"*Frasier*, of course."

"Of course."

Clay led Dane through a daunting downstairs foyer. Nothing so ostentatious as crystal chandeliers, but there *were* long, elegant hanging light fixtures that illuminated the entrance to the house. To the right sat a staircase that led up to a balcony, so anyone emerging from the bedrooms on the second floor could look over to the front entrance. And there was a fresco of swans painted on the wall behind the railing, in silver, gray, pale pink, and sage green.

"Damn, boy," Dane muttered.

In response, he could hear Clay's actual swallow. "The painting is a new thing," he murmured. "And we really did have chandeliers when I was a kid. Mom said they were showy."

Dane snickered. "This is still some flash. You grew up with this?" Clay had grown up with all of this…and still had to pay student loans? Dane wondered about that. He and Mason had college funds. It was true that his had long since dried up and blown away, but it was funny how Clay could feel so bad about going to college and getting a mysterious degree, when his parents could afford a small fiefdom on the hill.

"I don't want to talk about it."

"But why is it a bad thing?"

Clay grunted. "What was your house like?"

Dane had to laugh. "Small. Housing costs on the Bay Area peninsula are pretty high, so a teeny post-WWII house is worth nearly a million dollars. Mason and I had to share a bed—he snores like a band saw. But Mom kept it comfortable, a little cluttered. There wasn't much to clean, but she liked to be able to walk through it easily. They have this little postage stamp garden in the backyard—they both go out on the weekends and do things like crumple newspaper in pots to catch earwigs and individually mulch every chrysanthemum. Every two years they repaint the front—super-bright colors—and then wait for the neighborhood association to complain. It's one of their favorite games."

Clay chuckled and bit his lip. "Sounds perfect," he said softly.

"What's this one like?" Dane asked, feeling for the thing that Clay wouldn't say.

"Perfect." He pulled his lips in and looked around, and Dane noticed there wasn't a speck of dust anywhere. Yeah, the tiny house on the peninsula was cluttered, but it was friendly clutter. Sure, Dane and Mason had needed to share a bedroom, but they'd also talked almost every night until Mason went away to school. Mason had gotten in trouble a lot in school, not because he was a bad person, but because his mouth tended to say the one thing that would freak teachers and authority figures out the most. Dane had heard every detail about every teacher conference since he was old enough to pat Mason on the back and say, "It's okay. *I* don't think you're a freak," and Mason had been preciously grateful. They'd both known those were the days their mom spiked her Kool-Aid with a little bit of vodka, and maybe forgot the greens with dinner.

Not perfect.

But lovely.

"Perfect is hard," Dane said, realizing it for the first time. It was a lesson he should probably take to heart because he got locked in his head so often obsessing about the small shit. Maybe he needed to remember that being a good person was better than being perfect.

Clay shrugged. "You just gotta try harder," he said, and from the tone of his voice, Dane couldn't tell if he understood that was a lie—and a painful one—or not.

At that point, Clay led him to a partially opened door, where he knocked softly. "Everyone dressed?" he asked. "I'm bringing a friend."

"What's she—oh, Clay! A man?"

Clay's sister, Sabrina, was a midsized woman in her early thirties, pretty with an elegant oval for a face and Clay's big brown eyes. She looked as though she'd been sick—her chestnut hair was back in a ponytail, she was pale, and she was wearing a comfortably fitting sweat suit in navy, but she wasn't lounging in exhaustion, as Dane would have been. Instead, she was sitting upright in an overstuffed chair, her shoulders back in perfect posture as she used a laptop on a portable desk.

"He's my friend," Clay said, keeping his voice mild.

Sabrina grabbed the remote control and hit Pause. "Does Mom know you brought your friend home?"

"I thought she was in here where I was going to tell her," Clay said, stepping fully into the room. "Weren't you guys bonding over old television?"

"We did for an hour, but we both have jobs, Clay. We can't all take a whole sick day off, you know?"

"I took it off to watch your children, Brina. Give me a break."

She closed her eyes, probably to keep from rolling them, and nodded. "You're right. I'm… I wish I could just curl up and die, honestly." She gave a small, almost humanizing smile. "Mom is in her study, finishing some work for Monday. Apparently, she's meeting with an environmental committee and she wants to be ready."

"Okay. Well, we'll be downstairs with the kids if you need us."

"Aren't you going to introduce me to your buddy?"

Buddy? On impulse, Dane reached down and grabbed Carpenter's hand.

Clay looked at their twined fingers in mild surprise, and then rolled his eyes.

But he didn't let go.

"Brina, this is my friend Dane. He's a gamer with a science degree, going to vet school. You guys should talk sometime about the difference between dogs and people."

"So should you," she snapped. "You've got the same—"

"I'm gonna go find Mom." He tugged on Dane's hand and started toward the door, but Brina shook her head to stop him.

"How are the kids?"

"Well, they might need some help scrubbing the glue from the duct tape off their mouths," Clay said, mouth quirking at the sides. "And they both have bruises on their knees from being locked up in the trunk of Terry Jefferson's Toyota. Oh, and Jason's eyes were rolling back in his head—I think it was a sugar coma. He'll be okay as long as he doesn't foam at the mouth and seize."

"That's not funny," Sabrina said, and she sounded legitimately angry.

"That's *hilarious*!" Dane contradicted. "He spoiled those kids rotten! Do you know we're committed to doing jigsaw puzzles with your charming little… rug rats on Clay's dime?" God. Not even a thank-you?

Sabrina stopped short, and her eyes narrowed on their twined hands. "New phase, Clay? Is this like the pizza parlor job?"

Clay used his free hand to pinch the bridge of his nose, and Dane had the wistful thought that if he could hold Clay's hand all the time, he might be a little better about letting go of it. "Sabrina, please be kind to my friend, who sat with your kids while I played soccer today. He did both of us a solid."

She took a deep breath. "You're right. I just… you know, wish you'd take my parental guidelines seriously—"

"Clay, could you do me a favor," Dane said, using his best "I will blow you in the future" voice, even though Clay could not possibly know what delights that tone usually promised.

"Sure," Clay said, obviously excited to get out of this room. It wasn't a bad room—cream Berber carpeting, off-white comfortable furniture, a big-screen television, and some lavender-colored art—it was a very… tranquil place to chill. Not exciting, though, not to Clay with his love of bright colors and Disney prints and bold purple sunsets.

The room was perfect. When nothing about Clay was perfect… except everything.

"Could you go downstairs and see if Bridget has some chocolate milk or something similar?" He had the extra pink pill for the really bad days, and he had a feeling he was going to need that.

"Will almond milk do?" Clay asked. "Mom doesn't like keeping dairy in the house."

Dane nodded. Not his favorite, but not a bad choice. "Yeah. Could you go get me a glass of that? I'll be down in a sec."

"Sure." Clay smiled willingly, because he was that guy. The guy who would let Dane grab his hand and not yank it away, the guy who would go fetch him chocolate milk on a dime. "I'll find Mom on the way down. I wanted you guys to meet."

Of course he did. Well, they were both sort of mama's boys, even if Clay's relationship was a tad more problematic. "Sure. I won't be long."

Clay left, closing the door behind him, and Dane turned to Clay's sister and decided to make an enemy.

"Are you aware that your daughter heard you talk to your mother about Clay—and I quote—'getting off his fat ass and doing something'?"

Sabrina's eyes got big, and she swallowed abruptly. "Oh God, did he hear—"

"No, I did. I just wanted you to know that whatever… contempt you think you're hiding? You're not. And your brother's a good guy. The best. He called in sick to a job he likes, and he almost didn't play soccer just so he could watch your kids because he feels some sort of… I don't know, misplaced loyalty because you didn't flush his head down the toilet and give him wedgies in junior high. But I don't have any of that. And I need you to know that if you don't appreciate your brother, I do. His friends and coworkers sure as hell do, and you should maybe stop fretting about how Clay is dealing with your kids and start worrying about how you are."

He took a deep breath. Wow. He needed that pink pill more than he thought. Except he didn't feel manic or depressed or on any sort of mood swing. He just felt legitimately hurt and angry for the guy currently trying to figure out if there was chocolate almond milk somewhere in this palace.

"I'm sorry," she said, looking altogether wretched. "I'll—that's terrible. My children shouldn't have heard that. That wasn't appropriate—"

"It was bitchy as hell," Dane snarled. "And speaking of? Tell your kids to lay off the nutrition lectures. The next time they bitch at him for eating a protein bar, he's going to go for the donut box. And it's not that I give a crap if he eats a dozen donuts in your honor, but he'll feel awful about it when he's done, and that's not fair to *him.*"

She gasped. "Who are you to come here and tell me how to treat my family—"

"Lady, I'm the guy who's spent two days helping your brother watch your kids. And they're great. They're great kids. But they're not going to be, with you as an example."

He saw her huff a breath in outrage, and he rolled his eyes. "Yeah I know. I'm a terrible mean man and you're a frickin' saint—"

"I never said that." She crossed her arms defensively.

"No, but your brother thinks so—and your kids are judgy as hell, which is the kind of kids that saints raise. All I'm saying is that your brother's a good guy. The best. And he deserves better than to have a family look down on him because he had a passing fling with pizza and he's still repairing the damage."

"That's not the—"

"Or that he doesn't make enough money. Think about that. You have essentially tried to shame your brother because of his weight, which *does* make you a horrible person, and for his job, which makes you a mildly awful one. And he thinks you walk on water. How do you feel now?"

She swallowed. "Awful," she confessed. "Do my parents know he's bi?"

Dane's mouth twisted. "He barely knows. So maybe, if you really want to make up for being a flaming bitch, you can keep that one little detail to yourself." Not because Dane was ashamed, but because he had this sudden sense that Carpenter really *was* the odd duck out in his own family.

To his surprise, she nodded. "Thank you," she murmured, "for helping him with them. It…." She wiped her eyes on her sweatshirt, like a human being, and he felt another reluctant tug of sympathy. "It was kind."

"I was happy to do it," he said. "I'd love to help, anytime I'm free. And that's the truth." He really did like kids—even hers.

Her mouth pursed in at the sides. "Apparently so. You don't seem particularly afraid of the truth."

Dane grimaced. "Yeah, well, I'm very protective of your brother. I'll babysit for free, just don't hurt him."

"Understood," she said, and she looked exhausted, so he took that as his cue and left her there, shutting the door quietly behind him.

He wasn't sure if that was going to do any good—or any harm—but he knew it made *him* feel better.

An apple pastry and almond milk wasn't a bad combination. The kids were legit tired and buzzed after the morning, so doing the jigsaw puzzles afterward wasn't a bad thing—it calmed them down, made them Zen, gave them a mental reboot. They set up in the living room, the big puzzle on the maple wood coffee table, the smaller puzzles on some cardboard flats on the floor. The kids would show Dane and Clay pieces when they got stuck.

"See that one?" Clay said patiently. "That's an edge—now look at the color. Which part of the picture does it match?"

"Ooh," Holly said. "That's a good way to look! Thanks, Uncle Clay!"

"You're really patient," Dane said in admiration when Holly was absorbed in her task again. "I suck at giving directions." His contribution had been mostly, "Turn them all so the picture is facing up. Yeah, after that it's all luck."

Clay smiled a little. "Well, two years of listening to Skipper help people in IT helped. He will walk the dumbest people through the simplest steps. I'm like, 'Turn it off. Now turn it on again. Yup, magic.' And he's like, 'Now, if you do this, and then this, and then this, and then reboot, you could solve the problem completely.' Puts me to shame."

"Good teachers are hard to find," Dane said. "I had this one professor who pretty much told us we were all gonna fail because none of us were as smart as he was. Good times!"

Clay cocked his head and found his piece. "Did you fail?"

Dane shrugged. "No. For one thing, I was smarter than he was—and I had receipts. All that testing I did in school wasn't bullshit."

Clay snorted. "Genius. Excellent. I'll crawl in a hole now."

"Yeah, well, that's not why I passed."

Clay must have heard the thing in his voice that he'd put there deliberately, because he looked up from where he put the puzzle piece with wide eyes.

And parted his lips.

Dane waggled his eyebrows. Yes, he'd blown the guy into submission, and he wasn't ashamed. Prick. No telling how many people that guy had put off molecular biology for life. Dane considered ten sweaty, unpleasant minutes on his knees listening to the guy grunting, "But I'm not gay!" to be one of the finest acts of public service he'd ever performed in his life.

And Clay saw it—saw the sexual innuendo, the carnality, the complete lack of repentance—and didn't express horror. Didn't say, "Oh God, that's awful!" Didn't say, "You did not!" or "That's cheating!"

Nope.

Clay Carpenter saw that look on Dane's face, bit his lip, and blushed.

Dane couldn't deny the hopeful, sexual, insistent buzz that had started in his chest and warmed his skin. It settled in, like hot chocolate into your stomach on a cold day.

Way, way, way better than almond milk.

The kids fell asleep, facedown on the floor, the puzzles around their heads, and napped there for a good half hour. Right up until Clay's mother came down and tsked them all up.

"Come on, you two. Pick up your toys. Go lie down in your beds!" she urged, and Dane met Clay's eyes as the kids grumbled peevishly and started to do what she said.

"Holly, you missed a piece!" Cheryl Carpenter called as Holly trudged up the stairs.

"I got it, Mom," Clay told her. "I'll put it on top of our box after we clean up."

They were almost done, actually, and given it was one of those super-busy puzzles with a thousand tiny black-lined pussycats staring forward with that super-judgy look that cartoon cats got, Dane was reasonably proud of the two of them. Holly's puzzle was a bright pink Barbie abomination; there would be no confusion.

"Why would you let them nap down here, Clay?" his mother admonished. "They'll be hyper tonight—"

"We'll run them around before dinner," Clay appeased. "Here. Meet Dane. He's got the puppy-dog eyes. Everybody loves him."

And with that, Clay shoved Dane unapologetically at his mother, and Dane grinned and put on the charm.

Cheryl was a trim woman, with frosted hair pulled up off the back of her neck in an elegant twist. Like Sabrina, she was dressed in what Dane thought of as "mall sweats"—a pale blue leisure suit that would look appropriate doing something social and active. And yet she was wearing it in her home when she wasn't feeling her best.

Dane had seen some of Carpenter's "not feeling great" sweats when they were cleaning up his room. They'd been full of holes and hanging in tatters, and Dane was starting to see that entire scenario as Clay's giant finger in the face of his parents. Well, there was a cost to perfect. Dane could see that now.

"So nice to meet you," Dane said, prepared to lie his ass off in the name of love. "Clay thinks the world of you."

"Well, we're feeling very blessed. Clay brought his friend Skipper here for Thanksgiving, and now we're getting to meet another friend." She gave her son a look of gentle reproof. "It's like he's trying to prove he has them."

Clay's begging look at Dane said everything. "Well, he has a lot more—I'm just the only one who wasn't playing soccer this morning. Everybody else had to go home and scrub off all the mud."

"Why weren't you playing?" she asked, her lips quirking up, and Dane's stomach relaxed infinitesimally. That *was* a smile there. He'd obtained a parental smile. He was usually good with parents—had, in fact, been called back by the occasional hookup over holidays so he could appease a worried mother or overprotective father into thinking their dear, sweet little gaybie wasn't a complete and total disaster who would frighten a serial killer into running in the opposite direction.

Dane was pretty sure he'd dated every one of those guys the Bay Area had to offer. He told himself it's why monogamy hadn't been his thing in the last few years. Since the diagnosis. The last few years since the diagnosis. But he *had* dated a lot of jerks.

And he sure did know how to fool the 'rents.

"I'm more of a yoga and swim guy," he told her truthfully. He used the school pool every morning when it was open to the student body, and he had yoga tapes for his room. "Me and kicking the crap out of a ball—not really my thing."

That lip quirk deepened, and Dane was pretty sure he saw dimples. Oooh… how hard would Carpenter have to smile—and how clean would he need to be shaved—for Dane to see dimples?

But Clay's mother wasn't that much of a pushover. "Well, healthy competition can inspire us to push against our limits and excel, don't you agree?"

Dane almost did it. He almost sold his soul with that one. He smiled, and his eyes widened, and his mouth opened, and he said, "Oh God, no." Then he clapped his hand over his mouth and looked to where Clay had let out a snort that could have waked the dead. "No," he repeated, still horrified that this was what he was saying. "Healthy competition kicks my stress into high gear. It terrifies me. I either get unhealthily obsessed with beating my score or my performance or my original baseline or something, or I stress about how I'm failing at life and that makes my mood swings super radical, and then I have to quit. No. No, there is no such thing as healthy competition for some of us. There is only doing the things that are good for us to the best of our ability. Competition is a bad idea. Bad. No. Don't do it."

He looked wildly around to see if he should run outside and hitchhike home because he was no longer welcome in the palace-o-perfection, and was stunned to see Clay, eyes dancing above the hand in front of his mouth, staring at him with something like worship.

And Clay's mother was laughing in a mostly horrified way—but still laughing.

Oh, thank God, Dane hadn't lost his touch.

"Well, that's… unusual," she said. "Isn't that unusual, Clay?"

Clay dropped the hand in front of his mouth, and for a moment, he looked stricken, like a possum in front of headlights. Dane winked at him—he could do this! Articulating a real emotion in front of his parents was within his grasp.

"Uh, no," he said, the words sounding strangled. "That's actually how we play soccer."

Dane gave him a grin and a thumbs-up, but inside, he was thinking that he sort of wished *he'd* been the inspiration for that epiphany, and not big dumb Skipper's violent dumb game.

"What do you mean? Don't you play to win?"

Clay shrugged. "Well, of course. But mostly we just play to play. I mean, Mom—these guys aren't pros. They don't have scads of time to practice. They just like to get together and play. It's fine. We have fun. Dane's brother is our defender—or he will be in a couple of weeks after his ankle heals. He's not great. He's sort of…." He grimaced in Dane's direction.

"A gawky mess who fell over like a tall tree. Timber. Like—" Dane put his hands up to his mouth. "Tiiiiiiimbeeeeeeeeerrrrrrr…. It was amazing. I've never seen anybody fall like that."

Clay smirked. "It really was sort of amazing," he conceded. "But the best part…." His eyes darted quickly to his mother, and Dane grimaced. Well, he was in it now. Dane gave him a nod. "The best part was his boyfriend, who sort of wanted to ride to his rescue and get him off the field."

Dane couldn't help the guffaw that escaped. "Oh my God. Yeah. That was great!"

"What was so funny about it?" Cheryl asked, puzzled.

"Well, Dane's brother is super, super tall and like a tree, and Jefferson is about five foot six, and he drives this dinky little Toyota that was just barfing black smoke all over the field. So he rides down, and we have to fold Mason into a pretzel to get him into the car—"

"And the big moo was so happy to have a knight in shining armor!" Dane broke in. "He was like, 'Yes! This is fine! Isn't he wonderful! No, the super-swollen ankle doesn't hurt at all!'"

"And Dane's horrified, right?" Clay said. This was their rhythm, the part about them Dane loved the most. The way they talked off each other, like they shared the same brain. "He's like, 'We *have* a *Lexus*,' and Mason is not getting it. Not even at all."

Dane shook his head, the story winding down. "And you finally had to say 'Let it go, Dane. Just let it go.' And they went jouncing off the field, my brother's head hitting the ceiling of that damned car with every bump."

"But he was okay?" Cheryl said, and that's sort of when Dane got it. Fussy. Yes, she was definitely fussy. And obsessed with perfection. But she cared about Dane's brother, whom she had never met.

Sort of like when Sabrina had been horrified her brother might have heard what her children said.

These people weren't monsters.

But they were… difficult, if you were just a big solid guy who liked to play soccer and have a beer with friends after work. Sometimes that very simple thing was the lynchpin of civilization—or at least the cornerstone of a lot of other people. Trying to "refine" or "improve" that formula was like adding all those different flavors to chocolate chip cookies. Sure, that one batch was a lot of fun, but the next time Dane and Carpenter made cookies, they weren't going to throw in random shit again because they *liked* the tried and true.

Tried and true was what the world needed sometimes.

"He's at home right now," Dane said. "And his boyfriend is probably spoiling"—*fucking!*—"him senseless."

Clay made a suspicious sound, and Dane shot him a dirty look. Dammit, he was about to close this deal with the fussy mother, and he was about to have her approval so that Clay wouldn't have to work quite so hard to earn it for himself.

It was absolutely imperative that neither of them thought about what Mason and his squirrel-bait boyfriend were really doing right now.

"Is his boyfriend as nice as you are?" Cheryl asked, beaming.

"Sadly, no," Clay said, his eyes kind and sparkling as they met Dane's. "Dane is sort of special, Mom. I don't know if Jefferson can live up to that with anyone but Mason."

Dane cocked his head and gave his best coquettish smile while looking at Clay sideways. "Do you really think I'm special?" he vamped.

Clay rolled his eyes. "Do you really imagine you're not?"

Dane grinned and did a little dance as he sat.

"Well, I'm just glad Clay has friends like you and Skipper," Cheryl continued, puncturing Dane's happiness just a little. "It would be lovely if he brought a girl here someday, but I'm glad he seems to be happy."

Dane's eyes widened in outrage, and Clay covered his mouth again and chortled softly into his hand.

THEY MUDDLED through.

True to Clay's word, Clay and Dane took the kids out and played Frisbee and whiffle ball in the huge backyard for an hour before dinner. Dane wasn't sure about the kids, but he was good and tired by the time dessert had been served and he and Clay made their polite goodbyes.

"Oh my God," Dane groaned, collapsing into the front seat of the SUV. "I'm exhausted. How do parents do that all day?"

Clay snorted as he backed the vehicle out of the drive. "Well, Sabrina hires help, I think, but yeah. It's not for the faint of heart. Jason and Holly are sweet kids—"

"Well, they're kids," Dane corrected. Kids were often spoiled and peevish and selfish—but that didn't make them bad people. It just meant they didn't have a whole handle on that social niceness thing yet.

"Well, they could be worse kids. I went to their soccer games last fall. There were some absolute gems in that batch of entitlement, I shit you not. But Sabrina tries to keep them grounded." Clay let out a breath. "I mean, I don't know if she realizes what 'grounded' means. Yeah, she's an oncologist, but she also works in one of the swankiest hospitals with all of the experimental treatment. I mean, this isn't Cook County or LA General, you know?"

"Gotcha," Dane said, knowing what he was talking about. Clay piloted the big Ford Explorer easily through the Rocklin suburb toward Highway 65. "Can I ask you something personal?" He was only halfway kidding.

"Sure." Clay's voice softened.

"What's your degree in?"

"Nothing special," Clay evaded, and Dane scowled.

"You know, this is an absolutely stupid thing to shine me on about—" It had been obvious he'd cut Sabrina off before she could finish what she was saying.

"What did you say to my sister when I left?"

Uh-oh. "I told her what a good time the kids had," Dane lied, his sweetest smile on his face.

"Really? She looked really afraid of you when we were eating dinner."

"I don't think she felt very good," Dane temporized. But it was the truth—one of the reasons the two of them had bolted out of there had been that the women still didn't look like they were feeling wonderful, and Clay's father had been tired from work. They were welcome, but nobody was in much of an entertaining mood. Sabrina *had* given him a brief smile as he was leaving, though, and told him he was welcome to babysit anytime.

"Yeah, that's true." Clay sighed. "I'm just really glad nobody asked the kids about my soccer game. That would have been embarrassing."

"Why? You guys were great. It's not like it was a blowout or anything."

"Yeah, but… but it's kind of condescending, you know? 'Oh, Clay, bringing your friends here! How sweet! How's your soccer game, honey? When are you gonna get a real job?'"

Dane laughed like he was supposed to. "Yeah, but how else are they going to be? I mean, they're not going to get it—or you. Clay, you're… I mean, your parents are smart." They were educated and spoke really well about politics and current events. They'd reminded Dane of *his* parents in that way; they moved about in the world like they were part of it and had a say. "And your sister probably is too. But they're not as quick as you. Not as funny—"

"So I'm a smartass. So what?"

Dane wanted to shake him. "Because you're a *smart* ass. It's like… like with Skipper. You know that his tech certificate is a big deal to him. Yeah, we both think he's smart enough to do more, but you get, like with your heart, why you'd want to be careful explaining that to him. Because he didn't have the same shit you and me had growing up." Dane didn't know particulars, but Clay had told him that much. "It's… wait. I know what this is called." He closed his eyes and tapped one of his many, *many* psych courses. "Intrapersonal intelligence. It means you are really good with people on a one-on-one basis—"

"Not always," Clay said, self-recrimination harsh in the quiet of the car. "It… it took me a while. To look beyond myself, right? Like, I gave him gift certificates to my favorite donut place for Christmas as sort of a joke—I mean, work Christmas pool, right?"

"Who takes that shit seriously," Dane agreed. When he'd worked at the restaurant, he and his friends used to try to find the worst beer possible to give each other for Christmas.

"Well, it was the only gift he got that year, and I didn't know until recently. Because I'm an asshole."

Dane sucked air in through his teeth. "But everybody has *some*body," he said, not caring that he sounded like an old song.

"No," Clay said. "No. Everybody *doesn't* have somebody. So here I am, just… just *weird* about my family, letting every little thing they say get to me in a big way. And Skipper's got nobody, and he's still beating me at life."

"Skipper's got Richie," Dane said. "And it's not a competition," he added fiercely. He remembered his conversation with Carpenter's mom and got it, finally. "*That's* the bullshit you're having trouble with. There's no beating someone at life. There's just living your life the best you can. *You* can. I think you're doing okay, man. I really do."

Clay let out a breath. "Thanks, Dane. Seriously. Thanks for coming and playing with the kids and charming the socks off of my mom—"

"I sort of wish…." Oh no. He wasn't going to say it. He couldn't. "I sort of wish, you know, she'd seen me as… well, a viable candidate for her little boy."

Apparently, he could.

"Well, she doesn't know everything about me," Clay said softly. "I'd have to tell her first. You know. That it was a possibility."

"She'd be okay with it?" And oh, this meant more to Dane than he could possibly say.

"I hope so. I brought Skip over—they didn't bat an eyelash."

"Well, it's different when it's your own kid," Dane said, although his own parents had been more than supportive. Considering what Mason and his wayward mouth had put them all through, they were the patron saints for PFLAG.

"I'm not that worried." Clay shrugged. To Dane's dismay, he'd already gotten off 65 and was heading toward Fair Oaks through Roseville. It was late enough at night that traffic was minimal, and Dane knew they'd be at his house in a matter of minutes.

"Worried about what?" Dane asked. *C'mon, man. Give me hope. Give me hope. Give me hope.*

"That if I came out as bi, my folks would have an issue. I'm kind of sure they'd be fine with it. I mean, I think they'd rather I be flamingly gay and successful than fat and working IT."

Dane grunted, happy and appalled. "Can't they just be happy with you as you are?" he asked, a note of desperation in his voice.

"No," Clay said, so no-bullshit that Dane was forced to reevaluate his entire afternoon in that big elegant house with a mom who wouldn't let you drool on the carpet when you'd had a big day and had fallen asleep.

"You might be right," Dane said on a sigh. "But *I'm* happy with who you are. Doesn't that count?" He was so warm—and he was *right there.*

Clay's half smile did strange things to Dane's stomach. "It's like a Christmas present in July," he said.

Damn.

All else was forgotten. "That's impressive," he said, glowing a little.

"Not nearly as impressive as how much I want a hamburger right now."

Dane thought about it. Dinner had been delicious—vegan fare had been a big seller when he'd done restaurant work in the Bay Area. But yeah, he was hungry again.

"I could eat," he admitted. "How about a chicken sandwich instead? That way you won't feel guilty."

"Moderation," Clay grunted. "Compromise. That's some tricky thinking there, Dane Hayes."

"I do my best, Clay Carpenter. Find the nearest fast-food drive-thru, and let's moderately pig out." He paused. "And don't forget the cookies."

"Thanks, man."

"Anything for you."

And it was true too. Anything. Dane had dragged his sorry ass out of bed to be with Clay Carpenter when he'd been sure he'd never emerge again. But Clay had gotten him out of his abyss of self-doubt, into the world of perspective again.

Dane would die for him.

They pulled up into Dane's driveway, and Clay killed the engine, allowing some of the foggy cold of February to seep into the car. The river sat nearby, often trickling through a tributary in the ravine behind Mason's graceful house with the stucco arches and two-story tiled roof. For a moment, the air was filled with the inelegant rustle of fast-food wrappers and the munching of sandwiches, both of them quiet and tired and content just to be in the same space.

Clay swallowed and wiped his mouth, then threw half of his sandwich back into the bag before he turned slightly in his seat. "Tell me about this morning," he said softly.

Dane set his sandwich down. "Nothing to tell. Hit a rough patch, you know…."

Clay shook his head, his eyes bright. "I dragged my fat ass all over the soccer field in front of those kids—"

"You're not fat," Dane said staunchly.

"Every time you say that, I become convinced that you don't really see me. That you see some idealized version of me. I'm twice the weight of Richie Scoggins—*twice* another human being. Don't bullshit me, Dane. Not about any of this. What happened?"

Dane felt his eyes burn. Oh, sneaky, sneaky Clay. Talking about his problems, making Dane forget how badly the day had started, about being curled up in a ball and moaning to Mason about how he'd never get out of bed again.

"I… you know. Last night. I just—like any social situation, I replayed it in my head again and again, and the smallest, dumbest things just get bigger and bigger until I'm a freak who doesn't deserve to be around normal people."

Clay's look of concern—slightly bitten lip, furrowed brow, shadowed eyes—actually made Dane's chest swell and his breath come short. For him. That look was for *him.*

"School was super busy?"

Dane looked away. It was, but that wasn't why he'd neglected his meds. "It's just not fair," he complained bitterly. "I feel… indebted to a handful of chemicals. Like I couldn't live my life without them."

"You can't," Clay said brutally.

"But that's not fair!"

Clay just let his words ring there in the middle of the car. So Dane took a deep breath and went on.

"I'm living at home at thirty. I mean, I'm living with my brother, but that's because my parents are getting older and I'm exhausting them. If I didn't have… have these people in my life, I'd be in a care center, or homeless—I know this, Clay. *I know this.* And I'm so mad. My family has been nothing but awesome. Like, fantastic and amazing. What did they do to deserve to have me hanging around their necks like a millstone? Just once… I mean, wouldn't it be great if I could be self-sufficient? If I wasn't just a needy whiny bitch who falls apart without a handful of pills that…." And this was the frustrating thing. "That I can't even seem to remember to take?"

Clay sighed and—oh God—took Dane's bony, chilled hand into his big warm paw. The shivers that had started as Dane bared his soul eased up as that touch warmed him all over.

"My sister never buys cookies," Clay said out of the blue. "Doesn't bake them either."

Dane refrained from saying that's because no cookie would stay with her and any self-respecting cookie would run screaming into the night, but he thought that might be a little harsh. So instead, he settled for "So?"

"So, when I was a kid, my best friends—their mom—baked cookies all the time. They actually had batches of cookies go stale on them. Can you imagine that?"

"Baking cookies?" For a moment, Dane thought he must actually be crazy.

"No. Having them go stale. Not eating *every cookie* that was in the house, as fast as you can, because cookies are a rare and wonderful thing and you never know when you're going to get a chance for another one."

Before his diagnosis, Dane used to let entire refrigerators full of food go to rot because eating was just the last damned thing on his mind.

"Uh, yes? I mean… cookies. They're great but—"

Clay shook his head. "But I will *never* let a box of cookies go stale in my house. That's why I buy them for everybody else but not myself. It's not a *right now* thing. It's a *forever* thing. If I want to catch that ball or follow that friend across the mall—" He'd been frequently out of breath that day. "—or not die at forty-five because my body just can't take it anymore, I can *never* buy cookies. Do you understand? I am a slave to them. To potato chips. To white bread. There is no 'I'll just eat one cookie and save the rest for later' for me. I will make the batch of cookies, eat a few, and give the rest away—forever."

Dane swallowed.

"It's not fair," Carpenter said. "People all over the place can buy cookies and potato chips. They can get coffee without a truckload of cream. But I'm compelled to eat them all. There's a thing inside me that's broken. In my head. It tells me there are no half measures here. Do you understand?"

"Yes," Dane rasped. "So why—"

"Sure, I could ignore it. I had to *work* to eat half a chicken sandwich and one cookie. I had to practice that in my head sixty thousand times in the drive-thru so it didn't come out a double-quarter and three cookies with a shake. If I stop thinking that way, in three months, I wouldn't be able to walk across the parking lot. I couldn't fit in the car. This isn't heroin, where I just don't have it around. This is fuel—I *need* to eat. It's important for my body's function. And my other alternative is to *never* eat another cookie, *ever.* Are you hearing me?"

And Dane couldn't even pretend to fight it anymore. He clung to Carpenter's hand like a lifeline. "Yeah."

"So you're a slave to your body chemistry. What happens if you don't take the meds?"

Dane closed his eyes. "Well, when it was really bad, I did a demolition job on my dorm room, and then my boyfriend's house. I kind of spray-painted his apartment black." He shuddered. "Mason had to pick me up physically and haul me to the psych ward. They restrained me and shoved antipsychotics in my veins."

Carpenter moaned low and painfully. "And then you're really held captive, aren't you?"

"Yeah." Dane remembered that moment. Helpless. He'd been utterly helpless. They'd given him a drip of medication until he'd balanced out enough to remember why being in control was good.

Clay had been staring at the puzzle of their fingers for the past couple of sentences. Now he turned toward Dane as if he couldn't help himself. "So you see? We either control it, or it destroys us. That's how it has to work, you understand?"

"Yeah," Dane said, wiping under his eyes with the back of his hand. "But… but what do I get out of sanity? More work? You know, I told Mom and Dad and Mason I was going into the veterinary science program. Do you know I'm still in the prelim? I have another year of science before I even treat an animal. And then two years of the actual program. I mean, I'm volunteering in the shelters now, it's part of the requirements, but… but this? This is why I'm taking my meds?"

"No," Carpenter said. He let go of Dane's hand and reached out and cupped Dane's chin in his fingers. For a moment, Dane wondered if he'd actually done it, had his psychotic break and gone off the deep end.

"What—then why?" he desperately tried to stay on subject.

Clay moved closer, searching his eyes, close enough that Dane could feel Clay's breath against his lips. A small smile graced Clay Carpenter's mouth, and he brushed their lips together almost too gently for Dane to feel.

And then he did it again, a little harder this time.

And then again, hard enough for Dane to part his mouth, welcome Clay's questing tongue, to groan and grip Clay's shoulders, urging him closer. Dane moaned, not from pain, and pushed forward, surprised and hurt when Clay put his hands flat on Dane's chest and pushed back.

"What?" he panted. "What? Why are we stopping?"

"Because it's our first kiss, and I'm not doing the rest of this in the front seat of my Ford!" Clay's laugh invited Dane in on the joke, but Dane's entire body was heated, kicked into overdrive, needing more.

"That's it? We can go into my house. Mason won't care—"

Clay shook his head and put two fingers on Dane's mouth. "Take your meds tonight," he whispered. "And tomorrow morning. See me for who I really am. If I know you know who you're kissing, know me for all my flaws and fuckups and not for the wrong chemicals surging through your brain—"

"That's insulting." Dane pouted.

"That's my line," Clay said, his voice shaking. "Because you are special to me, and I think I'm special to you. And I don't want you to disappear because we hook up and suddenly you're terrified you did or said something wrong. If I'm your friend, you know anything is forgivable. Being lovers is harder. Let's get our shit sorted first."

Augh! He was right! How could he be right? "Are you sure this isn't just because I'd be your first guy?" Dane asked, not sure if he'd be disappointed or excited if this was the real reason.

Clay pinned him with hurt brown eyes. "I am *dying* to see what being with my first guy is like," he said, his voice raw. "But I've got friends. I've got you. Neither of us is going to lose the *us* we've been building because I can't keep it in my pants while I'm still too fat to even see it."

Dane's brain broke. "You can too see it," he said, looking at Carpenter's body and trying to figure out the line of sight.

"I couldn't a month ago," Clay said irritably. "Now focus. I want to be a better man for you—"

"Wasn't that—"

"Yes, it was a movie. But it's still a good reason. And I want you to see me as the man I am."

Dane let out a breath and told his traitorous body to stand down. When it became clear that Clay wasn't going to initiate another kiss, Dane grimaced. "I see you for who you are," he muttered. "But you want me on my meds so we don't self-destruct. I can respect that." His lips tingled. "One more? Just… just like a sweet kiss good night? Without all of the arguing afterwards?"

Clay's smile, soft in the moonlight, warmed even his fingers and toes in the cold of the SUV.

"Night, Dane," he murmured. "Text me in the morning. Maybe we can game."

This kiss was the sweet rasp of skin on skin, their mingled breaths, starlight and darkness, Clay's hand on his cheek.

Their tongues tangled, tasting, and Clay pulled back, cupping his chin, his neck, rubbing his thumb down Dane's jawline.

One more hard press of lips and Dane slid out of the SUV and slammed the door.

It was time to do the hard work, to do the baking that would get them the big cookie that wouldn't make anybody fat.

Hard Line to Walk

How's your leg?

Clay looked at the text and grimaced. *Infected. How's your brain?*

Full of spiders. Fuck.

It had been a little over two weeks since the kiss in Clay's vehicle. Two weeks of gaming and talking and being them, and the whole time, Clay's brain had been buzzing with "I kissed a guy! It was awesome! He's great! I want to do it again!"

But Dane was having problems. He'd needed two phone calls to talk him down in the past two weeks, and Mason had texted Clay, frantic, asking if Dane had talked to *him* about whether or not he needed to shift his meds. Because he'd been staying up too late, getting up too early, laughing to himself, and missing his meds by the week, and Mason knew it shouldn't be this hard.

In the meantime, they'd been helping Terry Jefferson fix his mother's house.

If Clay had thought he'd been educated about how people who weren't rich lived, putting on Teflon work gloves and cleaning out Jefferson's riotous and disgusting backyard had been an eye-opener, that was for sure. But also educating had been the way Mason, who was as bourgeoisie a guy as Clay had ever seen, had simply accepted the dead cats and the piles of dog shit and the blackberry bushes without judgment. The mess had started before Terry had been born. They were just both fixing it so Terry could leave his mother's house and not feel indebted.

Unfortunately, the education had come with a Weedwacker through a pile of old aquarium pebbles, and Carpenter had essentially been shot with the world's filthiest BB gun.

Dane had helped him clean out the wound, his hands warm and efficient over Clay's skin. They'd been surrounded by trash, by the other guys on the soccer team all swearing like sailors, and for a moment, it had just been them, Dane's eyes shadowed with insomnia and pain but still yearning.

Clay had wanted to kiss him then, so badly. But that hadn't been the place, and they'd both known it.

That had been a week ago, and one of those terrible phone calls, in which Dane was losing his shit on the other end of the line while Clay talked him down, had happened in the middle of that week.

But Clay would keep answering his phone, his text, his game unit, just to know Dane was on the other side.

He looked at Skipper at the desk across from him, playing with the squishy brain ball that was his favorite and deep into geek talk with some poor soul on the other end of the line who probably just wanted to turn their computer off again and on again and hope that did the trick. He could *feel* the tension throbbing from the other end of his phone.

He hit the Out-of-Service light that signaled he was on break and picked up his cell phone.

"What kind of spiders?" he asked, keeping his voice light. "The weird psychedelic ones that freak me out or your basic garden variety."

"They all suck," Dane sobbed, and Clay's heart shriveled in his chest.

Clay kept his voice calm. "Well, what are they doing in your head?" he sallied gently. "Come on, what do we do?"

"Close our eyes, think of a color," Dane said. "Blue."

"Blue sea," Clay told him softly. "Blue sky. Blue bells—"

"Blue *balls*," Dane said, voice harsh.

"Have you met my left hand? I have." Clay kept his voice caustic, because he didn't want to go there—not when Dane was hurting like this. "Blue lagoon."

"Blue lake," Dane breathed, and it sounded like he was slowing down.

"Blue bird of happiness."

"Blue raspberry slushy."

"Blue suede shoes."

"Wouldn't those pinch?" Dane asked. "I always thought they looked hellishly uncomfortable."

"Right? And oxfords or wing-tips?"

"Definitely wing-tips," Dane said decisively. "Blue velvet."

"Also a song," Clay said. Dane's breathing was easier, his voice a little steadier, but he wasn't sounding great. "Where are you?"

"At a gas station in West Sac," Dane said. "I… I sort of had to stop driving."

Carpenter inhaled hard. *Oh Jesus.* "Okay, so I want you to stay there, okay? I'll take an Uber—"

“That costs too much,” Dane wailed.

“Then I’ll take a Skipper,” he said. “I’m going to hang up for ten minutes. Don’t go anywhere, and text me the address, okay? I mean, go in and get a Slurpee or something so you can *see* the address, but—”

“Chocolate milk,” Dane muttered. “But I didn’t bring my meds.”

Clay breathed quietly in through his nose. “I’m stunned. I could have a heart attack and die from that surprise.”

“Don’t be an asshole!” Dane snarled.

“Don’t be a whiny baby!” Clay snapped back. “Now go get your chocolate milk and then get in the car and wait for me. I’ll be back on the phone in ten minutes. Set the timer. You need to have your snack and be back in the car in ten minutes. Understand?”

“God, you’re bossy,” Dane said, sulking. “I hope you know that when we finally make it to having sex, I call all the shots.”

“If you could get your act together long enough for us to do that, I would let you make a *list* of shit you wanted to do to me and sign off on every goddamned item. Now ten minutes. I have to kidnap Skipper.”

He hung up and without compunction invaded Skip’s cubicle and hit the Off-Duty light. Then, while Skip was staring at him in surprise, he texted Mason: *Skip’s taking me to get Dane. Get us out of work.*

Skip wrapped up his call, hanging up just as Mason returned: *Done. Go. See you at home.*

“What’s up?” Skipper said, standing up and getting ready to bolt out of his cubicle without any of his shit.

“Get your jacket,” Carpenter nagged. “Do you remember when you were sick in November, Skip? Because I remember. It terrified me. I thought you were going to die.”

“Yikes!” Skipper dutifully grabbed the work-logo hooded sweatshirt that Carpenter had stolen for him that week because Skip had looked like death and had been walking around wearing a polo shirt in the rain. “Fine. I’ve got my jacket. You’ve got *your* jacket. So why do we have our jackets, and where are we going, again?”

“We are going to your car, because I’m probably staying the night at Dane’s house after I drive Dane home in his car.”

“Car trouble?” Skip asked carefully. Mason called the two of them in to eat lunch with him about once a week. It was a nice little tradition. When Mason wasn’t trying to impress people, he was actually intentionally funny and down-to-earth and generous and kind. He and Clay had let slip a few things about Dane and his painful spiral since February.

"Dane trouble," Clay said with a sigh. He looked around, not wanting to broadcast Dane's problems to the world. "He—his program is really intensive, and he's just in the preliminary science part of it. He's not even in the residency part, where he apparently indentures himself for two years and we never see him. Ever. But he keeps forgetting his medication, and I'm not even sure it works when he *does* take it. It's hard to know, though, because he's so stressed, and then he skips it, and it stresses him out more and…." His voice rose and got wobbly, and he looked at his phone and realized he had to get himself back under control in time to talk to Dane again.

He took a cleansing breath. "He's not going to make it home. We're heading toward West Sac and some sort of gas station that you'd probably get to right off of westbound 80."

Skipper nodded. "I hear you. Get some particulars. I think I can get us there."

Just like that, Carpenter's eyes burned. "Thanks, Skip," he said gruffly.

"Yeah, well, remember, Richie's got a temper. Someday we may need to hide a body."

Carpenter had to laugh then. "I'll do some research so I'm ready. Nobody will ever find it, I promise."

"That's a good friend," Skipper judged. "Ask Dane for help. I mean, he knows science and shit."

It was on the tip of Clay's tongue to get defensive—didn't *he* know science and shit? But then he remembered that this sweet guy who had literally just bailed on the job he was so fiercely proud of to help Carpenter because he asked, didn't really know what Carpenter's degree was *in.*

And for the first time, really, he felt bad about that. He felt like he was living this life—this quiet, lower-middle-class life, where someone like Skipper would drop every-fucking-thing to make a forty-five minute drive on his say-so—as a lie.

It was stupid, really, to perpetuate the lie, but Skipper, Dane, Mason—he loved these people. He didn't want to lose them.

But that was a discussion for another time. Right now, he had to make sure Dane was okay. He limped out to Skip's car, panting more for the pain from the infected punctures on his leg than from exertion, and belted into Skip's painfully small Toyota, a little reassured when Skipper grunted himself because Skip was not short.

It had been the best thing Skip could afford when he cleared tech school—he'd told Clay that the first time he'd given him a ride. Beggars really *couldn't* be choosers, and Clay needed to remember that.

"Here," Skip muttered. "Lean the seat back and it won't hurt your leg quite so much. I'm sorry my car's so dinky."

"Not your fault," Clay told him, touched a little. "And the leg is all Mason's fault, so I'm blaming him."

Skip gave a strained chuckle. "Man, cleaning up Jefferson's house is the worst. But I'll tell you what—it sure did give Richie and me incentive to keep ours up so it doesn't get that bad."

"That's constructive," Carpenter told him, because of course Skip would think of it like that—and Skip still had healing scratches from the damned blackberry bushes that had seemed out to get him too. "It just makes *me* think of the joys of apartment living."

Skipper's chuckle bloomed a little. "You'll want a house," he said confidently. "You and…." He gave Carpenter a furtive sideways glance. "The person of your choice," he finished.

Carpenter sighed. He hadn't told Skip anything. But then, Skip had held Richie pretty close to his vest in the beginning too. Skip understood "reasons." But Carpenter had been hurt then, and now Skip was hurt, and the really good thing about all this was that Carpenter figured he and Skip were tight for life.

But other than that, secrets sucked, and Carpenter apparently had a lot of them, and he didn't have time for this right now.

"I'll…." He heaved a sigh. "I need to call Dane in a minute," he said. "He's really freaking out. I made him go get some food in the quickie-mart while we got out of work."

"Yeah. I'll pretend to be a fly on the wall, no problem."

"Thanks, Skip."

"You know—I mean, you *know* you can trust me, right? No judgments?"

Carpenter sighed. "I know. You're the best friend I've ever had."

"You too."

"Except Richie," Carpenter said, on automatic, because Richie had always been Skip's bestie, right up until they were lovers.

"Except Dane," Skip said with meaning.

Augh! Carpenter opened his mouth to spill—everything—the kiss, how suddenly weight loss meant a whole new thing, how he couldn't go to sleep without dreaming of Dane Hayes's bright brown eyes, when suddenly his phone buzzed in his hand.

"You were late," Dane said bitterly after Clay had pushed the button.

"I'm sorry," Clay said, looking at his timer. Twelve minutes. He was two minutes over. As wound up as Dane was right now, it probably felt like a zillion years. "We're on our way. Skipper's gonna drop me off, and I'll take you home."

"But you have work," Dane hiccupped, sounding very sorry for himself.

"Yeah, well, it turns out I know a super-big goober who's vice president of something important. We do lunch."

"Great," Dane muttered. "Mason knows."

"Yeah, Mason knows. Nobody told me we were a covert operation. I mean, are we smuggling state secrets? Procuring illicit substances? As far as I know, I'm giving a friend a ride home."

"What did you tell Skipper?" Dane wailed.

"I said, 'Get in the car, Skipper. We're going to West Sac,' and he said, 'Great. IKEA is in West Sac.' And that was pretty much it."

Skip snorted. "Fucking IKEA," he murmured, not loud enough to carry over the phone. He and Richie had bought a new kitchen table the week before. It was currently sitting in their garage in the box while Richie tried to figure out the directions and Skipper looked assemblies up online.

"Well, tell him I'm grateful." Dane's voice sank humbly. "I… I really need to see you."

"'Course," Carpenter said easily. "But you know we owe him a kitchen table assembly, right?"

"Man, I'll rip out his kitchen floor first and replace that shitty tile. Name a date. I'm good for it."

Carpenter chuckled. "I'm excited about this plan. Skip's having another gaming party before it gets hot. We should do it after that."

"Why before it gets hot?" Dane asked, and Carpenter could picture him, long legs pulled up to his chest as he rocked himself in his front seat. The movement—stimming—was something Clay saw him do that first time, after he'd gotten home. He'd put his head trustingly in Clay's lap and rocked himself until he'd calmed down.

Clay found himself rocking back and forth, infinitesimally, just to keep him company.

"Because summer sucks at Skipper's house. It's great for a couple of people to play games and stuff, but you put more than five in there and the air-conditioning goes on strike. Especially for gaming—last time we had a game day in June, all the PS4s overheated and we ended out in the backyard under the sprinklers, sliding through the mud."

Which was probably how the backyard had ended up looking so raggedy. But since it was Skipper's idea, he didn't hold any grudges.

"Sounds like a good time," Dane said, voice still shaking. "But, you know. Mason has a pool. He should be back on the field next weekend, at least to sub. I bet we could have people over."

"You guys are close to the field too," Carpenter said. "That would be great. Think he'd be up for it?"

"Sure. His last boyfriend had these super-boring wine-and-cheese parties and shit. I think Mason would love to have people over drinking beer and jumping in the pool."

"His last boyfriend sounds like a real douche."

"Yeah, well...." Dane let out a shaky breath. "Terry's better, because he looks at my brother like he's a god, but...."

"Your brother *is* a god," Carpenter said fiercely. Because Mason had just told them to go and covered for them like a diaper, and any guy who would do that for his little brother's nervous breakdown deserved naked porn stars in the pool. Clay didn't have any of those, though. So Mason would have to settle for a bunch of mostly in-shape guys who did their best but didn't skimp on the beer or the burgers, at least half of whom were heterosexual or married.

"Gods are hard to date," Dane said, and his voice was sinking, like he was falling into his own headspace and losing connection with Carpenter.

"Which gods have you dated?" Carpenter asked him, putting a little edge into his voice. "I mean, do you have Chris Hemsworth or Chris Evans on your roster? Seems like you've kissed a lot of guys, you know."

"Like you care," Dane snarled, suddenly right back in the present. Well, he was pissed because there'd been no follow-up to the kiss, but that was still better than that lost boy he'd been the moment before.

"Of course I care," Carpenter said. "Things won't always be like this. I need to know the competition. I mean, dating is like running from a bear, right?"

"Oh God—I don't even want to—"

"You don't have to run faster than the bear. You just have to run faster than the guy the bear catches. I don't have to be better than *you.* I just have to be better than the last guy you *dumped.*"

Dane started to chuckle. "You're already better than that guy. That guy told me I was a crazy bitch and if I'd just stop going to school and filling my head with ideas, I could sit on his couch and smoke weed and not worry about being productive with my life."

Carpenter grunted. "Well, weed has been known to help with bipolar—"

"He laced his weed with all sorts of random drugs," Dane muttered. "And didn't tell me. Besides, it was before I was even diagnosed. God—that was bad. That was when I started redecorating by sledgehammer."

"Okay," Clay said, his heart breaking. "So I'm way the fuck better than that guy. When was that?"

"About six years ago. I pretty much had to go to school all over again after that. I've got a year and a half before the residency, and that's going to suck, and isn't this hard enough? And I haven't even told Mason how much more I've got—"

"Sh… sh…." Because Dane was openly weeping now. "Why wouldn't you tell Mason that?"

"Because he thought I finally had my shit together! Getting into this school—it was like my family's reward for dealing with me when I was falling apart!"

"Jesus, Dane, don't be stupid. Dealing with you *sane* is our reward for dealing with you when you're falling apart!"

"Well, when's *that* going to happen, because this doesn't feel like it!"

Clay took a deep breath and realized he was getting sucked into the mood swing, which was a dangerous mistake. Everything—the anger, the panic, the self-recrimination—it was all part of what was happening in Dane's head. It was Clay's job to make Dane's life doable, not yell at him because it seemed out of his control.

"Look, we can fix this. I mean, you'll eventually have to tell your brother what your program is really like, and I don't think he'll care. But it'll be a load off your heart, brother, believe you me. Now let's not think about that guy. Let's talk about where you and me go from here."

"You could always kiss me again," Dane said miserably.

"I'd really like that," Carpenter told him, feeling just as wretched. "But I can't do it while you're crashing, man. You know that. That's no way for us to figure out how to be happy."

"But I'm going to have to talk to the shrink again tomorrow," Dane whimpered. "And I always feel like such an inarticulate loser and—"

"I'll come with you!" It was sheer desperation. "Tell you what. Mason got me and Skip out today, and tomorrow I'll come with you. We'll figure out a plan. We'll work together to get your shit together so it's not so hard to be on your meds, so you can make it through school. We can do that, right?"

"You'd do that?" Dane's voice still trembled, but as Skipper sped through the misty, overcast day down through Rio Linda and past Natomas toward West Sacramento, Carpenter got a feeling of hope.

"Of course I would," he said, his own voice as hearty and real and solid as he could make it. "Man, I'd do anything for you."

"Except blow me," Dane muttered, apparently still bitter.

"That's not off the table yet. But we're getting off the subject. Let's go back to blue."

It was possibly the longest conversation in his life—six or seven years crawled by with the scenery, he was almost positive. By the time they got to the address Dane had texted, Carpenter's hands were sweating, and so was the rest of him. As Skipper pulled off the freeway, he put his hand on Carpenter's and gave a curt nod.

"Sign off," he ordered.

"We're almost there, okay? I'm signing off so I can give Skipper directions. Hang on."

"I'll be fine."

Sure he would.

Clay hit End Call, and Skipper pulled off about two gas stations before the Shell where Dane said he was.

"Skipper—"

"Calm yourself down," Skipper said, his voice warm and no-bullshit. "He thinks you're his rock, and you're pretty watery right now. Three deep breaths, man."

Oh. "Yeah. Thanks." Carpenter rested his head against the window. "God, this is hard."

"Well, you're a champion at it. It's a good thing he has you."

“How much of that did you get?” he asked, because the jig was very probably up about his bisexuality and the way he felt about Dane Hayes and how he’d rather die than hear Dane in that much pain.

“We’re going to pretend I got none of it,” Skipper said irritably. “I thought we’d established that. Now you clear it with Mason that you’ll be gone for a couple of days, and I’ll tell our supervisor—”

“I thought just tomorrow!”

Skipper snorted grimly. “Three days. Minimum. Tell Dane it’s nice to be connected.”

“Ronnie’s gonna hate me,” Carpenter muttered. Veronica Haynes—petty goddess of the IT department at Tesko—tolerated neither slackers nor Y chromosomes in her realm. Unfortunately, Carpenter was a slacker, and Skip was very obviously a man.

“She hates us both,” Skip replied. “Her flaming bitchiness is not our concern. Maybe Mrs. Bradford will make us cookies again—concentrate on that.”

Mrs. Bradford was Mason’s administrative assistant, and she had apparently decided Skip and Carpenter needed adopting. The last time they’d eaten in Mason’s office, she’d brought them lemon iced sugar cookies, two apiece, and had given Skip two in a disposable container for Richie. The three of them had privately agreed that they would *die* for Mrs. Bradford.

“I’ll concentrate on that,” Clay said with a deep breath. He felt better. Maybe it was the thought of cookies, but most of it was Skip’s steadiness. “We can go, Skipper. He’s going to need me.”

“Yeah.” Skip pulled away. “Look, I get that you’re going to get out of the car and bail, but if you give me your keys, I can run and get your clothes, then have Richie drive your car to Mason’s house this evening.”

Clay had to work really hard to fight the burning in his eyes. “That would be the best, Skipper,” he said. “All my clothes that fit are folded in the big drawer right now. The stuff in the closet is too big or too small.”

Skipper pulled up in front of Dane’s obviously hand-me-down tan Pontiac Firebird, and Clay dug into his pocket for his key ring and his wallet. “And here’s money for gas—”

“That I will shove down your throat if you don’t get out of the car,” Skipper said smartly, snagging the keys. “Go. I’m going to go hug my boyfriend in the middle of the auto parts store and watch something sad on TV.”

"That sounds like a plan," Clay said, wiping his not-burning eyes with the back of his hand. "Thanks, man."

"Anytime."

He meant that. Clay wanted to hug him, but he just gave a hard nod and hopped out, then hustled toward the driver's side of Dane's sedan.

He tapped brusquely on the window, startling Dane from the fetal curl that was every bit as heartbreaking as he'd imagined. Dane rolled down the window and glared.

"What?"

"Scoot over. I'm driving you home."

"What about your car?"

"I told you—I don't have a car. I have a Skipper, and he's going to IKEA." Skipper would probably bomb the place first, but if it made Dane feel less indebted, that was fine.

"You lie," Dane said, trying for cheek and making it to tired snark. "Skipper would jump off a bridge before he willingly walked into an IKEA again."

"Richie wouldn't let him jump off a bridge," Clay said softly. "Now scoot over. We're going to talk about how much Skip hates IKEA and the next movie we're going to go see and what takeout we're getting tonight. That's the approved list. If you want to pick another topic, you need to clear it first, and I'm not feeling generous. *Scoot*!"

Dane hadn't been eating. His thin frame fit easily over the console, and his dedication to yoga really showed. He belted himself obediently into the passenger's seat and pulled his knees up to his chin again.

"If I tried that, they'd need the fire department and the jaws of life to get me out," Clay muttered.

"Nah-nah-nah," Dane returned. "Dumping on yourself is off the approved list."

"Well played," Carpenter ceded. He belted himself in and turned the engine over, checking his mirrors and making sure the wipers worked to take care of the rain that was finally being birthed by the pregnant clouds. It wasn't until he turned around to back out that he saw that Skipper was only just now pulling away. He'd probably waited until the car had started to leave.

"What?" Dane asked fretfully, chin resting on his knees.

"Skip. Watching out for us. Good guy."

"You should marry him," Dane snapped, and Carpenter wasn't surprised. Dane got nasty when he was in this much pain.

"I would, but Richie would shank me. Anyway, I've got my eyes set on the crazy goober with the crooked teeth who forgot to take his meds. Why is that, by the way?"

"I thought we weren't going to talk about it!" Dane said indignantly.

"Not the meds, moron. The teeth. I mean, don't get me wrong. They're charming as fuck, and I think you're totally adorable, but Mason's teeth are practically ruler straight. I spent my middle school years locked in an iron mask so my teeth are average. Why are your teeth crooked?"

Dane let out a grunt. "Because they're charming as fuck. Seriously!" He exclaimed at Carpenter's snort. "No—my mom kept saying, 'We need to get your teeth fixed, don't we? But they're so damned cute!' And by that time I was getting some action, and the other guys thought so too, so I asked my dentist if there was any other reason to fix my teeth. Like, you know, Mason had to fix his because otherwise his underbite would grind away at his top teeth. Dentist said, 'Nope, son—they're just a little crooked in the front is all.' So I kept them. They felt like me."

Carpenter chuckled. "Both adorable *and* vain as hell. How very you."

"I'm not vain," Dane mumbled.

"Are too."

"Am not."

"Why haven't you cut your hair?"

"'Cause the man bun looks good with the teeth. Goddammit, Carpenter!"

"And you use that super-fancy baking soda deodorant because…?"

"Because it makes my pits smell daisy fresh. You're killing me here."

"I'm just saying…." Carpenter eased onto the freeway, knowing that people drove like assholes in the rain, particularly when he passed Truxel. "You're a little vain. A lot adorable. I can live with the vain because I also get the cute and the snarky. So whatever spiral of self-hatred you're currently dealing with, know that I really do see you for who you are, and you're fine."

"Aurgh!" It was a sound of exasperation, but it was also a last stand. Dane leaned his head against the window after that and made small talk about how hot all the Marvel stars were and how he might even do the raccoon if he got desperate enough, and somehow, they managed to make it home.

They spent the evening doing normal.

First, Clay made him go upstairs and shower. Then he fixed a snack of whole-wheat crackers and cheese, because he was pretty sure Dane hadn't eaten. By the time Mason got home, they were watching old Cary Grant movies on TV and reciting the lines before Cary could get to them. The empty plate was on the coffee table in front of them, which felt like the ultimate indulgence to Carpenter, and Dane was sleeping, his head in Clay's lap.

"How is he?" Mason asked softly, checking to make sure he was really asleep.

Carpenter just shrugged and shook his head. "He called his professors so he doesn't go in tomorrow, and has an appointment set up at the shrink's office. I told him I'd take him. So, uh, if you could get me off work…?"

Mason didn't even blink. "Yeah. Sure. I'll tell Veronica I've co-opted you for something special. It'll make her insane."

Carpenter flashed him a smile. "Yes, yes it will. Maybe send Skip out to lunch or something too—I want to watch her hit on you again, because that was hysterical."

Mason's ears turned red. "The only woman in my entire life," he said, sounding panicked and a little nauseated. "I don't understand it at all."

Against his knees, Carpenter felt Dane's breath coming a little faster, like he was just awake enough to laugh. "I was going to wake him for dinner. Did you bring takeout?"

"I brought better," Mason said. "Don't worry. I'll bring it in." His limp was hardly noticeable, and as he made himself busy in the kitchen, Carpenter realized he'd brought groceries.

About half an hour later, an amazing aroma filled the air—one Carpenter was familiar with, but for once, it didn't fill him with horror and self-recrimination. Shortly afterward, Mason came in with a plate for each of them, and as Carpenter urged Dane to sit up so he could eat, Clay realized what Mason had done.

"Oh God, Mace—I love it when you do this!" Dane moaned, smelling the doctored pizza. "He gets one of those big fresh-made ones from the grocery store and then adds extra pepperoni and sausage. It's a-maz-ing!"

Carpenter looked at the thing on his plate—it had extra Romano and Mozzarella too—and tried not to groan.

"It looks awesome," he said, his voice weak. In fact, it looked like the thing he'd been craving but hadn't eaten in six months, but he didn't want to crush Dane's high.

"I only gave you one piece," Mason said, putting a gentle hand on his shoulder. "And I used turkey pepperoni. Also, the salad is vinaigrette."

Carpenter blinked and remembered the days when he'd devour a large pizza, by himself, in his apartment alone. No salad, no turkey pepperoni, no friend who'd made dinner.

"Progress, not perfection," he said gamely. "Thank you."

He ate his slice slowly, appreciating every bite, and *really* appreciating that he had friends who got it. The pizza was for Dane, and he would have dug in and pigged out, but Mason knew that wasn't what was good for any of them.

It was a reminder—if he could keep up his calorie diary and continue to exercise, he wasn't eliminating pizza from his diet. He was just moderating the entire package.

Dane ate two pieces and ignored the salad, but came out of his funk long enough to offer to help clean up. Carpenter was just about to wrap the pizza in plastic wrap when there was a knock at the door.

"I've got clothes," Skip said, holding up Carpenter's gym bag. "And keys."

"Oh man, that's great." Carpenter pocketed the keys and ushered Skip and Richie in. "Come in, guys. Have you eaten?"

"Feed them the rest of the pizza," Mason said, coming into the kitchen. "We owe you guys."

"Not a problem." Skip closed his eyes and sniffed appreciatively. "But we'll take you up on the pizza." He grimaced. "As long as it's quick, because we left the dog outside in the backyard, and he starts to eat the fence when we do that."

"You mean chew on it?" Mason asked, smiling, but Carpenter and Dane had actually seen the beast.

"Nope, I mean, he, like, eats it," Richie said frankly. "Like kindling, because he's the size of the fuckin' porch."

"But he's only a puppy!" Mason blinked. "That's right, isn't it? You guys only got him what? A month ago?"

"He's doubled in size," Skipper muttered. "We have to buy two bags of kibble at a time and hide them in one of those locking garbage cans in the garage. We learned that the hard way."

Dane chuckled weakly. "Do you guys run him in the evening? That dog had a lot of go."

"Every day," Richie confirmed. "Either we go jogging and take him with us or we throw him the stick until he passes out. It's like I used to think Skip's backyard was perfectly sized, but when Ponyboy gets full grown, he'll be sailing over the fucking fence."

"You should bring him here," Dane said, giving his chin a nod. "We're sitting on a couple of acres, if you count the ravine and the woods behind the patio. You could run that dog until he drops."

"That would be a blessing," Skipper said, after Mason nodded and seconded the offer. "Thank you."

The guys sat down and ate the pizza and finished the salad, shooting the shit politely but not extensively. About halfway through, Dane sort of drifted into the living room and curled up in front of the television with a vacant stare, and Mason's shoulders sagged. Carpenter felt his own expression melt, the happy social mask slipping for the moment, and it took a couple of heartbeats before he realized nobody was talking.

"Rough day?" Skipper asked, all gentleness.

"It's going to get worse," Mason said, and he sounded tense, like he knew.

"Let us know how we can help." Skipper polished off his pizza, and Richie stood and took their plates to the sink. "Right now, it looks like we can help best by going. I'll give your regards to Ronnie."

"Just don't let her grab your ass," Mason said glumly. "She'll give you anything you ask."

Richie stared at him. "Skip, can I bring the dog to work?"

Skip rolled his eyes at Mason. "You just had to, didn't you? Just had to bring that up."

Mason scrubbed his face with his hand. "Sorry, Skipper," he said repentantly. "Do you still want me at practice?"

"Sure. Wrap your ankle and we'll have you stretch and scrimmage, as long as it's not still raining." He looked outside, where the rain pattered, and probably would continue to do so for the next three days. "The field's gonna be shit. Bring your mud gear."

Richie blew a raspberry. "Fuck that, Skipper. I'll just sit on your ass and use you like a toboggan. Rest of the guys'll push. It'll be great. And whatserface won't be grabbing it."

Skip crossed his eyes at Mason. "Now do you see what you've started? Come on, Richie, let me explain to you why Veronica Haynes is just lonely and not really a threat to our happiness, okay?"

Richie shook his head, but he followed Skipper out. "Skip, some guy could be on his knees with your dick in his mouth, and you'd be telling me that he didn't really have evil intentions; he was just pining for his girlfriend. Then you'd put your dick in your pants and buy the guy a beer and send him on his way. And the whole scene could have been totally avoided if you'd just let me kill him from the get-go, you understand?"

Skip broke into a cackle of totally delighted laughter. "You're all talk. As long as I'm putting my dick back in my pants, you totally wouldn't kill a soul!"

Richie sent them a dark look over his shoulder and put his hand in the small of Skip's back. "You just keep believing that, Skipper. That's fine with me. Night, guys!"

Skipper turned his beaming, besotted smile back over his shoulder and called his goodbyes as Richie shut the door behind them.

As soon as the door closed, Carpenter and Mason met horrified gazes.

"He would so totally kill someone who moved on Skip," Carpenter said, with no irony whatsoever.

"And then he'd use the body as mulch," Mason confirmed. "We really have to get a handle on your guys' supervisor. That's a disaster waiting to happen."

The phrase fell between them, and they both turned worried eyes to where Dane sat, staring sightlessly at the television.

"You'll stay with him tonight?" Mason asked. "I mean, you don't have to, but he's got a king-sized, and you guys don't seem to worry about boundaries and—"

Carpenter held up a hand before Mason's awkward mouth could get him in any deeper. "Yeah. That's fine. I told Dane I'd take him to his shrink appointment tomorrow. I meant it."

Mason closed his eyes. "It's going to get bad," he said frankly. "I counted his pill calendar. He's missing about six days. He's going to say all sorts of super-ugly shit he doesn't mean, and then he's going to hate himself for it later. I just… don't want you to hate him for what's going to happen over the next two weeks, okay?"

It was a classic bipolar spiral—the pills didn't feel like they were working, the patient resented taking them, so the patient didn't take them. So they didn't work. This was going to take all of them to fix.

Carpenter swallowed. It was Dane. Seriously. How bad could it get?

Lost Spring

"SO HELP me, Clay, I will beat the shit out of you if you don't get your sorry whiny ass out of my room!" Dane snarled. He heard the words from far away, like an animal screaming in pain. In his heart, he was sobbing, "Why won't you love me!" but his mouth? It was a rabid shrew trying to draw blood.

"Please do," Carpenter said shortly. "Please do beat the shit out of me. Take a swing. I'm looking forward to it. We can both swing away, and then I'll sit on you, tie your wrists, and make you bathe. It'll be exercise. I mean, I've been making it to the games and practices and shit, but you haven't left your room in a week. Cardio, man, it'll be great! That'll burn the fat off!"

"*You're not fat*!" Dane sobbed. Oh, he wasn't. He wasn't. He was magnificent. He was massive and furry and warm. He'd slept in Dane's bed for the past couple of… days? Was it a week? Was it two? Just so he'd have someone. Someone to help Mason get him up in the morning. Someone to wheedle him into taking his pills. Someone to get him to do his homework, or to talk to his professors about why he wasn't going in. He should have been flunking out—he knew it. But Mason had gotten on the phone and woven Mason magic about mental illness. Thanks to Dane's big brother, that illusive hobgoblin—hope—was still being used as a flog to get Dane the fuck out of bed and to his shrink's appointment and to the occasional class.

And Carpenter, who was his… companion? Was that what they were? The guy he'd known barely six months was now lodged solidly in Dane's life, taking no shit and giving no quarter and generally not giving up on Dane when Dane would have crawled into a corner long ago and willed himself to die.

"I'm not fat?" Clay was saying now, the bitterness like a slap to the face. "Oh, you think I'm not fat? That's fucking rich. Someone finally finds me attractive and he's actively working to be crazy. Thanks a fucking lot for *that* compliment, Dane Hayes. You want to convince me that I'm not fat, *work for me*, you fucking asshole! Get out of fucking bed, shower, get dressed, and let's go see your shrink so he knows for real that your meds aren't working!"

"How's he supposed to know that?" Dane practically wept. "What are we supposed to do to convince him?"

"Take them!" Clay practically laughed. "Man, this is the seventh day in a row, and look at you. If you're this bad after taking your meds for a week, something is *wrong*!"

Dane sucked in a breath. "I've taken them for a week?" he said, feeling wobbly with hope. "Really?"

"Yes," Clay said, his voice suspiciously rough. "Yes, Dane. We've been doing this for a week. And it hasn't been a picnic, but today's our payoff day. Today's the day you, me, and Mason go in and show them all our paperwork and how the meds aren't fucking working and see if they can get you something else."

Dane sucked in a sob. "Something else?"

"Yeah, baby. Something that might work."

Dane sank down onto the bed, in tears and hating himself for it. "We could find something that would work?" God, he hated to hope.

"Yeah." Carpenter sank next to him, a thinner, scruffier Carpenter than the one who'd taken Dane home two weeks before. Three weeks before? He didn't remember much of the week after that, but somewhere in there, Mason and Clay had done some research and come to the conclusion that Dane's new meds weren't suited for Dane at all. The psychiatrist said that he needed to take them regularly for an entire week before he changed them, just so they knew for sure.

Dane remembered some ripe words from both Clay and Mason about that, but he'd been chasing a YouTuber down a rabbit hole and he hadn't been able to focus. He *wanted* to game, but Clay and Mason had hidden his gaming system because apparently, he'd disappeared into the PS4 for three days without eating sometime in the last couple of weeks, and they said that was bad.

He had dim memories of Clay and Mason trading off to sleep on the couch, because apparently when Dane *did* sleep, he was restless as fuck, and there were a couple of nights they'd spent in Clay's apartment so Mason could get some time with his boyfriend, which, Dane dimly recalled, might be the one thing holding Mason together right now.

Dane had begged him not to call their parents. Sobbing. God, he was fucking useless—and Mason had agreed, on the condition that Dane came to

Thursday night practice and game days, even if all he did was stare moodily at the field from the car.

Maybe it had been more than two weeks.

"How long?" he asked hoarsely into Clay's shoulder.

"What?"

"How long have I been like this?"

Clay hummed in his throat. "Three weeks, give or take," he said quietly. "I tried to spend a few nights at home. That didn't go over so well."

"Jesus," Dane croaked, rubbing his face on Clay's shoulder. "You must hate me." Because right now, he hated himself. So much. After all his talk about wanting to stand alone…. It had made him worse of a pain in the ass than ever. He should probably just walk out of their lives forever.

Clay's arm tightened around his shoulder. "No," he whispered. "Not even close." And for a moment, Dane was confused.

"No what?" They didn't want him to leave? That was probably a polite lie.

"We don't hate you. Don't be dumb. We wouldn't do this for someone we didn't care about, Dane. Now come on. Today's the day things change for the better, okay? You're going to get your meds changed, and then you'll remember to eat and sleep, and make it to school every day of the week, and you and me…." He bit his lip and looked away.

"What?" Dane begged. "Come on, man, finish that fucking sentence." Because suddenly, things weren't all lost. They still cared about him—and he owed it to them to get his ass out of this hole.

"You and me can… can maybe see where we were going before your train derailed. But that's not for a while, you know?"

Dane felt… empty. Hollowed out. Suddenly incapable of thought or emotion or even words.

"God, Clay," he said. "I've got to get my train going again. You guys… you can't live like this."

And Clay's shoulders started to shake. He tried to stand up—he probably meant to chivvy Dane to the bathroom and into the shower some more. And God, Dane's mouth tasted like monkey ass, which meant a toothbrush and a hearty flossing would probably not be amiss. But Dane kept his arm over Clay's shoulder and held on tight.

"I'm sorry," Dane whispered into his hair. "I'm so sorry. I didn't mean to put you through all of this."

Clay shook some more, rocking back and forth against him in complete helplessness, and Dane had a terrible moment of realization.

Clay had *made* himself this vulnerable. Not like Dane, who had his dignity and his self-possession ripped away by a terrible accident of chemical imbalance. No, Clay had *given* those things up *voluntarily* in the past three weeks.

At one point, Dane had wet the bed. He remembered Clay's gentle hands, shoving him toward the bathroom while he changed the sheets and sprayed the mattress, and then… Jesus.

He'd shoved Dane into the bathtub and washed his hair and his beard.

Clay had wrecked himself this hard.

For Dane.

Dane would keep getting up. He would try this round of meds, and if it didn't work, he'd try the next one. And he'd keep going. He had to. Because look what this man—this perfect, wonderful man—had done for him.

And he still cared. For the first time in forever, Dane saw his life as an embarrassment of riches.

"Don't worry," Dane whispered, heart aching and bloody—but still beating. "Don't worry. I won't fight you anymore. Not today. Let's get in there and restart my medication. Let's find some hope, okay?"

Clay nodded, still sobbing, rocking back and forth in Dane's pretty room, the one he and Mason had redecorated, standing side by side, because Mason wanted him to have some color and some joy in his life.

Dane lowered his ear to make out what Clay was saying.

It sounded like "Please get better, please get better, please get better…."

And Dane closed his eyes and steeled his cynical heart and prayed.

DAY BY day. Later he'd try to figure out how he'd gotten better, and he'd realized it had been day by day.

That day, they'd started him on a new regimen; then Mason had gone to work while Clay had taken him out to lunch. He'd gone home and napped, then woken up, voluntarily, taken a leak, seen his reflection and, God help him, trimmed his beard. His hair was super long—longer than man-bun length—but he wasn't going to fuck with that.

He brushed his teeth because he'd felt human that morning after he'd brushed and flossed, and he'd remembered he liked that feeling. He'd gone downstairs and eaten the grilled chicken teriyaki that Clay made for him and Mason, and then taken his pills voluntarily with dessert.

He'd been exhausted then, and he'd looked at his brother and his… friend. If nothing else, the best, closest, most loyal friend he'd ever had, and said, "Nobody needs to sleep with me tonight. You guys are beat."

Mason met his eyes and swallowed. He was such a handsome man—clean-cut, strong jaw, fine brown eyes. They were sunken now, and he looked like he hadn't slept in… well, three weeks.

Their parents were getting older—and fragile. They needed a break. It was just Mason and Dane, and Dane had just drained his brother of all his color, all his joy.

Dane needed to be a better brother.

"I hope you don't mind if we don't take that at face value? Tonight's my turn. If it goes well, Clay can maybe visit his apartment, check his mail, that sort of thing."

Clay nodded, and Dane wanted to howl. No! No—don't cut him loose! God. Clay had obviously been the only thing holding him together.

But he'd seen the tired anticipation on Clay's face, the willingness to accept "no" and keep doing what they'd been doing.

He wanted Clay for so much more than holding him together. He wanted Clay for *Clay*. But how was the guy supposed to know that when he'd been a human woobie/zookeeper for most of the last month.

"Yeah," he forced out through a raw throat. "Let's give Clay some room to breathe."

And he knew the look on Clay Carpenter's face for what it was.

Relief.

THE NEXT day he woke up and called his professors, surprised at how functionally he'd kept up with his homework, and even more surprised by how much they professed to want him back. Well, that was progressive. He didn't think playing the "crazy" card would get him that far—it felt about played out by now—but he was grateful. Redoing the entire year would have sucked.

He spent the day resting, catching up, doing laundry, *taking his meds*, on time, every time.

He put together his own pill calendar so he could have Mason double-check it later.

He texted Carpenter around lunch. *How you doing?*

Fine. Skipper and I are having lunch with your brother in ten. His turn to buy. He goes fancy.

Sounds fun. And it did. Normal.

Usually is. I think your brother's worried about Terry.

Dane blinked. Terry, who came over after the games on Saturdays, when they went to Carpenter's and hung out. Dane had visited Carpenter's parents one other time—that had been one of his better days.

There had been workdays at Terry's house, getting it ready for Terry to move out, and Dane was starting to realize this meant more to Mason than it had to him.

What's to worry about?

The guy's gonna go squirrelly as soon as he's out of the house. Mason's gonna let him. It's gonna hurt.

Dane stared at the words, knowing what he'd seen of Terry Jefferson, knowing what he knew about his brother.

Mason didn't want to be another parent. God, didn't he have enough of that with Dane? He wanted an equal.

Aw, Mace....

Yeah. Gotta go.

Dane stared at the words. He couldn't ask Clay to come back. Not so soon. *Game tonight?* But probably not. He wasn't sure he'd be good to game for a while. It was too seductive, too much like its own drug. His phone pinged.

Text tonight. Promise.

He stared at the screen, feeling both bereft and proud.

Thanks.

THE NEXT day he went to school, taking his medications at strict intervals. It was odd, this new medication. It made him feel hollow and clean—not too extreme on the inside, and not too happy.

Even.

And a part of him mourned. Because that moment when Clay had kissed him had been luminous. Transcendent. Beyond even. The high end of the roller coaster. He was pretty sure that wasn't the old meds—and he was pretty sure that wasn't because he'd been on an upswing. And he wanted that moment back again.

Could he get it back like this? Careful, clear, lucid in his own head? His resentment at taking his medication had faded in the last few days. Whether that was the new medication lessening the mood swing or that terrible realization of what he'd put Clay and Mason through, he didn't know.

He just kept remembering Clay, talking about cookies in the house.

Some adjustments you made for life because you wanted to *have a life.*

He'd have to have faith that the moment in the car, where Clay had looked at him with all that was hope, had been transcendent because it had been him and Clay—not because he'd been on the chemical roller coaster, clicking up for the crash.

And if he wanted a reminder, all he had to do was look at his phone. It said April was on the downslide. He *thought* he'd spent Easter Sunday at Clay's parents' house, helping the kids search for food-colored cardboard eggs on the lawn and sneaking real chocolate into the kids' hands instead of carob, and hopefully indebting the little bastards for life.

But so much of that time, he'd been in his own head. Coming out of himself long enough to spend that time entertaining youngsters might have been the most real thing he'd done in almost a month.

He'd spent three weeks with the chance to have Clay Carpenter in his bed, and all he remembered was that big body, that gruff voice, calming him from dreams that ripped him open. No spooning, no tenderness, no banter.

He wanted that back. He wanted the way Clay's eyes had glinted in the dark, the way he'd seemed charmed and enthralled by Dane's every move.

The high of the roller coaster was nothing compared to the surety, the joy of having Clay in his life when Dane wasn't a raving mess.

He'd forsake his gaming system, leave the computer alone, read a book, talk to his brother, take his meds, eat his veggies, drink his milk, trade that roller coaster in for real life.

He missed Clay in his real life.

ONE DAY at a time.

Two weeks after the change of his meds, Dane was eating his lunch on a spare patch of grass in the quad, his face turned up toward the sun. Dr.

Klein, oh she of the dreaded lab practical that Dane would have to face the next year, suddenly dropped down next to him.

A severe white woman in her fifties, she had a long gray plait down past her bottom that Dane suspected she only braided once a week, but she did it so tightly, in fishtail formation, that it didn't dare come loose.

"Mr. Hayes," she said pleasantly.

"Dr. Klein!" He'd been texting Clay, and he hurriedly set the phone down. Clay would understand—he wasn't sure his professor would.

"Good to see you back among the living," she told him pleasantly.

"It's good to be here."

And then, oh God, her severe expression—the one that seemed to never relax, even when she was with her peers—grew gentle. But what she said next was unexpected.

"Do you know," she said conversationally, "that I didn't get my degree in veterinary medicine until I was forty-two?"

Dane gaped. "Uh… no?"

"Yes. I had all of the other things done—the degrees in biology, in husbandry, in chemical science—but the veterinary program was known to suck up your life, and I'd had my twins right after I got my first BA. I went to school nights, got my other degrees, taught high school part-time, but I waited until my girls could drive before I applied for veterinary science. My husband, dear man, was incredibly supportive, but I didn't want to miss out." She smiled in a way that almost made her pretty. "I only got to see them young once, you understand?"

Dane thought of his own mother, who had worked hard and put away money so she could be a stay-at-home mom. She'd been older before she'd done that, but she'd done the same thing. Put off one thing for the other so she could enjoy the life she'd chosen.

"I do," he said softly.

"You have a double major in biology and chemistry—that's what you came here with, am I right?"

"Yes, ma'am."

"And most of your master's classes revolve around those two areas. I'm right there, yes?"

"At the moment, yes, ma'am. I haven't started the program proper, though. I'm still finishing off the preliminaries."

She nodded. "You know, when people think of veterinary medicine, they very often only think about taking care of the animals. That's why I started. I loved animals. I wanted to help them."

"Animals are better than people," Dane said loyally.

"But do you even have a cat?" she asked.

Dane swallowed. "Too busy for a cat." Also, asking Mason to take care of his cat when Mason had a full-grown Dane to look after was just too much.

She cocked her head, and he knew he could do better. "I'm worried about taking care of a cat until my meds are completely balanced again," he said with more truth.

She nodded, like that satisfied her. "Dane, you're very bright. Your test scores are great, and your work—especially under the circumstances of the month—is amazing."

"Thank you, ma'am," he said humbly. "But?"

"But there are a lot of things you can do in the realm of veterinary medicine that don't involve the actual program that lets you be a veterinarian," she said. "Things that come with less pressure. Things that will get you a job in the field, so when you're actually ready, you won't have to retake your classes."

Dane stared at her, mouth opening and closing, and tried to put his thoughts in order. "Are you saying I can't—"

She pursed her lips. "I'm sure you can," she told him. "But ask yourself—do you want to? I mean, life's short, Mr. Hayes. Is it too short to live without a cat?" Her voice sank to something she knew was probably too personal. "Or a girl or boyfriend?"

"Boyfriend," Dane clarified, because he'd never been anything other than out.

"A boyfriend, then?"

"I'm already thirty," he told her, as if the fact that he was a good three to six years older than his peers in the graduate program might have escaped her notice.

"I'm sixty-two," she said amicably. "Isn't it amazing how much we both have in front of us?"

He swallowed and wondered if she could see how near tears he was. "It would be nice," he said softly. "You know. To get a cat."

"Not a boyfriend?" she probed.

"I… I have a candidate in mind," he said with as much dignity as he could muster. "I just need to…." He turned his face up to the sun. "Stay in the light."

"Hold still—I'm going to use your shoulder to hoist myself up," she said, and he grinned at her while she did just that. She gave his shoulder an extra squeeze. "So thin," she said softly. "Please think about what I said. We've got an opening in our research and development department coming up the year after next. You'll have all your prerequisites done after next year, and you could be a valuable member of our faculty and our team. And in the meantime…."

"I could get a cat," Dane said softly.

"Or a boyfriend." She winked saucily, and then her face settled back down into her usual lack of expression. She walked away, her wiry body full of purpose and youth, and Dane watched her go, pondering.

HE CALLED Clay on his way home from school, partly out of habit and partly because he just wanted his opinion. His guilt-meter kicked to about a thousand when Clay answered the phone immediately, his voice an uneasy mixture of panic and forced calm.

"Hey, how goes it?"

"Fine!" Dane said hastily. "I'm fine. You need to know I'm fine. I just… you know. Wanted to talk to you."

"Oh. Sure. Not a problem." Off phone, he could hear Clay say, "I'm hitting my Out-of-Service for ten. Do you got it, Skip?" Right after that, Clay picked up again. "So—it's all good?"

"Yeah. I—well, a professor talked to me, and I wanted to tell you what she said and, you know. Bounce it off you before I talk to Mason and my parents and see what can be done."

"Oh!" He sounded genuinely thrilled. "Hit me with it!"

And Dane did, getting more and more excited as he went along. It wouldn't be another four years in school. It would be another year plus what he was finishing up now. He would have some leeway—very little, but some—in his grades, since he wasn't competing for a spot in the practical program, but going into research instead.

"And we could get a cat," he said breathlessly before he tried to rein his enthusiasm in a little. "You know. *We* could get a cat. In a couple of months. Maybe August. You think August?"

"Sure," Clay said, and before Dane could think Clay was humoring him, he added, "Or maybe a dog. Not a monster dog, like Skip and Richie. But maybe a small dog. Something that cuddles. A cat-sized dog."

Dane had to think about this. "Or a dog-sized cat?" he suggested.

"Well, I wouldn't mind a Maine coon cat," Clay said, thinking hard. "But I would want it to come with a dog that he could dropkick over the kitchen table."

Dane felt it bubbling up before he even let it loose. A laugh, as pure as spring water, untainted by sadness or bitterness or sarcasm. "How much *Garfield* did you read as a kid?" he burbled.

"Obviously enough to shape my younger self irreparably," Clay returned with dignity. And with a smile—a real one. Dane could hear it in his voice.

"I've got homework Thursday night," Dane said. "But I could come see your game on Saturday."

"Sure." Clay's voice had enthusiasm Dane had forgotten. "And then we could go catch a movie, maybe? There's a *lot* out. Man, we could even catch two."

Dane felt it, a soaring in his heart. "Maybe watch one in the theater, one in your apartment," he said. "My brother probably really needs his time with Terry."

"Yeah. They're finishing up with Terry's house next week. I—" Dane could almost picture him looking around. "I'll gossip with you about this later," he said. "Hi, Veronica, I'll be off in a minute. An emergency came up." He paused. "We were worried about my cat."

Dane snickered and bid Clay a quiet goodbye.

Better Than Cookies

"WHERE YOU guys going?" Skip asked as they walked out to their cars on Friday.

"What, after the game, you mean?" Clay squinted at the overcast clouds. He didn't mind overcast *or* clouds, but he could do without the humidity that was making him remember that losing sixty pounds didn't mean you weren't fat anymore.

"Yeah. I asked you over afterwards, remember? To play PS4? And you said, 'No, me and Dane are doing something,' and you said he was doing better, so I assumed it was a date."

Clay stopped in the middle of the parking lot and stared at Skip. "You assumed… you assumed it was a…."

Skipper cocked his head. "You said he was doing better."

Clay nodded. It had been almost three weeks since the magic "change the meds" date, and Dane was most assuredly doing better. But Clay was never going to forget those weeks, the way Dane, the sweet, goofy, snarky guy he'd been… really attached to had just… disintegrated before his eyes.

Mason had seen it coming and had a plan. It was funny, because Mason didn't *look* like a superhero to anyone but Dane—but he sure had some spectacular moves where his brother was concerned. Clay had watched his devotion—everything from getting Clay days off with pay to running out in the middle of the night to get the extra medication that the doctor had thought would help at first, but then really, really hadn't.

And then reversing course in the middle of everything so they could prove this wasn't fucking working.

He'd even produced medication journals and research to make their case, whereas Clay was just impressed that he'd been able to tie his shoes that morning.

And puzzled as to why they'd been like his pants—loose and sloppy and a pain in the ass.

Almost three weeks wasn't long enough—a part of him was screaming that. Two weeks to trust that his friend would be there after watching him be replaced by an angry animal, lashing out in pain, was not enough.

But Clay couldn't help it. He *missed* Dane so bad.

"The doc said to give it a month at least," he said, his eyes unfocused.

"Well, why are you going on a date, then?" Skipper asked. "You could just bring him to our house and we could game."

"We were going to the movies." Clay still felt dazed. Dane was doing better. *He was doing better.* "I mean, once he sort of picked himself up, I've been staying away. I think we all needed…." He flailed. "Space."

"That's understandable," Skipper said, pausing at the door of his Toyota. "Carpenter—*Clay*—what's the matter?"

"He's better," Clay said, a slow smile at war with the worry lines that threatened to take over his forehead.

"Yes."

"He might stay better."

"Yes—that's the hope. So?"

"So what happens to us when he's better?"

Skipper smirked. "Well, Clay, I assume you're going to want to try his kisses on for size and see where that goes?"

Clay wasn't sure what his expression was, but Skipper put his keys back in his pocket and came forward to take Clay's out of his hand.

"You know what? I think you need a beer and pizza. We'll get salad—don't worry, we won't revert back entirely. But I think my friend Carpenter needs some comfort food and a little bit of alcohol, then to fall asleep on our couch, watching Marvel movies with the dog. What do you think?"

"What about your car?" Clay asked, even as he got into his own passenger's seat.

"We'll get up early and come pick it up before the game," Skip soothed. "You need to go to your apartment for your gear anyway."

Clay sagged back into his seat, suddenly too tired, too shorted out, to even think for himself.

"Thanks, Skip," he said softly. "I… I'm not sure why I freaked out there."

"Because you're really in love with the guy," Skip said with half a laugh, turning over the engine. "And now he could *really* fucking hurt you." There was a pause, because Clay couldn't answer, so Skipper blithely continued, as if he hadn't just exposed all the big shit in Clay Carpenter's soul. "God, I love driving this thing. Do they still make these? Do you think I could get one used?"

"I'll help you look for one," Carpenter said. "You really are too big for that Toyo, you know."

"Yeah. And we make more now. I could afford it too."

Skipper should have been captain of all the things—Clay believed that. But knowing that he'd settle for a used Ford Explorer and call himself lucky was sort of one of the most marvelous things about him.

This man would be happy.

Clay wanted the same for himself.

"CARPENTER, GET that!" Mason called. "C'mon, man!"

The ball was coming in fast, toward the corner of the goal, and they were tied, three-all with maybe two minutes left in the game. If Clay missed this fucking shot, he'd have to wait until next week to find redemption, and he was *tired* of waiting. Besides, their next team was pretty much unbeatable, and this one was pretty much the worst team in their division. A loss here would be humiliating.

Besides, Dane was watching.

With a Herculean effort, one he didn't think he could have mustered six weeks ago, much less six months earlier, Clay Alexander Carpenter threw himself at the ball as it tried to sail through the goalposts.

He got there first.

He pulled up, trying not to gulp air, and nailed his best dropkick ever over the midfield, straight to Terry Jefferson. For once, Jefferson didn't dick around with the ball and show off his footwork. Instead, he passed it to Skipper, who powered it in for a point.

The game was no longer tied, and his team hooted and shouted in excitement.

"Nice!" Menendez said, giving him a low five before he ran into position.

"Well done!" Mason grinned, looking dusty and tired, his eyes on Jefferson, who, true to predictions, had been breaking dates and forgetting to call, the closer he got to moving out, which they were slated to do tomorrow morning. Apparently his only anchor in the land of adulting had been his mother, who'd been drowning him too. Mason was right—Jefferson was going to have to be out on his own before he decided if he wanted a Mason in his life.

"Are you looking to take over permanently?" Singh asked, but he was smiling kindly. They often switched off, with one of them subbing defenders for one half and working as goalie as the other.

"Not on your life," Clay panted. "This job's harder than it looks."

Singh cackled, and they turned toward the ball, because there was no way that fucker was getting through in the last five minutes of the game.

They took the win, and Dane jumped up and down on the side of the field cheering, coming in for a whirlwind hug at the end.

Clay laughed and set the dorky goober down, somehow keeping his hands on Dane's hips. "We won," he said, stating the obvious.

Dane's smile turned sober. "The rest of the day is ours. Let's get you cleaned up."

They participated minimally in the after-game discussion—most of it was who was doing what to move Jefferson to his new apartment, anyway. Right before they left, Dane grabbed his brother's keys and ran to the car to get something, and Skipper dropped quietly out of the conversation and edged over.

"So, going to the movies?" he asked casually.

"Shut up," Carpenter said.

"I'm just asking." Skip didn't get mad because that's not what Skip did. "Have a good time. Take things slow. And don't you dare miss tomorrow, because…." He cut his eyes to where Jefferson was giving scattered directions to the guys who were helping with the move and Mason was trying to look supportive.

"Yeah," Carpenter said, and they exchanged glances. *Oh, Mason*. Man, this was so not looking like it would cut his way. Dane was still rummaging around in the car, so Clay took his courage in both hands. "It was worth it, right?" he asked. "Going from friends to something else?"

Skip nodded. “It’s like your favorite blanket as a kid. It’ll give you comfort if it’s small, but if you want it to work for you as a grown-up, you’ve got to find a way for it to grow.”

Clay patted his back. “You’re very fuckin’ wise, Skipper.”

“You only say that because you know I’ll pick up the pieces if things go south.”

They both watched Mason steel himself for the moment Terry ran away.

“Yeah,” Clay said, heart aching. “I know.”

AN HOUR later, Carpenter was standing in front of the mirror in his tiny bathroom, shaving and trying not to look at himself as he was doing it.

“Jesus, Clay!” Dane hollered from outside his door “What the hell is taking you so long!”

“I’m shaving!” Clay snapped back. “What do you think I’m doing?”

The door popped open, and Clay clutched the towel around his hips tighter. “Jesus! What—”

“Stop being a baby.” Dane tsked. “C’mon, do you have an electric shaver?”

“Yeah, but there’s a lot of scruff here for that,” Clay muttered.

“Well, you don’t kill it with the whole enchilada!” Dane looked around, probably for a towel, and his eyes fell on Carpenter’s hands, which were clutching the only one in the bathroom—a tatty old beach towel, because it fit easily around Clay when he was at his biggest.

Clay tightened his hands convulsively around the thing, because, oh God, he was standing here shirtless, his hairy chest exposed, belly flopping forward, the fat under his arms in full view.

“Uh….”

Dane shook his head and passed his hand along Clay’s clavicle, and something tremendous happened.

Clay’s blood surged.

Everywhere.

Nipples.

Face.

Thighs.

Cock.

Oh, dear God. Oh my giddy aunt—Clay Alexander Carpenter had a *sex drive.*

"Dane…," he said in a small voice. "No offense, buddy, but I really only ever wanted you to see me naked in the dark."

Dane rolled his eyes and put his palm square in the middle of Clay's pectoral muscle and rubbed. Clay's nipple was right in the middle there, and he shifted uncomfortably as his entire body changed alignment.

"Uhm—"

"Sh…." Dane put his finger very softly over Clay's lips. "I know you think I'm looking at your fat, but I'm not."

"But, uh—"

"And I'm not touching your fat either."

Clay closed his eyes and thought, *Then what do you see? What are you touching?* But he was too afraid to ask.

"You keep telling me I don't see you," Dane whispered, stepping closer until Clay could feel his heat and the rasp of his cargo shorts along his belly, the whisper of his fine mesh T-shirt by his chest. "I know what I'm touching. Please believe me."

For a moment, there was just his heat, permeating the air-conditioning in Clay's apartment. His smell—he used a super-subtle male body wash that was really turning Clay's key right now—surrounded Clay, like the steam from the shower had worked as an atomizer, vaporizing that scent throughout the room and into Clay's sensory input.

Clay swallowed. "We were gonna go see a—"

Dane's lips stopped him. He closed his eyes, surrounded by steam, by Dane's smell, by heat, and Dane's mouth moved softly, making him crave.

The rush of air on his face as Dane moved back was almost cruel.

"Here," he said softly. "Let me shave you. I want to see your dimple."

Clay blinked slowly, surprised that this was not rejection. It was, in fact, a form of foreplay. "What dimple?"

Dane turned and found the aerosol shaving cream, sprayed some into his hand and smoothed it onto Clay's cheeks. The intimacy of the moment, of having Dane's hands on his skin, of their proximity was both choking and liberating. Clay struggled to breathe and prayed for the strength not to back away.

"I know there's one in here somewhere," Dane said, his mouth quirking ever so slightly. "I saw one on your mother's cheek, and I'm pretty sure you've got the same kind of face."

Dane leaned in closer, seemingly absorbed in the job.

"That's a little creepy, you getting all close to me because you think I look like my mother."

"There's nothing wrong with your mother," Dane said, not fazed because Dane just didn't get that way. "She has lovely bone structure, and I'm pretty sure you're a handsome boy under all of this scruff."

Clay's eyes got big, and he took a step back. "It's a good thing you like my mother because you just turned into her!"

Dane snickered and took a step and a half forward, right up against him.

God, they were standing chest to chest—or, well, stomach to stomach. Clay usually didn't let people get close enough to touch his stomach because it stuck out a little farther than his chest. Except it had gotten smaller in the past months—particularly March, which had sucked donkey farts, and Clay didn't like to think about it. They *were* mostly chest to chest, and Dane didn't seem to mind the contact with Clay's tummy.

"I'm not your mother," Dane said, making sure the foam was everywhere. "I just think her baby boy is beautiful, that's all."

Clay bit his lip, suddenly at a loss for words, and Dane took the opportunity to rinse off the razor sitting next to the tiny apartment basin so he could turn back and edge it smoothly down Clay's cheek.

Dane rinsed the razor again and looked at him. "No words?" he asked playfully.

"No words," Clay said, voice gruff.

"How about 'thank you'?"

Clay closed his eyes as Dane swept off another swath of beard. "Sure," he said when Dane was finished. He was vulnerable here. His body was exposed, his skin was being exposed. And now Dane had just exposed the biggest, most tender part of his psyche.

"You think I'm lying?" Dane asked, his tone as careful as the razor on Clay's skin.

"I think you're biased," Clay answered, mouth quirking. "You seem to like me. I think that gives you the wrong kind of glasses."

"I like mine rose-tinted, thank you very much," Dane said, his demeanor mild. "And if I want to look at you with my heart, who's going to stop me?" He paused, and Clay peeped at him through his lashes. "You?" Dane pressed, making sure they had eye contact.

Clay swallowed. "No," he rasped.

Dane made another pass with the razor, and Clay waited until he was done to spread his feet and plant them again, the shift bringing Dane closer.

"I'm losing my balance," Clay said weakly, because it was true, on a whole lot of levels.

"Hold on to my wrist," Dane said, "and stop trying to back away."

Well, that was easy enough. Clay did, and closed his eyes, waiting for Dane to bare him to the world.

A millennia later the planets had stilled and all the worlds had stopped to listen to the beating of Clay's heart. It was pounding so hard he knew Dane must have felt it through his skin. Dane pulled back, his own breathing a little harsh. "Here, let me towel you off."

Clay kept his eyes closed for that part, and when Dane was done, he felt the surprising rasp of Dane's lips on his cheek, near the corner of his mouth.

"Wha—"

"There," Dane whispered in his ear. "Your dimple. I knew it was right there."

He pulled away and turned Clay toward the mirror. The steam had long since vanished, and Clay saw his perfectly average, clean-shaven face and neck, looking a lot leaner than the last time he'd seen it, his eyes just a little bit more hopeful.

"You really want to date that?" he asked Dane with complete sincerity.

Dane's lips moving next to his ear this time made him shiver, made him ache. "I want to *devour* it," he promised. Then he pulled back and bussed Carpenter lightly on the cheek. "But slowly. I've never been anyone's first before. I sort of want you to stick around."

"Ditto," Clay said.

Then, as though knowing Clay really needed his space, Dane backed away. "Now go change. I'll get our movie tickets while I wait. By the way, when you move in with me, can we burn the couch?"

"I'm moving in with you?" Clay asked, befuddled.

"Yes, eventually." Dane said it with such confidence that Clay figured he must be kidding, and then walked out of the bathroom, leaving Clay to wander into his bedroom to get dressed.

When he got there, he discovered that the "thing" Dane had needed to grab from his car was really a shopping bag full of new clothes.

"When did you have time to get these?" he asked in pure astonishment, because he couldn't think of anything else to say.

Jeans in his current size, button-down shirts in his current size, everything with just a hint of stretch in it, just in case Clay lost his mind and went back to Oreos as a staple. There had to be a week's worth of clothing spread out on his bed, with some sci-fi themed T-shirts and pajama bottoms thrown in for good measure, as well as a ten-pack of boxer briefs that *weren't* full of holes and *wouldn't* hang off his currently leaner ass.

"See this handy little computer in my hand?" Dane asked. "It has Wi-Fi, and I know all the Twitters. Now try some of it on so we can go."

Clay flailed his hand, realizing his other hand was cramping from holding on to the towel for so long.

"But… but Dane—"

"But what? Jesus, Clay, they're clothes. Put them on. We're burning the others with the couch, just so you know."

"But what if I get fat again? Er. What if I get fat*ter* again?"

Dane shrugged. "Then we buy more new clothes. I don't see a down side. Now say 'Thank you' and get dressed."

"Thank you," Clay said automatically. "But—"

"I'll be in the living room. You have ten minutes or my feelings are going to be hurt." Dane smiled coquettishly. "Also, I figured we'd go to Rubio's for lunch. You could have a salad or a California bowl or whatever, and then we could share some candy at the movie theater. Do whatever you have to do in your phone to make that right, but get a move on!"

"No candy during the movie," Carpenter said, a little desperate for control. As Dane turned around with his mouth wide open to complain, he finished the thought. "There's this dessert place that puts ice cream between donut halves. I figured we could split one." He bit his lip shyly. "I, uh, figured it out on my app and everything."

"Nice." Dane gave him an approving smile, and Carpenter's panic at seeing himself cared for eased a little.

"Thanks for the clothes," he said softly. "It's… nice."

Dane's smile went sly. "Oh, honey, you know I'm motivated by self-interest. I want the world to see who's holding my hands at the movies."

He sauntered out, and Clay picked a lightweight collared shirt in a pretty sage green and a pair of cargo shorts that would *not* go past his knees and hoped for the best. He was dressed in five minutes and spent the next five putting the rest of his clothes away so his bed was clear.

He resolutely didn't think about why it would be a good idea if his bed was cleared off.

"So help me—" Dane muttered, coming into the room as he hung the last of the shirts. "Oh! Okay. You're dressed. Good choice. I like green on you."

"It looks good on Mason too," Clay told him. "You're gonna be surrounded by plants."

"Green things are good. Now let me take a look." Dane turned Clay forward, then stood dutifully back, looking him up and down. "Oh, for heaven's sake. Lift your arm."

Clay raised his arm obediently and Dane yanked on the sleeve. They both heard the popping of the tag, and Clay grimaced. "Sorry," he said. The one on the shorts had been chafing into his waist and easier to spot.

"Nope, no sorry." Dane wrapped his arms around Clay's shoulders from behind and nuzzled his jaw, and Clay relaxed happily into the hug and made a realization.

"If we're gonna do this, this is gonna be us," he said, thinking about Dane's warmth, his happiness, the way they always seemed to entertain each other, even when things sucked and they were barely holding on.

"What is?" Dane asked, seemingly fascinated by his earlobe. He played with it for a moment, until Clay let out an unconscious moan.

"You're killing me. I'm going to die from a permanent erection, and people are gonna go, well, he may have been a fat guy, but at least he had a chubby." Dane nipped his earlobe, and he gasped this time, not wanting to lose contact. "All the touching. You like to touch. You will be touching me all the time." He remembered being a kid, when hugs were doled out like carob, as a reward.

"Is that going to be a problem?" Dane purred, and Clay turned around so they were in each other's arms.

"No," he said, and this time *he* initiated the kiss, capturing Dane's somewhat pouty mouth and shoving his tongue inside, liking the way Dane melted against him, as if he was helpless, and let Clay take over.

Dane made Clay feel like he had control, over the touching, over the kissing, over his life. Clay loved the control, but he wanted to use it to make Dane happy, so there was a lovely, blissful little feedback loop going on there, much like this kiss. Clay pushed forward, Dane accepted, Dane pushed back, Clay opened his mouth and let Dane in.

Long and deep, passionate and wet, their hands just holding, soothing, roaming but not intruding, until Dane pulled back and rested his forehead against Clay's.

"We have a plan," he panted.

"It's a good plan," Clay agreed.

"Healthy lunch."

"I like this plan."

"Movie."

"Great plan."

"Dessert."

"Still good." Clay took a deep breath through his nose because everything in his body was trembling and trying to tell him to fuck the plan, fuck the date, and fuck—

Nope. Nope, nope, nope.

"We've got to go," Dane murmured, taking a step back.

"I want you." It was a revelation, in its way. He'd known it back in February, when he'd kissed Dane that one night. But then, as Dane had spiraled into not-Dane, the angry, pissed-off, bitter dark version of himself that tried to hurt people and drive them away, he'd stomped on it.

"I've wanted you since we met," Dane said, the strain of making that light obvious in his voice. "We can wait through an actual date to make out on the couch."

Clay blinked and swallowed, then reached for the end table where he'd left his wallet, phone, and keys. "Since we met?" he said, pausing before he turned around.

"You said you weren't gay," Dane told him. "And my heart sort of disintegrated. And then you said, 'But Skipper and Richie didn't know until a couple of weeks ago,' so I hoped."

Clay swallowed. "I'm so scared," he admitted.

Dane's hard breath told him he took this seriously, even as his hand on Clay's urged him on. "I'm terrified. Let's go watch a superhero movie."

Clay nodded and followed him out.

We Can Be Heroes

DANE SAT in the movie theater with his head on Carpenter's shoulder and watched the screen dreamily. He had no idea what was happening in the movie, but his body was humming in excitement. He had to check his pill calendar three times to make sure he was up on his meds—this physical reaction to his endorphins was beyond his experience.

The memory of Carpenter, mostly naked, staring at him with those enormous eyes and letting Dane render him bare and vulnerable had been possibly the most erotic thing Dane had seen in his long and distinguished list of sexual encounters.

That wasn't just sex—although Dane couldn't keep his hand away from Carpenter's thigh as they watched the movie, because he wanted to glut his palms on Clay's skin—but trust.

This man had seen him at his absolute worst—so bad that Dane couldn't remember most of it.

And he'd somehow seen Dane as he wanted to be, instead. They shared the same snark brain, and Dane wanted to learn from his kindness. They shared the same loyalty for Clay's friends and Dane's brother. They shared the same belief that being happy was the best form of success.

And they seemed to share a deep and abiding hunger to feel the other one naked.

Dane wasn't sure what the other shoe would look like, but he knew it was coming. He wanted to get Carpenter naked first. He hadn't had many—any!—truly successful relationships, but he knew that if it *was* a relationship, sex made it harder for both parties to walk away.

That was partly bad. That last real relationship—the one that had led to his boyfriend's destroyed apartment and a dorm deposit his parents would never get back—had seemed so much more entangled because they'd been having sex. The sex had been seductive, and Dane tended to be hypersexual when he was on an upswing, anyway. The itch had been ever-present, the need all-consuming, and whatever Anthony had asked for, Dane would give, as long as he'd "do me baby one more time."

But in this case, with Clay, Dane knew it would be different.

For one thing, Clay wouldn't hurt him—not on purpose.

For another, the few hints Clay'd dropped about his sex life—or his ex of about two years before—said that he took sex seriously. Well, of course. Letting someone see him naked—or without a shirt, even—was an act of trust. He just wouldn't trust someone to get that close. And why not? His parents doled out approval like starvation rations. Carpenter wasn't going to trust that someone he cared about would unconditionally accept him with all his little quirks.

Sex was important—to both of them. Which was why they had both insisted on the date, probably. Dates were… formal. This right here, Dane's head on Clay Carpenter's shoulder, their fingers twining as their hands rested on Clay's meaty thigh, that was a public announcement right there. Clay wasn't going to deny their relationship and Dane wasn't going to just wander off with some other guy.

Amid the banter and the crosstalk and the hipster snark, this relationship had been serious from the get-go, because they'd started out as friends, and then they'd become *important* friends, and then they'd let each other see the places inside where not even friends were allowed.

Confidence by confidence, emotional support strut by securing rope, they'd become naked in each other's hearts long before this moment, when all Dane wanted was to touch Clay's naked body with his own.

Ten years ago, he would have grabbed Carpenter's hand and blown him in the bathroom—he wasn't even ashamed of that. Ten years ago, his bipolar had gone untreated, and his body had craved, and his self-awareness had been nil, and he hadn't really had anyone in his life he wanted to keep badly enough to make it important.

But this was special. They weren't having candy so they could have dessert afterward. Clay was wearing new clothes that looked damned good on him, just for Dane. Clay had cleaned his apartment—really, really well—and bought a new sheet and comforter set, one in muted blue and beige, that Dane really liked.

Things were special because they *mattered*, and in Dane's whole life, nobody had mattered this much besides family.

So Dane, who was known for being restless as fuck during movies, didn't even twitch. He just soaked in the presence of the nicest guy he'd ever known and enjoyed the explosions. Eventually, he even settled in and figured out the plot.

THE DONUT ice cream place really was as good as Clay had advertised, and they cut the donuts in half so they each got a super-decadent ice cream sandwich with salted caramel ice cream and almond slices and chocolate chips.

"God," Dane said, licking the last of the ice cream from his fingers. "That was stunning! How come nobody knows about this place?"

"They had a line to get in—*somebody* knows about this place!" Clay had finished his half off as well, but then, he'd saved up for it.

"Okay. How come *I* didn't know about this place?"

Clay's smile deepened—and yes, his dimple popped when he did that. "Because we've never been on a date before."

Dane gave him a smile that was all teeth. "You ready for the date to continue?" Outside, the sun was getting ready to set, and Clay nodded.

"Do you want to go watch the sunset first?" he asked. "I mean, there's a park near my place, or the river—"

"We can stop at the park on the way back," Dane allowed. "Maybe tomorrow, we can go to Sailor Bar after we help Terry move in and see it by the river."

But he'd said the magic words—*Terry move*—and even as Carpenter stood up and pulled Dane's chair out in an unconscious moment of chivalry, Dane became aware of the savage melancholy of tomorrow's approaching move… and of his worry for his brother.

"You really think Terry's going to bolt?" Dane asked, hating the quaver in his own voice.

Clay grimaced and grabbed Dane's hand to pull him out of the ice cream shop. "Yeah, baby. I'm sorry. I think he has to. He hasn't really been living, you know? For all he knows, grown-ups don't get a Mason in their lives."

"It's stupid," Dane muttered. "Mason was with his ex-douchebag for four years. Four years! But Ira was… well…."

"A douchebag," Carpenter supplied. "Yeah. Anybody who would cheat on your brother and make him feel bad about himself is the biggest douchebag around."

"But you know what? As much as I hated Ira, I wasn't as… as…." Again, his hands did that flailing thing. "As *hurt* by their breakup as I am thinking about Terry bolting like a scared Yorkie."

Carpenter sputtered. "*That's* what he looks like—my God. I've been trying to figure out where I've seen those eyes before, but you're totally right. But yeah, I get it. I mean, we *like* Terry. And we get him. He's not going to hurt your brother out of a lack of respect or because he thinks he can do better. He's just trying to figure himself out, and he hasn't had a chance to do that until now. I mean… it sucks, because it's Mason, and we love him, but it's not like we can slash Terry's tires over it or anything."

"Would you slash Ira's tires?" Dane asked, completely serious. "Asking for a friend."

"I'd have no idea how to slash someone's tires. You'd have to ask Richie. But I'm down for the road trip alone. Where's this Ira jerkoff live?"

Dane grinned at him, feeling all sunshiny inside. "You're the best," he said in complete sincerity. "I'd *marry* you."

Carpenter let out a low chuckle, and Dane leaned into him as they walked through the parking lot. "But first…," Clay said, dropping a kiss on the top of Dane's head.

"First," Dane supplied, "we have to have a first night of kisses."

"Is that what it is?" Carpenter murmured. "I like how that sounds. By the way, when am I getting you home?"

Dane almost stopped, which would have been disastrous because that would have made Clay fall. "You're getting me home?"

"Well, uh…." Clay frowned. "This is a date? Did you bring moving clothes and meds for tomorrow?"

Dane scowled. "Goddammit," he muttered. "Apparently you're bringing me home around one in the morning, but only if you pack your own clothes so we can drive your SUV."

"Why? What's wrong with your car?"

"You wouldn't be in it. Damned meds. I brought tonight's dose but not tomorrow morning's. Shit. It's a good thing I brought rubbers and lube or I'd have to kick my own ass."

He pretty much heard Carpenter's eyes click to their widest setting.

"You brought, uh…."

Dane looked sideways just to see him blush. "Yeah, Clay. I brought rubbers and lubricant. Although I'm pretty sure if we both compared health screenings, the rubbers might be unnecessary."

"I haven't had sex in two years," Clay said ruefully. "My last employee physical ran the test and my screen was clear."

Dane had suspected as much. "I haven't had sex in almost a year," he said, because he'd banged pretty much all comers when he'd been working at the restaurant. "I used condoms faithfully, and the PrEP protocol is part of my medication." He paused and swallowed. "I've been absolutely on target for my meds all month."

"I know that," Carpenter said, and Dane knew he did.

"And my health screening was clear in March when they were testing my med levels."

"Oh," Carpenter said, like that had just occurred to him. "So, uh, we don't really, uh—"

"No, Clay," Dane said softly as they drew near the SUV. "We don't."

"Why are you on PrEP?"

Dane blew out a breath. "Because sometimes hypersexuality is among the symptoms of bipolar disorder. I was not particularly careful before my diagnosis, and let's just say that when I'm lucid, I remember how lucky I got. I went on PrEP in case I ever got sloppy again."

Clay let out a breath. "You are so… so strong," he said after a moment. "You'll, uh, let me know, right? If, uh—"

Dane felt the flush of embarrassment creep up his neck—not from his sexual history, but from his medication past. "I promise," he said softly. "If I'm ever out of my mind enough to cheat on you, you'll know. I want to be well—I want to *stay* well—so I can be the sort of man you can count on. And if my meds stop working again, I promise that me cheating will be the rock-bottom of the spiral, okay? You'll be in the loop a long time before it gets that bad. You were last time, right?"

Clay nodded, turning his head toward the freeway, where they could both see the sky turning pink. "I trust you," he said, his eyes distant. He turned back to face Dane, and Dane caught his breath. He really did look serene. "I just need you to not run away after tonight, you understand?"

Dane nodded. "Yeah. I get that. I've got nowhere better to be."

THEY SKIPPED the park, watching the sun set as they drove back toward Clay's apartment with the windows down.

"What movie do you want to watch?" Clay said, walking toward his bottom floor apartment. "I can make us some salads for dinner if you're hungry again, and I've got cubed chicken in the refrigerator we can put on top—"

Dane stopped right in front of Clay's door and turned, capturing his mouth in a blatant gesture of possession, and then keeping it until he felt a definite wobble in Clay's knees. Ah, God, yes—he wanted this taste.

"Carpenter?" he said, when he pulled back for air.

"Yeah?"

"I don't give a shit about the movie. And the salad might be nice later. But right now, I've wanted one thing all day. It's like you and that ice cream sandwich. You were a good boy and you got your treat. Haven't I been a good boy?"

"You've been the best," Clay breathed, and this time *he* pressed the kiss, pressed Dane back against his door until Dane's knees wobbled.

Clay pulled back, and for a moment, Dane was going to pull him down again because how *dare* he, and then Clay held out his key and let them both in. They tumbled into Clay's front room, hands everywhere, mouths only separating under the direst need.

Clay moved with a sort of exquisite grace, an absolute care, probably born of the awareness that he was bigger and heavier than the person he was with and didn't want to hurt or crush anybody.

Dane appreciated it at first, but as Clay backed Dane gracefully to the arm of the couch, he'd had enough of it.

"Bed," he demanded, and then shoved at Clay's shoulders. "No couch. No necking. Bed. I want naked, and I want bed, and I want *you.*"

"Wow! You're a pushy bastard!"

"And you're still dressed, and we're still in the living room! Now move!"

"What if I *want* the couch and the necking like teenagers and the no naked yet," Clay asked, but he was following Dane into the bedroom, albeit reluctantly.

"Then I say get a couch that isn't a hide-a-bed and built like a dinosaur skeleton trying to skewer me. But I'm not waiting for a new couch to be delivered. I want you *now.*"

The warmth of Clay's laughter did nothing to ease the urgency driving Dane into the bedroom.

But once they hit the doorway, Dane managed to stifle the urge to turn on the light. It wasn't that he didn't want to see everything. It was that he wanted Clay to be perfectly comfortable, especially this first time. Dane wanted sex with him—Dane, a male person with a penis—to be so stunning, so amazing that Clay would have it anytime, anywhere, in darkness or in the light. So no, he wouldn't put up a fight, this first time, Dane, he would not hex, he wanted Clay to love the sex!

He started to giggle a little at the rhyme, just as Clay started to kiss his neck. Clay pulled back. "What? That tickles?"

"I'll tell you later," Dane breathed. "Keep sucking on my neck!"

Clay would apparently do anything he asked. Down his collarbone, he paused at Dane's Adam's apple and hummed, making him giggle again. "What?"

"This is new. It's like your stubble. Let me appreciate it."

"Later!" Dane stepped back and stripped off his shirt and shorts, the briefs with the shorts, and toed off his loafers. "You savor a fine wine after a meal. You *devour* the first meal you've had in two years!"

"Stop," Clay said gently, and he stepped forward again, fully clothed, to slide his palms down the outside of Dane's arms. "*You* are wonderful. I've been waiting my entire life to touch you. Just slow down and let me do that, okay? We're in *my* apartment. I'm not running away."

Dane cocked his head suspiciously. "Would you run away if we were in *my* house?"

To his dismay, Carpenter shifted his feet. "Maybe. But you're naked, and your body is doing this"—he waved his arms in the direction of Dane's erection—"thing! And I'd really like to touch that. Can I touch that?"

Dane let that fear dissipate. This was a first step, not a final one. "Come here," he murmured. Clay stepped back into his arms, and Dane took over the seduction. He kissed Clay's newly shaved jawline, down his neck, unfastening the new shirt one button at a time, kissing the newly revealed skin. When it was open, Dane pushed it back off Clay's shoulders and started kissing his bear-y hairy chest, delighting in every kiss.

"I'm, uh, a little furry," Clay panted, and Dane hated the note of apology in his voice.

"For some of us, that's a turn-on," he muttered, stroking it some more. He cleared a little path to Clay's nipple and felt the smile stretch his cheeks. "Pink!" he said happily, before bending his knees so he could suckle.

"Oh damn!" Clay sucked in a breath and knotted his hands in Dane's hair, dislodging his bun. "Dane, baby, what're you—"

Dane pulled in his flesh a little harder, because he needed it, needed the taste and the smell and the feel, and Clay gasped. "I need to lie down," he said in wonder.

"See?" Dane urged. "*That's* what I'm talking about! Now take off your pants!"

"Sure, sure." Clay stepped away, breathing fast, and started fumbling with his belt. His cargo shorts fell to the floor, weighted by keys and his wallet and phone, but Clay just sort of toed his shoes off around them and stepped out. "I should pick those—mmmf!"

Dane had bought him the clothes; he didn't care if they got rumpled. They were *naked.* Wholly, completely, fantastically *naked*, and Dane wanted to feel his body everywhere. He loved it, the solidness, the pale skin under the hair on his chest, the way Clay's newly shaved cheeks turned pinker every time Dane did something new. He took Clay's mouth and Clay wrapped his arms around Dane's shoulders and Dane almost melted. Oh, his body, all of his body… Dane belonged *next to all of his body.*

He took Clay's mouth again, thinking maybe Clay had the right of it. They should kiss more. They should kiss more naked. They should—

"Oh wow," Dane breathed, thrilled. "That's your penis!"

He reached down between them and felt him, hard, surprisingly long, and decently thick, loving the silkiness of it and the fact that it was Clay's.

"Mmf…." Clay grunted and spread his legs a little. "I really gotta sit down." He reached behind him and pulled back the covers and sat down on the bed. Dane stepped into the shelter formed by his thighs, gratified when Clay started kissing his tummy and rubbing his newly smooth cheek on Dane's soft skin.

"You like?" Dane asked shyly. Nobody talked about his body, the weight he'd lost, the fact that he was not muscular, just flexible and thin.

Clay looked up at him, biting his lip. "I like. It's, like, exciting because you're a guy, but it's awesome because you're Dane my friend and I love that guy. So you put them together…." He lowered his head and kissed below Dane's absurdly prominent navel. "You get magic," he said, and then he lowered his head a little more, stuck out his tongue, and licked a bead of precome off the head of Dane's erection.

Dane whimpered. Just like that. No guilt. No, "Oh my God I'm licking a guy's cock!" Clay just… just… oh God, now he wasn't just licking it, he'd opened his mouth, he'd taken the head in, he was….

"You're sucking me!" Dane gasped in excitement. "And you're *good* at it! Oh my God!" Clay pushed his head forward and pulled back, again and again. He was doing that swirly thing with his tongue when he pulled back, and every time he did that, Dane's knees would decide to buckle, only he couldn't sit down now! Not when Clay Carpenter was *sucking his cock.*

"Oh God," he moaned, knotting his fingers in that rich brown hair, not close to coming but not sure how long his legs would hold out. "Oh, Clay, could you… could you maybe let me lie down and do that some— *Yes! Do that some more*!"

Clay had moved one of his hands from cupping Dane's thigh to the front. He cupped Dane's balls gently, rolling them delicately between his strong fingers, driving Dane insane.

"Here," Dane grunted, widening his stance. "Between my legs. Go to town. Grope me and keep doing that thing with your tongue. *Oh my God, teach me, sensei*!"

Clay chuckled, which made everything on Dane's cock just swimmier and more lovely, but he used his hands as requested, feeling behind Dane's balls, stroking tentatively along his taint, and every inch, every investigation, made Dane crazier with desire. He was getting close, so close, and then—oop! There went Clay's finger, tapping at his slutty little pucker, and Dane almost blew his load, right there.

"Wait," he begged. "C'mon, Clay, let me do something."

Clay pulled back, eyes big, and wiped his face off with the back of his hand. He looked debauched and a little bit dazed, and Dane could eat him in one bite. "Yeah, sure," he said. "Can't I just suck your dick for, like, ever? 'Cause I could do that for a super-long time and—"

"And I'd never get to touch you!" Dane supplied, indignant and breathless. Carpenter's skin was electric satiation—he never wanted to stop. "Now lie back in bed and let me do that thing to you, see how you like it!"

"I don't think I'll mind," Clay said, sounding a little desperate. He squirreled back on the bed, putting his head on the pillow and spreading his legs before looking at Dane expectantly in the dark. "How are we doing—"

Dane pounced on his cock, taking it firmly in his hand and sucking the head—the rather bulbous head—into his mouth.

Mm…. He tasted wonderful. A little sweaty from being out and about in the May sunshine, but mostly clean. He was leaking precome too, and it was salty and sweet—mostly sweet, which probably came from his meticulous diet, although Dane would have sucked him down if he'd tasted like hops and bitters.

Clay started to massage his scalp, pulling his fingers through it gently. "That feels really good," he whispered. "I'm… I'm getting close. Can I see your face? Please?"

Dane nodded and then sucked Clay to the back of his throat hard, keeping him there and swallowing for a minute, partly hoping for Clay's come, and partly hoping he'd hold off because Dane had a plan for his orgasm that he thought Clay might enjoy.

Clay moaned, bucking his hips off the bed and jerking at Dane's hair—not hard enough to sting, just hard enough to prompt Dane to let go of him.

Dane pulled up from his dick and turned his face toward him, smiling in a way he knew for a fact was utterly debauched. "I know you want all the things," he whispered. "But I want to taste you super, super bad. How about let me have my way now, and you can have your way afterward, okay?"

"I'm gonna come in your mouth," Clay said, and he sounded like that would be a bad thing.

Dane had to change his mind about that. "Yeah, I know—it's gonna be great!" And then he slurped Clay into the back of his throat again and played with his balls, a little firmer than Clay had played with his. Clay's hips arched and retreated, the motion unmistakable and raw and carnal, and Dane wanted more. He hollowed his cheeks and sucked, down and up, knowing this was one of his strengths and so excited about using it—here, on Clay.

He sucked down one more time and held there, gulping like mad to massage Clay's cockhead, and Clay let out a yell that probably rattled the windows before moving one of his hands up to cover his own mouth… and orgasming, pumping come into Dane's mouth, glorious and creamy and proof, right there, that Dane had done this one thing, this one magical thing, absolutely right.

Carpenter made a little sound of "done" and Dane pulled back, scooting up the bed to kiss him. Clay didn't back away or make a face, even though Dane knew his chin was dripping in come. Instead he stared at Dane thoughtfully for a moment, his brown eyes huge and luminous, and then he kissed Dane reverently, so gently Dane almost cried.

Then the kiss went deeper, taking in more of his own taste, and then dirtier, licking Dane's lips, the scruff on his chin, before moving down Dane's chest.

"So, returning the—oh, damn. Damn. Damn!" Clay's mouth on his nipple was exquisite, and it was Dane's turn to spread his knees and arch his cock to the heavens, wanting all the things.

Clay suckled, sliding his hand down Dane's concave stomach, running his fingers through Dane's happy trail while Dane arched his hips a little more demandingly.

"Oh, come on," he begged. "Just a handy? Squeeze? Just a—"

"You are so pushy!" Clay laughed, after releasing his nipple with a pop. "Oh my God, do you give *all* your lovers explicit instructions?"

"No!" Dane muttered, hips still undulating against the bed. "Just the slow ones. Oh my God, I will explode all over you. It will be terrifying. You'll be sucking my nipple and suddenly my cock will just spew all over the place and you will run away…." He keened as Carpenter wrapped his hand around him and squeezed. "Screaming!" he squeaked.

Carpenter laughed and moved down his stomach, pausing for a moment to tongue his belly button. "You have an outtie!" he said happily. "Why do you have an outtie?"

Dane hissed, because his little nubbin of a belly button was sensitive, and until right now, nobody had ever appreciated the benefits of that.

"It's practice for my dick," he moaned in frustration. "Now could you… you know… hurry it up a little?"

"You just promised me your cock will explode and I'll run away screaming." Carpenter chuckled, tightening his grip and stroking while he continued to explore. "I thought you were looking forward to that!" He continued to nuzzle his way to Dane's hip bone and lick experimentally, and Dane forced his hips flat against the bed and let him. Clay thought Dane was worth the time, and Dane… well, Dane hadn't really ever been one to *take* that sort of time with a lover.

But he'd never enjoyed himself quite this much with one before either, and he figured it would be worth the wait. He put his palm flat on Carpenter's wide shoulders, stroking, loving the smooth skin under his fingers, the way he could feel the muscle groups bunch and release as Clay leveraged his body up and down the mattress. God, he was beautiful. Not "hey, look, you can see every shred of muscle" beautiful, just solid and warm and comforting and lovely—and reverent.

For all their banter, his every touch had been filled with a sort of wide-eyed excitement, a holy joy that even Dane, as impatient as he always was, could appreciate.

"I'd be okay," Dane gasped. "You know, if there was no screaming and running away."

Carpenter *hmmd* in the back of the throat, and finally, *finally*, took Dane into his mouth again.

All the way into his mouth. As far back as he could.

Dane moaned and tried not to thrust up, and Carpenter "hmmd" some more, the subtle vibrations sending frissons of excitement dancing along Dane's skin.

"This… this is amazing," Dane murmured. "You can grope some more—you know, like… yeah. Ah…."

Dane spread his knees farther, naked, exposed. It was the only way he knew how to be during sex, and sometimes lovers touched him like he wanted and sometimes they just sucked his dick like that was the only part of him that worked. But Clay was apparently fascinated and happy with *all* the things.

He kept up that delirious pressure with his mouth, pulling back, rocking forward, way forward, pulling back again. He fisted the shaft firmly and maneuvered his body between Dane's legs, filling up the empty air, exuding warmth and exploration.

Ah, God! He used his free hand to stroke—just stroke—Dane's backside, palming his thighs, his glutes, and the sensation of being touched in those rare and faraway places sent Dane into floaty-floaty land, where, hello, he could get blown forever and simply make yummy-yummy noises.

"I hope," Dane gasped, "you're ready to do that all night, because I'm pretty sure I can."

Carpenter chuckled, making his lips vibrate around Dane's cockhead and upping the ante just a tad. "Are you hinting at something?"

Oh, this was sort of embarrassing. Most guys did this on general principle, probably because Dane had "slutty bottom" written all over him. He *was* the guy who got his ass creamed—or fucked and jizzed on, pretty much standard.

But Clay wasn't going to do that to him. Clay was going to *pleasure* him, so this thing he wanted was something he had to ask for so Clay knew it was pleasurable.

"Finger me?" he begged, breathlessly. "A little spit, a little poke-e-ta poke-e-ta? Please?"

Clay's laughter filled the room and vibrated against Dane's dick and his abdomen. And then, oh bless him, he did what Dane asked. He let his spit trickle down between Dane's meticulously cleaned cheeks and played with his pucker, pushing in a little, pulling out, not even to the first knuckle. In some more, out, the subtle burn enough to push the blowjob from "super-pleasurable haze" to "increasingly urgent stimulation."

"Mmnangh…." Dane thought he was going to make a word there—something like "more" or "yes" or "please God keep going!" But no word could be made. Instead he hunched his hips lower, impaling himself deeper on Clay's careful finger, and moaned.

Clay pulled his mouth off Dane's cock and laughed softly. "You are not subtle, are you?"

"Mmangh?" he pleaded, and bless Clay for reading his mind, he added another finger there, stretching him further, and then squeezed his cock, stroking up and licking the head.

Suddenly Dane wanted to be on his hands and knees, where Clay Carpenter's oh-so-perceptive gaze couldn't rest on his face, watching him enjoy this so much. He was barely comfortable asking for things when it was a faceless cock, nameless hands, a boyfriend he didn't intend to keep. But Clay was watching him, taking notes on how to make Dane come undone, and for a moment, he wasn't entirely comfortable with that.

And then—oh! Oh! Clay's fingers were thick, capable, and that third one in his backside made him as wide as a cock, stretching his entrance. And now he was beyond shy, beyond hazy, pounding the bed with one hand and Clay's back with the other.

"*Yes*!" he cried. "God yes! Oh please don't—don't—don't—" Orgasm swept him, everywhere, sweating from the soles of his feet to the back of his neck, turning his body into a big central nervous system earthquake and shooting white light from his fingers, toes, eyes, mouth, and his ridiculously sensitive little outtie belly button that had so charmed Clay Carpenter in the first place.

He also dumped come down Carpenter's throat, a thing he couldn't even *think* to regret until he heard the protest noises Clay was making as he tried to swallow.

He would have said, "Sorry! So sorry! Was going to warn you!" But his language centers were still on hold. His limbs flopped out, and his frenzied pounding on Carpenter's back turned into a desultory stroking, and his entire body melted into the mattress, the excess come dripping from Clay's mouth sliding off his abdomen and onto the sheets.

He felt *amazing.*

"Dane?" Carpenter said anxiously, pulling himself up the bed and grabbing a tissue to wipe all the things. "You okay?"

"Kiss me," he mumbled, wanting the warmth, the earthiness of come in Clay's mouth, Clay's body covering his own.

Clay didn't say anything, just framed his face with gentle fingers and touched his lips to Dane's. Dane closed his eyes and let him in, the taste of the two of them glorious, Clay's warm body just amazing as it moved against his.

His lassitude started to fade as he ran his hand down Clay's backside, along his hips, over his waist, and he was not surprised—but a little hurt—when Clay backed away.

"Stop it," he commanded, grumpy. "The ship has sailed. I've touched your stomach and your chest and your back and your cock, and I've found it to be all good. Delicious even. You can't suddenly go, 'Oh, wait! He's seen my fat!' Now come back here and kiss me some more!"

Clay regarded him soberly. "You need to know," he said. "You need to know that, as awesome as what we just did was, I'm not going to be okay with you seeing my body right away. I'm… I'm gonna keep towels on until you worry them off of me. I'm not going to swim in your brother's pool if the whole world is there to see. This—" He smiled, the expression making his plain face transcendent and beautiful. "This thing we just did, it was awesome. But it was private. I feel like I can fly—but I'm going to remember sometimes that only small elephants fly."

"You're not an elephant, you big dumb jerk," Dane said, his eyes burning. He rolled over and draped himself on top of Clay, playing with the hair between his pecs and not looking him in the eyes because he was vulnerable too. "But since that was in all other respects, a really sublime sexual experience, and I don't want to do that with anybody else but you ever again, I'm going to let that bit of self-deprecation slide."

"Really?" Carpenter said, face lighting up.

Dane managed to meet his eyes. "Which part?"

"The part about only doing that with me for a while—"

"Ever again."

"Yeah?"

"Yeah."

Clay's expression reached a serenity that Dane had to appreciate. "Good."

Dane kissed him again, and again, and their blood started to thrum and their urgency increased. He took his time, since Carpenter seemed to enjoy doing that, and stroked everything—Clay's upper arms, the sides of his neck, the spot behind his ear. Clay mapped Dane's skin in return, like a path to the holy land, both of them completely avoiding the erogenous zones which were still delightfully sloppy and used and swollen from their first orgasms.

Dane finally felt down to Carpenter's cock and realized he was dripping precome, and he shuddered.

"Lube?" he panted, stroking Clay hard.

"What?"

"Do. You. Have. Lubricant." He enunciated carefully, because what he really wanted to say was "Fuck me! Fuck me now! Fuck me dry! Fuck me raw!" But he figured it might be a little soon for that.

"Uh, oh!" Clay rolled toward the end table near the bed and reached inside the drawer. He came out with basic lube, two steps above KY, and Dane reached out imperiously.

"Give me!"

Clay did, his bemused expression indicating absolute trust.

Dane slid to the side and pushed on Clay's shoulder. "Lie back," he commanded. "Spread your legs a little."

Clay took a deep breath, like he was fortifying himself, and did what Dane asked.

Dane dripped a dollop of the silky lubricant on Clay's cock and spread it around with his fist, while Carpenter took a deep, surprised breath.

"What?" Dane asked absently, snicking the cap closed and handing him the bottle back. Carpenter just sort of dropped the bottle next to his hip, and Dane pushed up on one knee and threw the other around Clay's hips, straddling them and scooching back until his asshole was immediately over Clay Carpenter's thick and amazing penis.

"Just… I don't know… thought we were doing this the other way?"

Dane snorted and reached behind him, positioning Clay just… right. "Seriously?" he breathed, settling down with that large, delicious head at his entrance, just starting to stretch. "When you went…." He slid down a little, shuddering as Clay's cock widened him, the head pushing at his dilated opening enough to burn… oh-so good. "To all that trouble…," he continued. "Oh!" Clay popped in, and he kept lowering his ass, because the glide was just too damned good. "To stretch… oh yeah. Yes. Oh my God. Stretch me out?"

Oh damn. He settled himself down completely, full in ways he didn't think he could be. He paused for a moment, his face tilted toward the ceiling, back arched, ass thrust out, and just breathed, shaking all over with the need to move.

"Dane?" Carpenter's voice quavered a little. "Uh…."

"Touch me," he said throatily, keeping his eyes closed and rocking forward. Clay's tentative fingers skating on his cockhead were pure torture. "*Fist* me," he begged, although if Clay had wanted to just palm his inner thighs, he wouldn't have minded that either.

Then Clay wrapped his fist around Dane's cock and Dane let out a groan they could both feel where they were joined.

"Dane?" Clay said uncertainly, and Dane started rocking back and forth a little faster. And a little harder. Oh God, his thighs burned, and his knees ached and… "I can't go fast enough from here!" he complained.

Carpenter grunted, grabbed hold of the outside of his thighs, and in a move of unprecedented smoothness, rolled them both over until he was on top and Dane was where he loved to be best, his knees pressed to his chest being *fucked through the floor.*

And Carpenter wasn't holding back.

Hard and fast and deep—it was like he'd read a manual or something, because every thrust hit hard and hit home. He wasn't rabbit fucking, but that was fine. Rabbit fucking made Dane's ass numb. He was just… solidly fucking Dane until Dane felt another solar wind of orgasm rushing up his body. He reached down for his cock, needing and not caring at this point if Clay saw him stroke himself.

Everything was tingling, and damn if Dane didn't need to—oh yeah! More! More! More! He shuddered, gripping his cock hard enough to hurt, and this next orgasm didn't explode so much as roll out of him, slowly, powerfully, both helped and hindered by Clay inside him. As his muscles clamped around Clay's cock, Clay cried out in surprise.

"Holy *wow*! Jesus—*oh my God*!"

His voice cracked on that last word, but Dane was still spasming too hard to laugh. Clay shuddered and fell forward, catching himself on his arms and sliding out of Dane as his angle changed. Dane moaned and came again, rolling to his side so Carpenter could spoon him from behind.

For a moment, he heard nothing but his own heartbeat and harsh breathing.

Then he heard Clay's.

Clay's hand rested lightly on the outside of his arm, and Dane reached over and pulled it tighter across his chest, shoving back hard against Clay's chest and stomach so that meaty, muscular arm could wrap all the way around his shoulders and keep him safe.

"Clay?"

"Yeah?"

"In case you're wondering how that went, it went really fucking well."

Carpenter laughed weakly. "I *was* wondering. Thanks."

"Well, don't. I'm not sure if anyone ever told you this, but you're an amazing lover."

Clay grunted. "Nobody has *ever* told me that."

Dane rolled over to look at his face and make sure he was serious. "For reals?"

Dane's hair had come loose from its bun and was falling in his eyes. Clay shoved at it with the palm of his hand. "Only you, Dane Hayes."

"The rest of the world is stupid," Dane said thickly. "You need to stick with me because I'm the only one who appreciates you."

They dozed for a little while then, and Dane startled awake about an hour later.

"What? Who?" Carpenter sat up, confused, and Dane saw the exact moment he recognized who was in his bed and what they'd done together.

He pulled the coverlet up to his chest in maidenly modesty and tried to be a rational human being.

"Uhm, was there something we forgot?"

Dane held his hand over his mouth. “Yeah. I need to take my meds and we need to go sleep at my house.”

Carpenter frowned. “Are you sure you don’t want me to just drop you off—”

Dane regarded him with deep disgust. “Do I *look* like I’m sure? Now drop the damned quilt, get dressed, and let’s find some chocolate milk. I *liked* sleeping in your arms, and God willing, I shall do it a lot more in the future. Now move!”

“Yikes,” Clay muttered, rolling out of bed with the cover still wrapped around him and scrambling on the floor to find his underwear. “Somehow I thought when I fell in love again there would be fewer orders and more flowers.”

“I’ll send you flowers next week. Right now, obey me, okay? We’ve got to get going!” Dane paused. “And what do you mean, ‘again’?” He widened his eyes. “Wait! What do you mean *love*!”

“There were girls,” Carpenter protested, sliding on his underwear with his back to Dane. “Relationships. You’re my first guy, not my first *person.*”

Dane grunted. “No, I beg to differ.” He plastered himself along that broad back and kissed Clay’s neck softly. “I’m your first *person*, because *nobody* knows you like I do. So I’m the only one you ever loved. And what do you mean by love?”

Carpenter kept his face turned away. “Are you dressed yet? I was very close to sleeping, and I’d like to get back there. Get dressed and let me get some shitty clothes for tomorrow.”

“No, seriously, what did you mean, ‘love’?”

“Dane, pack your stuff so we can go to your place and hope Mason and Terry are done having their own Saturday night.” He paused. “I mean, they’ll still be together, right?”

“As far as I know,” Dane said. “What did you mean love?”

Carpenter took a deep breath, pulled up his shorts, and turned to face him. After fumbling with the button and the fly, he wrapped his arms around Dane’s waist and pulled him close.

“Dane, do you like this?”

Dane melted a little. “Mm?”

“Yeah, me too. Can we… can we just do this for tonight? Tomorrow, we have to move Terry, then we’ll probably sleep in our own beds tomorrow night—”

"Says who?" Carpenter frowned, and Dane tried to fix his wayward tongue. "Says who? What do you mean? Why would we not sleep together again?"

Clay took a deep breath. "I have work. You have school—"

"I don't care."

"I'm well aware you haven't done relationships, Dane—"

"That doesn't matter."

"We'll definitely have sex again—"

"I mean sleep together. Why would we not sleep in the same bed tomorrow night?"

Clay cocked his head. "Because I have an apartment and you have a house," he said slowly. "But let's get to your house, get some sleep, and discuss it tomorrow."

"And get my meds, you mean," Dane said without heat. "But this is not me being crazy. This is me being… well, me. I am bipolar, but this isn't the cray-cray talking. This is the guy who hasn't had a boyfriend since—" He stopped himself, because the end of that sentence abruptly contradicted the first part, when he said this wasn't the cray-cray.

"Since your diagnosis," Clay said softly, but he didn't let Dane go. "I am aware. One thing at a time, Dane. Clothes, meds, your house. Terry's move, tomorrow night, who sleeps where. Next week, your finals, what comes next."

"When do we get to the part about you love me?" Dane asked suspiciously.

"When it doesn't freak you out."

All of Dane's muscles relaxed at once, completely, not just the little bit that had happened when Clay first hugged him. He rested his head on Carpenter's shoulder like they were dancing, and let that magnificent powerful body support his weight a little. "It doesn't freak me out," he mumbled, not sure how to catch the tiger's tail that his brain had become.

"Sure, it doesn't."

"Much."

"Yeah, baby, I know."

"The sex was good?" Dane brightened at the thought.

Clay chuckled a little. "The sex was fucking amazing."

"So that's a win."

"Oh yeah."

Dane had to nod, wanting nothing more than to rock like this in Clay Carpenter's arms forever. "One thing at a time," he said. "We're taking the win. Okay. I can do this. We can do this." Suddenly he frowned and stood up. "But you love me best. If that word's hanging between us, I have to be the one you love best."

Clay's eyes grew suspiciously bright, and he was doing something with his mouth that suggested he was squashing his initial emotional response. "I love you best," he confirmed.

"That's more than Skipper."

Clay's eyes narrowed. "I'm going to point out here that I wouldn't ask you to pick between Mason and me, and then I'm going to leave this subject alone."

Dane felt it welling up—felt the tantrum, the pout, the desire to pick a fight that Clay couldn't win, not if he wanted to keep his self-respect intact.

And for once—oh dear God, for once—Dane got a handle on that bullshit. Maybe it was the new meds, which had been working astoundingly well. Maybe it was that he'd never felt like the stakes were this high. He wouldn't just lose Clay, the guy he'd been rolling around naked with an hour ago, he'd lose Carpenter, the buddy over the intercom when he was gaming and the gentle man who hadn't let him be alone during that weird lost month when every breath he'd pulled into his lungs had hurt.

Carpenter was already family. If Dane didn't get a handle on his demons, he'd lose more than just a fuck buddy.

"Okay," he said, his concession obviously taking Clay by surprise. "That was a twatty thing to ask of you. I'm sorry. I just—"

Clay kissed him with so much tenderness, he thought his heart would stop. "Call me your boyfriend," he said, smiling a little.

"You're my boyfriend," Dane said, and the wonder of that hit him. Not a fuck buddy. Not a one-night stand.

"Good. I'm taking my boyfriend home so I can stay the night, and we need to get a move on."

Dane nodded. "Okay. That's a plan."

Finally—*finally*—they got dressed and out of the apartment.

Safety and Caution

"OH MY God." Dane yawned. "Am I glad that's over with!"

"It wasn't that bad." Carpenter shrugged. "Jefferson looked so proud—I mean, you know. First apartment. Big deal." The apartment was dinky. In Fair Oaks, in a small apartment block that sported a grass-covered quad and minimal air-conditioning. Carpenter figured the one outstanding feature was that it was close enough to Mason's house that maybe—*maybe*—Terry Jefferson of the teeny-tiny attention span and the limited knowledge of human relationships *might not* forget about the truly decent guy who'd fallen totally in love with him.

"Did you talk to his friend? Rude?"

Carpenter snorted. "Rud-*y.* It's a name."

"Short for Rudolph. The red-nosed reindeer. The rude nob rounder. Whatever. He was a total prick to my brother. Let's shank him."

Carpenter couldn't fault Dane for the sentiment. Mason had made excruciatingly polite conversation with Jefferson's friend, and Rudy had pretty much told Mason that he was a relic and should piss off. Of course, Jefferson didn't see it. Jefferson thought Mason was invulnerable, a fortress of solitude.

It seemed like only the rest of the world could see that Mason wanted to be a duplex of duality, and it hurt to watch him hope.

"Skip says Jefferson wants him on the team," Carpenter warned him.

Dane practically choked. "Over my dead body!"

Clay rolled his eyes. "You don't even play on the team. You get no say until you have bruises under your shin guards and a pair of cleats that live in your car."

Dane pouted, and Carpenter let out a sigh. He'd been doing a lot of that today, and Clay got the feeling Dane hadn't really "forgotten" about his little slip the night before.

Stupid. So stupid. Clay knew about Dane's past—Dane had been more than candid. And while Dane hadn't said it in so many words, Clay knew, as sure as he'd sky-written it, that Dane had been avoiding a real relationship since his diagnosis as bipolar, six years earlier.

Clay got it.

After following Dane down the rabbit hole that spring, Clay could see how people could be scared off. Clay wasn't afraid—he saw the darkness and the light so evenly blended inside Dane, he didn't want to think about separating the two.

You had deeply cynical Dane, who would blow a professor into giving his class a break, and then you had the bright and shiny Dane, who would play with Clay's niece and nephew for an entire day without blowing up about the two entitled little punks who possessed every game system known to man. That was the guy who could make Clay laugh during the shittiest day.

They were twisted together like rose bushes, and Clay wouldn't unwind the red from the white for fear of completely destroying either part.

But Dane couldn't see that. Couldn't trust it. Not right now. Clay knew it. They'd just changed their relationship. Dane needed to see that the other parts of them—the snark, the banter, the balls-out honesty, the gentleness of friends—all of that would remain intact and fully functioning while they progressed to making that amazing and wonderful thing they'd done the night before into part of their repertoire.

After some time in which "making love" became part of their comfort zone, Dane might be readier to hear that Clay wasn't just "making love." Clay had long since "fallen in love"—probably from their first meeting in the fall. Because God, if Clay hadn't been in love with him through that dismal and bitter spring, he wasn't sure they would have survived.

"It would kill Mason," Dane said unhappily. "Kill him to see that little prick on the same team with Jefferson, whether or not they break up."

Clay made a disbelieving noise. "I don't know—your brother seems pretty grounded, Dane. I don't think he'd get too upset over…."

"You don't get it," Dane snapped. "When his ex split up with him to shack up with his boss—his *boss*, Clay, the guy who took potshots at Mason's self-esteem for four years—*they* got all the friends. Mason got left out in the cold because he hates wine-and-cheese parties and is lucky he knows how to find a suit, much less one that fits him. He's not smooth. But for some reason, he's all fucking excited about your Holy Church of Soccer, and if he sees it… *desecrated* by another asshole who wants to get in his boyfriend's pants…."

Dane trailed off and settled into blistering funk on the other side of Carpenter's SUV.

"I'll talk to Skip," Clay said softly. "Skip loves your brother like a… well, a brother. So I think Mason gets a say. Anyway, we'll see. There's a two-week hiatus after the next game, so anything can happen."

"I think we're having people over next week," Dane said with a sigh. "Mason's sort of excited about it—he's inviting mostly soccer people. God, maybe that Rudy kid will have to come too."

Clay sighed. "Well, we can try to poison him, but if we get one of the guys we like, that'll sort of suck. Maybe we could just say shitty things at his expense."

Dane actually smiled, and then he roused himself. "Wait! Why are we going this way! You need work clothes for tomorrow!"

Clay grimaced. "I thought I was going home tonight."

"No, I don't think so. Mason's going to sleep at Terry's tonight. We need to try out my bed to see if it's more comfortable than yours."

Oh brother. "It is, Dane. Remember? I slept there most of March."

"Well, I don't really remember that, so I think we're going to have to repeat it."

"As you wish," Clay muttered, spotting a mini-mart where he could turn in the parking lot. "If I ask you if you took your meds this afternoon, will you get upset?"

"No," Dane said, scaring him badly. "I mean no, I didn't forget them—and no, I'm not upset. I know I'm sort of out there, and you're probably wondering if I'll even notice you, but…." He let out a frustrated sound, and for the first time since they'd gotten in the car, Clay felt like Dane really knew he was there.

"I'm worried about my brother," he said frankly. "And yes, I'm off balance because you and me did something big last night. But… but I'd really like you to stay, even if we don't do the same big thing tonight. I just… I feel like if I let you go home right now, we'll never have sex again."

Clay's eyes got wide. "I think you do yourself a disservice," he said. "And I'm wondering if you were even there last night, because my mind was seriously blown. If you think I'm going to pass up the chance to do *that* again, you have been sleeping with some seriously freaky assholes."

Dane chuckled, the sound easing some of the tension between them. "I wouldn't know about their assholes. I don't top."

Clay thought about that for a moment. "I am a little disappointed," he said. "I won't lie."

The silence next to him grew increasingly unnerving. From the corner of his eye, he could see Dane staring at him like he was a rare summer bird who had flown into an open fall window.

"What?"

"So… you'd be interested in bottoming?"

Clay shrugged. "I won't rule it out. *You* seem to enjoy it."

"Oh, I do. I enjoy it *very* much. But for some guys, it's a control thing. 'Yes, I'm gay, but it's okay, I put the dick in the hole, so I'm still a man!'"

Carpenter blinked and then widened his eyes, and the view was still the same dusty hot suburb with outrageously narrow streets and steep hills. Apparently, half the world was watering their lawn tonight—go figure.

"*That's* not very progressive," he said, trying not to be horrified. "Tell me people don't think that."

"Well, they did six years ago," Dane muttered. "I have no idea what they think now."

"Well, does it really matter what they think? You're not sleeping with *them.* You're sleeping with me! Doesn't it matter what *I* think, because *I* think you do what feels good and nobody shames you for it. I thought that's what you thought, too!"

Dane let out a frustrated sound next to him. "It is. It's just… you know. We never actually *talked* about what we would be like when we started having sex with each other."

Carpenter half laughed. "You lost me. How else would we be?"

For a moment, the silence on the other side of the car lightened up. "I have no idea."

"Well, how about we *not* be freaky and weird… more than usual I mean. Dane, don't you know there's not much I wouldn't do for you?"

"Would you come out to your parents for me?"

"God, you suck."

"See?"

"It's not that I won't—or haven't been planning for it, honestly. But Jesus, do you have to go for the jugular in every skirmish?"

He pulled into his apartment complex, finding his parking spot by braille because parts of his brain sure weren't working, and pulled in. For a moment, they sat there, the blistering heat of late May already seeping past the coolness in the SUV.

"Yes," Dane said softly. "And I don't know why. I… I have to keep myself from sniping at you until I drive you off. I don't know what's wrong with me—"

"Really?" Clay asked, wrinkling his nose.

Dane sighed and rubbed his eyes. "Really what?"

"You really don't know what's wrong?"

"What's that supposed to mean?" He bristled.

"It means I'm your first big relationship since you tried home decorating by sledgehammer and spray-bomb. It means I've seen you naked—not your body, but your person—and it scares you. If you think I don't know I'm a big deal for you, *you* underestimate *me.* So you're trying to bitch me away so you can control it. That's how you've dealt with your other hookups, right?"

"No," Dane muttered. "I just… didn't engage."

"Well, I'm honored. Lucky me that you're trying not to run away."

Dane's eyes went narrow. "I can't tell if you're being sarcastic or not."

Carpenter just looked at him, eyes soft. "Really? Can you really not tell?"

Dane swallowed. "Last night meant so much to me. I'm so afraid that if I hold on to it too tight, it will slip away."

"That makes me really happy. Now let's pretend it didn't happen."

"*What*?"

"Until we're in the bedroom, doing the thing, we're going to pretend it didn't happen. That way, you don't have to be any different. We can just be us."

Dane swallowed and wiped his eyes with the back of his hand. "Okay," he rasped. "That's a good idea."

"Excellent. Come inside with me. I need to pack, and it's hot as balls out here."

Clay threw together some of his new clothes, making sure Dane saw, and some boxer shorts and a sleep tee. He wasn't sure how excited Mason would be if he caught Carpenter stumbling around the coffeemaker in his boxer shorts, so he added sleep pants, and was not surprised at Dane's pouty little grunt behind him.

"It's a billion degrees—"

"I need something to make coffee in," he said with dignity. "I think Mason and I will continue a relationship based on respect, kindness, and taking care of you and Skipper, as long as we don't have to see each other in our boxers more than absolutely necessary."

Dane thought about it for a moment. "That's fair," he finally concluded. Then he took a deep breath. "Uh… you, uh… you know that…. Never mind."

Clay shoved everything into a duffel with his toothbrush, remembering when he lived out of this duffel when Dane was in his spiral. "Never mind what?" he asked, trying not to let that dredged-up memory fill him with shivers.

"Nothing," Dane said, too quickly.

Clay didn't let Dane see him sigh. It was going to be a long, long, long miserable night.

It was a good thing Clay had already concluded that living without this asshole was really not an option at all.

"Nothing sounds like something," he said brightly. "Hit me with it in the car." As he and Dane made their way out again, he paused at his door and looked around. He'd added more prints to the place—and liked them—and was looking into replacing his couch. Generally, the place looked better, homier, than it had back in December. Dane had helped him make those changes, and they were good ones.

But the place still wasn't really in his heart.

His parents' place still gave him hives, but next to Skipper's place with the tile they were slated to replace sometime in the summer, the one house he'd ever felt at home in was the one they were going to now.

Because Dane was there.

God, he hoped Dane could adjust to their new relationship. Carpenter wasn't sure he had anywhere else to be.

THEY MADE dinner when they got back—whole-wheat pasta and marinara with a salad—and then gamed for a couple of hours. The gaming was a relief, actually. Sitting next to Dane on the couch, touching as they had been for the past few months, swearing at the screen, felt familiar. There was no "we just had sex" when they were annihilating small planets in cyberspace.

Dane's ten o'clock alarm came as a bit of a shock, but Clay shut down his control immediately. One of the things they'd determined during that miserable March and April was that putting a timer on the gaming system was a good thing. Besides snapping Dane back to reality, it helped him remember his night meds, and that was necessary.

"Guess Mason's staying with Terry," Dane murmured as they made their way upstairs. Natural as breathing, Clay put his hand in the small of Dane's back as they neared the door, so Dane would go inside.

"That's a good thing," Clay assured him, although his heart was troubled about that too. Dane paused just inside his door and turned, looking at him with limpid eyes.

"Can we be the guys who do the thing now?" he asked piteously.

Clay let out a breath he didn't know he was holding and relaxed into his body. "Yeah," he whispered. "Yeah."

Dane met his mouth midway, and this kiss was… exploratory. Patient. A little tired, but growing more urgent by the second.

Clay opened his mouth wider and pushed, backing Dane up toward the bed, enjoying Dane's hands on his skin under his shirt.

Dane made a greedy little whimper, and they both paused to strip to their underwear before burrowing under the covers. When they got there, Dane pulled his sheet over their heads and whispered to him, as if they were naughty children, still playing after their bedtime.

"It's warm enough to do this on top of the sheets!" Clay protested.

"Yes, but I want you more to myself," Dane told him. "I just want to kiss you." Dane started by kissing his neck, which was always sort of tender, then his shoulder, then his nipple. Clay gasped, enjoying this more with Dane than he ever had with a girl, maybe because Dane got that it could be just as much a part of the playground for men as it could be for women.

"Dane," Clay gasped. "I am going to come in my shorts!"

"Then take them off," Dane ordered, and then went back to work.

Carpenter put his thumbs under the waistband of his boxer briefs and started to push down, but Dane didn't help him in the least. He continued his seduction of Clay's nipple, and added forays with his hand to any flesh Clay exposed during his efforts with his underwear. The result was a heaving, thrashing mess that not only shoved off the underwear but also all the covers and left Clay exposed on the top sheet, naked, spread-eagled, and *hard.*

And Dane took the lack of covers as an excuse to move to the next nipple.

"Augh! You are not helping!"

Dane turned his head, cheek still resting on Clay's chest. "I'm not going to help you hide under the covers when I want to eat all of you!"

"I thought we were going for the quiet pity hand job tonight!" Clay argued, not sure if he was ready for "extraordinary" and "amazing" after the night before.

"Why do we need to be quiet? My brother's two miles away?" And with that, Dane actually *lunged* down the bed to engulf Clay's erection in his hot, busy mouth.

Clay made a noise previously unheard in human history and spread his legs wide to give Dane access to any part of him Dane wanted to fondle, grope, or suck—including his soul, should his soul reside among any points south, especially, *especially*, his cock.

"Augh! God! Dane! What are you—why? Oh my God!"

It was like Dane had been taking it easy on him the night before, and this was what real blowjobs were like, and Clay needed to man up and enjoy!

"This is good, right?" Dane panted, coming off Clay's cock with a pop. "Like you love this and want more of it?"

"God, yes! But can I recipro—wait, what are you—"

Dane took him in, all the way to the back of his throat, while thrusting a gentle finger in through the back way.

Clay came. Hard enough to see stars. Hard enough that the pressure on his cockhead was just a little too much. He cried out in pleasure, his fingers tightening in Dane's hair, and then whimpered, rolling sideways, trying to remember he had fingers and lungs and eyes and things.

Dane pulled up, draping himself over Clay's back and peering down at him. "Good?"

"Yes," Clay moaned. "But over too fast. Can I do something? Why would you not let me do something?"

"Because I was paying you back for being such a whiny asshole. Did it work?"

Clay swallowed, then took a deep breath… and decided he was furious.

With a heave, he rolled off the bed, grabbed his underwear, and said, "I'm going downstairs to sleep on the couch. We'll talk about this in the morning."

"Clay?" Dane scrambled to sit up, but for once, Clay wasn't about to make him feel better.

"I love you, you stupid jerk. This thing we're doing in the bedroom is part of that. If I'm in bed with you and naked, that means we're square." His cock hurt. His *heart* hurt. "God, Dane. I know shit gets squirrely up in your head, but you need to say that shit out loud before we get naked."

"But I'm a mess! My emotions are all over the place. Why would you even want to sleep with me when I'm a weird whiny baby!"

"*Because I love you*!" He shouted it—for the first time in his life, he shouted it. "But I'm already afraid you're touching me out of pity, so if you don't love me back, spare me the power blowjob!"

And with that, he managed to put on his underwear and stomp out.

He grabbed a sheet from the linen closet and used the afghan from the couch to protect him from Mason's overzealous air-conditioning, and tried to make himself comfortable. God, what a mess.

He got it. He got that sex would be different for Dane than it would be for him. He got that while he was fantasizing about tender lovemaking, Dane was remembering years of careless hookups because he was afraid of rejection.

But Carpenter had waited too many years to kiss his dream boy—and not have him disappear—to deal with "Let me be your sex god because I'm too afraid to let you love me!" He didn't *need* a sex god. He needed a friend and a confidant and a lover.

Perhaps you should have told him that.

But he didn't think he could say the words without crying.

Changewinds

DANE POUTED for a good hour.

Clay was walking out on him for delivering a world-class blowjob? Really? The actual hell?

But as he sat up in bed, knees clasped to his chest in the still-darkened room, several things hit him in succession.

The first was that Clay had been patient with him. He'd been floundering, and Clay had accepted him for what and who he was—even when he was a writhing bundle of contradictions.

God, Dane hadn't deserved that, but it seemed what Clay was willing to give.

So maybe he had a point about talking things out before he went for the dick.

The other thing was that Dane was still in his briefs.

And Clay had been naked and vulnerable in front of him, and Dane had been in power-blowjob mode so Clay wouldn't *have* to see him naked.

Clay had very much enjoyed his body the night before. Apparently there was no *have* to about it. Dane hadn't seduced a straight man. He'd fallen in love with—scratch that—slept with a bisexual man.

It wasn't fair, keeping himself all layered under armor, emotional or otherwise, while Clay, who was openly sensitive about his body image, exposed himself.

Oh God.

Dane really wanted him back.

He made his way down his brother's carpeted stairs and saw Clay stretched out on the couch with the blanket over his shoulders, eyes closed.

"Clay?"

Those dark eyes opened almost immediately. "What's wrong?"

"If I promise not to be a complete disaster, will you come back to bed?"

He saw the grimace, the flicker of doubt, and remembered the underwear thing again.

"I promise not to go all sexual predator on you again—for real. I… I just wanted to make you happy. And I wasn't doing it with my stunning personality. It was a fallback maneuver. I… you and me work because we're honest, but you gotta know, I've never really had that before."

He contemplated getting on his knees, but Clay was already swinging his legs off the couch and gathering up the sheet. Dane folded the afghan and draped it across the back.

"Thank you," he said, as they turned to go back up the stairs. "I… I don't deserve this, but I really, really was looking forward to sleeping with you. Just sleeping, I mean."

"Me too," Clay said, a little sadly. "Maybe next time, we feel free to say that, okay?"

"Yeah. I'm sorry." They got to the foot of the stairs, and Dane paused, feeling it in his bones. He turned to Clay in the dark and captured his mouth softly, pulling back before the kiss could go anywhere. "I'm, like, really sorry," he said. "I really want to get this whole emotional honesty thing right."

Clay gave him a brief flicker of a smile. "Talking's a start," he said.

"Well, we can't do that when you're on the couch, right?"

"No. And I have to say, I'm sort of relieved you came downstairs."

"Why? I thought the couch was comfortable."

"It is, but…." He made a sound of embarrassment. "Man, I think your brother and Terry have been having sex on that thing, because it is starting to smell like fabric freshener with an undertone of come!"

"Oh dear God," Dane muttered. "That's horrible!"

"Right? I mean, it's sort of making my apartment look better and better."

Oh shit. Talk about being emotionally honest. Dane sighed, wondering if he was about to say the thing that broke Clay, right here in the hallway, in the dark, in their underwear.

"Clay?"

"Yeah?"

"Remember that thing I told you to never mind?"

"Yeah."

Shit. He had to. It was his biggest fear, maybe. The thing that had driven him to push against his meds, that had driven him into the veterinary science program to begin with.

But Jesus, maybe this was what he really did owe Clay after their shitty evening, after his squirrel-brained emotional manipulation.

"I may never move out of my brother's house."

Clay's eyes widened so much in the dark that Dane could see the glint of the whites around the brown parts. "Really?"

Oh God. "I… I was living with my parents, you understand? They kept me on my medication and kept me sane. And I get that you want to be that guy for me, but I'm afraid…. It's going to take both you and Mason, and me, and maybe an army, don't you understand? I… look at me! One sleepover and I'm a mess! What if I need my brother and he's not here because he thinks I don't need him because—"

Clay put two fingers gently over his mouth. "We're just going to stop that train right now," he said, voice level. "I won't make you go anywhere you don't want to. I'll stop saying things that imply I need you to move out to have you. It's been one night. Let's make it to a week. A month. A year. It's going to be okay."

Dane nodded and swallowed, his throat tight. "Sorry," he said, his relief so acute, it hurt. "Sorry." He sniffled. "I'm sort of falling apart. I don't know why. I'm all medicated and fed and slept and—" He dragged the back of his hand over his eyes, feeling about twelve, and suddenly Clay Alexander Carpenter did the most magical thing.

He hugged him. Hard and without any bullshit, he wrapped his big arms around Dane's shoulders and held on. "You've had a big weekend," he whispered. "I know the feeling. Now come on. We both have adulting to do tomorrow. Let's try this again."

Dane nodded but stood for a moment, resting his face on Clay's shoulder. "You really are magic," he muttered thickly.

"Sure I am. Can we go to bed now?"

"Yeah."

This time, Clay spooned him from behind, keeping those marvelous arms right where Dane needed them, up until they fell asleep.

THE NEXT morning was surprisingly normal. Up, shower, let Carpenter have his turn. The only different thing was the touches, small and personal. Carpenter's hands on his hips as Dane was combing his hair and Carpenter was moving to the shower. Dane's kiss on Carpenter's shoulder as he buttoned up his new shirt.

The kiss they shared before they went down to coffee.

They sat quietly, eating toast and fruit, before Clay said, "So, do you want me to stay home ton—"

"No!" Dane shouted, breaking the almost wordless rapport they'd shared all morning, and then clapped his hand over his mouth.

"Jesus fucking Christ! Could you calm down?"

"No," Dane reiterated, keeping his voice level this time. "No, please, Clay. I would like very much for you to be here tonight so I don't think we're a hallucination."

"You don't have hallucinations. Why would you—"

"Look, not for real—just, you know. I want you here. As often as possible. I know you have to go get clothes and stuff sometimes. And there may be nights when you stay at home because you need a Dane break. Do you need a Dane break?"

Clay thought about it, which was actually reassuring. "Not as long as you don't shout at me again."

"Good. Because I… I'm going to be off-balance with us for a while, and I'd really like you here until it starts to feel real."

Clay swallowed, and to Dane's horror, his eyes got red-rimmed. He held out his hand and took a sip of coffee. "Just remember that I love you," he said gruffly when he was done. "Just—no matter what else happens, remember that I love you."

Dane took his hand and kissed his knuckles. "I'm pretty sure I won't forget," he said. "Just… you know. If you can't for a night or two, say so. I'll demand a lot. I shouldn't get my way all the time." Oh God, Dane was so afraid. He knew it was irrational, but when had rationality ever entered into it?

"No. I'm good." Clay *was* good. He was the best guy Dane would ever know. Dane had to remember that before he wigged out. "I know you'll find this hard to believe, but I really don't mind staying over. I…." He glanced around Mason's kitchen, which had been recently remodeled before they'd moved in and was pretty and sparkling, with tan tiles and a sort of mellow gold counter and paneled cabinets. "Your brother's house is a nice place. I just… I don't want to get on your nerves either. But—*unless you're yelling at me*—I want us to get back to being comfortable."

"And also more sex," Dane said, hoping to make Clay smile. After the night before, he was starting to feel, in his bones, that sex may have been a big thing—but it had never been the only thing.

"Of course."

"Good. We have an agreement. You'll pretty much move in here and only leave me when we let you escape from carelessness or you've chewed your paw out of the manacle."

Clay cracked a tired, rather emotional smile. "God forbid."

At that moment, Mason came crawling in like a slutty college boy. He walked into the kitchen and eyed them both assessingly, trying to figure out the mood. Clay gave Dane a determined look and asked for a ride to work, which meant he was coming home that evening. Dane knew a message when he saw it. Of course Mace agreed, because he was the world's best brother.

He went upstairs to shower, and Dane walked over to Carpenter and kissed him, hard, wanting, and tender. He pulled back and kissed his cheek. "I'll leave before he gets out. He won't have to watch us get weird."

"Have a good day," Clay said earnestly. "Text me if you need anything."

Dane popped a grin. "Or if I feel like messing with you."

"Of course. Love you."

Again. There it was. The third—or was it fourth time? Did it matter?—Clay'd said it, and Dane hadn't responded. He kept whining about never being able to be a grown-up. Maybe it was time he ponied up in one of the few places he could.

I love you too, he thought, and walked thoughtfully out of the kitchen.

THEY DID okay, really. Clay stayed over every night but Wednesday, because he had to pay bills and he didn't want to drag all his stuff over.

There was lovemaking in between—hand jobs, blowjobs—Dane taught Clay Carpenter the finer points of squeezing, of spitting, and of very gently grazing with his teeth.

Clay taught him how to edge without even knowing he was edging, just by kissing Dane for what felt like hours before he even moved on to grabbing Dane's cock and working for the big *O*. Yeah, Clay said it was "lovemaking," but Dane knew it for potential blue balls, even as he let Clay do it.

Clay was just so earnest about everything they did in the confines of the bedroom that Dane was starting to think of it as holy too.

"HEY," DANE said quietly as Clay brought him a drink. "Do you see?"

Clay nodded, both of them having a full-on conversation with only the flicker of their eyelashes so that none of the other people at Mason's pool party noticed.

The full-bore heat of summer had hit that week, and Mason had offered his house—and swimming pool—after the last game of the spring season.

The entire team—plus significant others—were there, including Skip and Richie and their giant fucking dog, who had lived up to his promise of that winter and had turned into a Volkswagen with a lethal weapon attached to his ass.

Mason's squirrel-bait boyfriend, Terry, had gone off to throw the stick to Ponyboy, and Mason had followed. Clay and Dane watched the entire interaction from the shade by the pool and worried. Terry had been distancing himself from Mason ever since the move, and their body language—Mason holding himself back from getting too close, Terry practically turning away with every step—didn't look promising.

Apparently they weren't the only ones who noticed.

"Ya think?" Skipper asked, casually wandering up to the two of them.

"Yeah," Clay replied, and part of Dane was pissed that Skipper apparently spoke eyeball too. But most of him was just glad somebody loved his brother now like he did and would be watching out for him. Mason spent so much time watching out for Dane—he was happy to see someone had Mason's back now, as well.

"K-k. I got a plan."

Dane looked at the big blond god with a little bit of awe. A plan? It was more than he'd had!

"Thrill me with it," he practically begged.

"We wait until everyone leaves, we get him drunk, and we watch movies with him until morning," Skipper said sagely.

"That's a plan?" Dane's brother was doomed.

Skipper regarded him mildly. "He lost all his friends with the last breakup. This way he knows he's got us."

"Yeah, sure he's got you," Dane snapped. "Didn't you tell Terry you'd let that Rudy kid play on the team?"

Behind him he heard a low chuckle that sounded like it came from Satan himself.

"I hate that little puke," Richie said, and Dane regarded Skipper's boyfriend with a little bit of awe.

"You do? Why?"

"Keeps sayin' snide shit about Mason. Whose house does he think he's in? Don't worry. Terry we like. He's one of us. That kid'll be gone next week."

Skipper shrugged, like it was a done deal, and suddenly Dane was *very* interested to see what they had in mind. "Okay," he said, feeling a little better. "If they break up, we've got ourselves a plan."

Next to him, Clay went in for the fist bump, and Dane returned it. And then the four of them watched beyond the gate to the ravine, where Terry had gone to throw sticks to Ponyboy and Mason had gone to talk.

Terry came back first, the dog trotting at his heels. He walked to the far end of the pool, avoiding the entire little shaded corner where Dane and the others sat. His eyes were noticeably red-rimmed, and when Mason came back to man the grill some more, he avoided eye contact with pretty much everybody.

The minute Terry left, Skip walked around to the stragglers by the pool, looked at Mason, then looked toward the door, and the place was cleared out in twenty minutes.

Dane was reasonably impressed—even more so when Skipper brought his brother a beer and made him a hamburger and generally took care of him while Dane and Clay cleaned up and Richie ran the last of the go out of the dog.

"What?" Clay asked, as they were taking a couple of loads to the recycle bin. "You look surprised."

"They really do have his back," Dane said softly.

"That surprises you?"

"It's nice, is all." Dane shrugged. "It must be how my brother felt when you came to help with me."

"Mm. Yeah, you Hayes boys look like you got shit all figured out, but you're pretty high maintenance." Clay winked, but Dane could only manage a small smile.

"We're worth it though, right?" Oh my God, the sixty-four-million-dollar question, wasn't it? All of Dane's weirdness, his insecurity, the crazy that had nothing to do with the bipolar depression—he was worth loving, right?

"Are you kidding?" Clay looked out into the night, the dark purple of twilight settling around them like a stifling blanket now that they were out on the street instead of by the pool. "It's like guarding princesses," he said, dropping his bag of cans into the bin, then taking Dane's from him. "Yeah, sure, there are lots of battles. But you know, you're *princesses.* Totally worth it."

"I'm a princess?" Dane asked archly, batting his eyelashes.

Clay didn't let him down. He kissed him instead, not afraid of prying eyes, just… quietly. Dane was starting to feel a sort of heat in his chest when Clay did that, treating what they were doing, who they were, with that sort of quiet tenderness.

"You're the prettiest one," Clay said, and even though he'd let his scruff grow in this last week, Dane knew where it was now. He could still spot the dimple. He'd never felt more at peace.

Of course, that was right before Dane found out what Clay had been hiding. Then he was a sucky sucko that sucked—and not in the good way either.

They returned to the backyard and the coolness of the shade and the pool, and sat around the patio table with beer, telling Mason their own breakup stories in the time-honored tradition of making a brother feel better.

And then, instead of talking about his breakup history, Clay Alexander Carpenter dropped a bomb on all of them.

DANE GAVE himself props.

He got a little mad at first when Clay told them he had an MBA—that humble Clay Carpenter from the IT pool, who had been gently schooling Dane on how not to be such a snobby tool about people's education, actually had an MBA and a science degree to go with it. But Clay had made the revelation with a purpose—to make Mason feel better. He wanted Mason to know that he was special, not just because Mason was rich or because he was smart, but because he was a good person with an eclectic bunch of hosers as friends, and he believed the best of all of them.

Dane was all for that—the entire reason they'd lingered outside in mosquitoland was to make his brother feel better about his stupid breakup with his even stupider boyfriend, who had left because he "didn't know how to be a boyfriend." The only reason Dane didn't roll his eyes at that was because the last week with Carpenter had proved that there was a learning curve to relationships, and Dane had yet to reach peak proficiency as well.

So he could let Carpenter get away with a smack on the head from Skipper while Dane kept his pout to himself in the background, but as the full implication of that MBA began to sink in, Dane's funk got worse and worse.

Carpenter hadn't trusted him. Dane had thought they'd known each other's secrets—he'd confessed his deep, dark, "I may never move out" fear, and this was such a stupid bullshit secret to keep!

And because he was Dane, he brooded.

They eventually moved inside and watched movies until everyone fell asleep, and Mason woke them up by cooking waffles, and Dane had to hold his tongue for another hour.

It was obvious his brother had been crying. The guy Dane had worshipped his entire life—and who had held Dane together over the last year of it—had been crying over some stupid kid who had seemed to, for the first and only time, get the absolute glory of Dane's brother. Dane wasn't going to make it worse.

Breakfast. Cleanup. Skipper and Richie went home. Mason went upstairs to nap.

Dane sat on the couch and waited until he heard the quiet echo of footsteps at the end of the hallway to turn a fulminating glance at the guy who'd just sort of revealed to everybody they knew that he wasn't who they thought he was.

"So?" he snapped.

"Uhm…." Clay gave a near approximation of a smile.

"Do you care to explain?"

"It's not like it's something I'm proud of!" Clay protested, and the fact that he didn't have to ask what this was about just proved that he knew it was a big deal. "God, it's hot outside already. Do you want to go swimming? I brought trunks. Now that there's not a thousand people out there, I can go swimming."

"So help me, I will hide your trunks and make you go swimming naked," Dane snarled, standing from his curl on the couch. "We're going to talk about this!"

"Why? So you can use it as an excuse to break up with me?"

The naked hurt on Clay's face was tough to take.

"No!" Dane fought the temptation to stamp his foot. "I don't want to break up with you!" He frowned. "I just, right this minute, got used to the idea that we're actually together. We're not a hookup. We're boyfriends. Go us. Now back to the subject! Why wouldn't you tell—"

"Because Skipper and I can't work together if I tell Tesko I have an MBA. I mean, your brother's great and all, but he works long hours and shit, and he's all serious about his job and… and that's not the life I want. I want to work with *people* and do something *real.* Skipper's talking about getting his degree and teaching. Maybe I could do that. We could do the program together. Anything, you know? Just not walking into an office and wearing a suit and focusing on how to make a company grow when I… I just can't. I can't think about making a company do anything. But one person at a time, or even a class or something—*that* I can do."

"But you and Skipper could still be—"

"Dane, I love you—and it's great that you're not wincing anymore when I say that, by the way—but everybody loves you. You've got Mason eating out of the palm of your hand. Random professors stop by and offer you your dream job on a platter with a minimum fix to your paperwork. You just offered to take Mason's place in the Holy Church of Soccer and Skip didn't bat an eyelash."

He hadn't either. Dane had rather been hoping to be worshipped for that gesture, but, well, he *had* been on the sidelines a lot. Maybe it was time to play.

But Carpenter hadn't stopped his rant. "So everybody loves you. I love you, so that seems totally legit. But my own family thinks I'm like a zit—yeah, sure, I'm part of the basic genetic makeup, but if only they could pop me a little so I'd shrink. I finally find a place I fit in, and the one thing different about me is a totally worthless piece of paper that I regret going to school for and I'm embarrassed to have."

"But… but why wouldn't you tell me?" That's what hurt. "And seriously, what the hell? What was your BA even in?"

"It wasn't a BA. It was a BS, as in it was another piece of bullshit but this one had to do with science. I think it was microbiology with a minor of molecular chemistry. I'd have to look it up. Seriously, my evaluator did my paperwork for me because by then, I practically burst into tears just thinking about another goddamned science class. So there you go. I got through college as a total loser with worthless pieces of paper to my name. At least you *like* what you're studying." The look of self-hatred on Clay's face was hard to bear—and so was his out-and-out dismissal of all the work he must have put into something that gave him nothing but self-loathing now.

"I'm a veterinary science student who doesn't even have a cat!" Dane argued, at a loss, then finally understanding. This was the part of himself that Clay hated—all wrapped up in one convenient piece of paper. "And if you hated it so much, why did you get it? Why didn't you get a degree in something you loved? I mean, you still have student loans, right?"

"Because every time I tried to talk to them, they were like, 'So, molecular biology isn't your thing. You can still save the world doing something else you hate just as much, but that you seem to have an aptitude in. Here, take more classes! We love you, honey—and stop eating sugar; it's starting to show!'"

"Aw, man—Carpenter!"

He turned away. "I don't want your fucking pity, Dane. I… I just want what you give me. Whatever you can manage, however you're doing that day, you give me what you can based on who I am. Not the better person you want me to be, or the person I'm trying to be, but who I am that day. That's what Skipper gives me, and Richie, and even the fucking Holy Church of Soccer. But I never got any of that from school or those fucking worthless pieces of paper. I wish I'd done something useful after high school, like go on a mission or join the Army or something. But I didn't. I tried to make myself into someone I really loathed, and I'm still trying to wash the taste of that person out of my mouth with donuts."

"That's not true," Dane defended staunchly. "Not anymore."

"Whatever." Clay took a few random steps toward the pool, which glowed in the sun outside the sliding glass door like a jewel against the darkened living room. "Do you want me to go home? Are you that mad about it? Or can I swim? I love swimming. I feel like a god in the water. It's not until I climb out that I feel like a manatee."

Dane sighed, completely out of anger. In fact, before Mason's love life unspun, he'd been hoping this would be celebration time—and that Carpenter would be with him. He'd finished finals last week. He really wouldn't mind hanging out by the pool and reading something that had nothing at all to do with his major.

"Yeah. Let's go put our trunks on and swim. Then maybe a nap." He felt the corners of his mouth curl up. "But I think there's more to say about this whole MBA thing—"

Clay looked over his shoulder at him. "Please, Dane?" he begged. "Can we just… drop it? Pretend like you've known all along? Like… like it's just a part of me, but not one we have to deal with?"

"But why wouldn't you tell me?" Dane said, feeling like a broken record. Then again, wasn't that his biggest problem? Not letting things go. "*Me.* I mean… shouldn't I be the person you can tell anything to?"

Clay's face did something painful, something that looked like he almost cried. "Because that's such a shitty part of myself," he said. "And I'm… I'm so much happier now."

He turned without words then, heading up to Dane's room, probably to change. And suddenly Dane didn't want to swim anymore.

Dane wanted to *give.* Clay had said he loved Dane for giving what he could to the man Carpenter was *right now.* Well, right now, even when Dane was still a little pissed, he thought Carpenter was an *amazing* man. He had all of that to give.

He followed Carpenter up the stairs and into the bedroom, noting that they'd all been leaving the lights off just because it made the already air-conditioned rooms seem even cooler. Carpenter was standing, shirt off, unselfconsciously rooting through the duffel he'd brought over after the soccer game, since he'd spent Friday night at his place.

Dane needed to touch him, palm his skin, be close to him, so badly. His stomach shook with a visceral need to be taken.

He moved quietly to the bed and planted a gentle kiss on Carpenter's shoulder. Clay looked up from his duffel bag in surprise. "Weren't we—"

Dane kissed him, soft at first. Then, when he made a little "Oh…." Dane pushed the kiss further. Harder. Clay moved his hands to Dane's shoulders and started to massage, like a cat.

Dane pulled back just enough to turn around completely in his arms—and purred.

"What's this?" Clay asked breathlessly.

"I want you," Dane hummed, bumping his nose along Carpenter's jawline. "Outside it's hot and bright and hard and loud. In here, it's cool and safe and you."

Carpenter let out a little "Oh!" and Dane captured it in his mouth, humming back.

Carpenter moved from that thrilling little rub up and down Dane's arms to wrapping his arms over Dane's shoulders, engulfing him, protecting him from all the bad things in Dane's own head.

That protectiveness, that solid kindness, was the sexiest thing Dane had ever known.

Carpenter moaned, rucking up the back of Dane's T-shirt and sliding those gloriously wide palms along the skin of his back. Dane took his turn to rub Clay's stomach under his button-up—and then to undo the buttons with trembling fingers.

Clay brought his hands up to cover Dane's and the shaking got worse. "Hey," he whispered. "What's wrong?"

"You're wonderful," Dane said, eyes burning. "You're so wonderful. You told us that thing about the MBA for no other reason than to make my brother feel good—and you knew there'd be fallout, but you did it anyway. How do I… how is my love supposed to be good enough?"

Carpenter made a hurt sound, then captured Dane's scruffy chin on the edge of his forefinger. "You love me?"

"Oh God. I really do. I love you so much."

Clay took over the kiss, the undressing, until they were naked and Dane was beneath him, and their bodies and hands were undulating, searching for contact, looking for an effortless way to become one.

There was no effortless way to join. Joining two human beings requires trust and preparation and careful, careful touch. Dane kept kissing him, kept arching his groin against his, while at the same time fumbling for the lubricant under the pillow.

He pulled it out and slid out from under Carpenter, wriggling down until his mouth was level with Carpenter's cock. He paused for a moment to lick Clay's abs first, because he didn't ever want him to think he'd skip that part, whether they were in six-pack formation or apple pie formation or, as they were now, a soft pillow top over some fairly solid muscle. Carpenter moaned softly and stroked his hair back from his face.

"What are you doing?" he asked, voice all breath.

"Giving a blowjob?" Because if Carpenter didn't know that at this point, Dane had been doing things all wrong.

"I know that, but—"

Dane held up the hand with the lube and clicked the bottle open, dumped some lube over his fingers, and handed it off to Clay to shut it.

"But—"

Then he reached behind himself and thrust his messy slick fingers toward his cleft, taking Carpenter's cock into his mouth just as he breached his own entrance with one finger.

They both moaned this time, and Dane started to shudder with want. God, he loved that feeling, full, aching, burning. He always wondered if he should donate his asshole to science or something, because he seemed to have extra nerve endings right… oh God… oh yes… *there.*

And at the same time, Carpenter thrust deep in his throat, making greedy little grunts as his hips arched forward and retreated. For a moment, Dane closed his eyes and fought the urge to come.

He pulled back instead, rolled over to his stomach, and spread his legs. "Fuck me!" he begged. Then, in case Carpenter missed the hint, he put his hand back, spearing himself with two fingers and spreading them.

Clay grunted and wrestled his hand away. "Oh my God, you're impatient."

Dane whimpered and wiggled his ass.

"And shameless," Clay said with a laugh. He paused to nibble on Dane's asscheek, and Dane buried his face in the bedding and screamed in frustration.

"Too bad," Carpenter growled. Dane felt the maddening tickle of one—*one*—of Clay's fingertips tracing a pattern on his backside in the excess lubricant. "Did you leave any in the bottle?"

"So help me, Clay Carpenter, I will—*nungh*!" Three thick blunt fingers speared into him, and he wanted nothing more than to flop about the bed orgasmically, like a fish spewing come. But that would have been a waste of a perfectly wonderful fuck, so instead he drove himself backward, the thickness spreading him, driving out his demons, his doubts, taking his greed and making him willing, a submissive, wanting nothing more than Carpenter inside him.

Clay kept going, forward, backward, curling his fingers until Dane begged for a fourth and got it. "Oh God! God! Yes! Oh my God! More!" He wanted it all, and he wanted to scream for more—scream for a thumb, for a fist! But that wasn't what he really wanted. What he really wanted was the length and girth of Carpenter's cock. He wanted the joining, vulnerable nerve to vulnerable nerve, and he was just fumbling for the words to beg for that when Carpenter pulled out his fingers, leaving him practically weeping with emptiness.

Clay's cock, still dripping with Dane's spit, thrust hard into him, filling him. Better than a fist—a *cock*—and still Dane wanted to cry.

It was perfect. Wonderful. Taking him over, hitting his sweet spot. He howled into the mattress, gibbered, keened. And Carpenter had found his footing now. Their last week taking it slow, with tender touches, giggling through hand jobs, perfecting the blowjob—that had given him confidence, and he fucked like a master now.

Dane felt the first wave washing up from the backs of his thighs, and it swept him hard, but not hard enough to come. The second wave, from his groin, down his spine, tightening his nipples, God, even his *forehead* tingled—*that* wave made him orgasm, and he fell into the sheets howling, body thrashing, all self-control gone.

And still Carpenter kept thrusting as Dane lay spread-eagled on the bedding, his soft pants of exertion still quieter than the slap of his flesh. He groaned, low in his throat, and slowed, using Dane's asshole with excruciating precision, catching the ridge of his cock right… there… oh God…. Dane shuddered one more time when he wasn't sure he could still *breathe*, and in the aftershock, Carpenter orgasmed, climaxing mightily, filling Dane up and more, until come gushed copiously, leaving a glorious mess.

When he collapsed, sliding to Dane's side and breathing hard, Dane could barely turn his head, but he managed to raise his fingertips to trace the scruff on his face.

They were quiet for a moment, and Carpenter moved to kiss Dane's bare shoulder.

"Think we woke your brother?"

"Don't know, don't care," Dane slurred, eyes drifting shut. He wasn't tired so much—just spent. Every nerve ending felt deliciously used, unable to fire, done.

He wasn't sure how much time passed before he felt the washcloth along his backside, taking care of his bits. A strong hand rolled him over and washed the come off his stomach, and with some fiddling, repositioned the sheets so that one was on top and one was on bottom.

"So busy," he mumbled, completely lost in subspace. "How can… so busy…."

Clay chuckled lightly and climbed in next to him, not so close that they were mashed together and sweating, but not too far away either. Close enough to touch.

"You're super out of it," he said softly. "Wow. This happen a lot?"

"No," Dane said, enjoying one moment of lucidity. "No. Gotta trust…." Because that was the thing, right? Bottoming was great if it was just nerve endings, but you had to trust the other person not to hurt you. Dane had perfected the art of wiggling, scrunching, and flexing to keep himself from being hurt—but with Clay, he'd just… relaxed. Because Clay wouldn't hurt him. He hadn't the first time, he wouldn't do it now. "Never trusted like that, before you."

He closed his eyes, wondering how long the world would be so gorgeously swimmy.

"Well, I'm honored," Clay said softly. "Why me?"

"Because," Dane told him. "You're Clay Alexander Carpenter. That's really all you need."

Eventually they'd get up and make that swim and spend a decadent Sunday not doing very much. But every so often Dane would catch Carpenter looking at him like he was brighter than the sun and wonder what he'd said.

Becoming the Quiet Bright

SKIPPER COCKED his head. "Do you hear that?" he asked.

Carpenter nodded at the murmur of voices coming out of Mason's office, and they both looked at Mason's assistant, Mrs. Bradford. "Same guy?" he asked quietly.

Lilian Bradford had graying hair styled into wide curls around her head and worn back with the prim efficiency of a '30s film star. She was level-headed, nonfrivolous, and extremely competent.

She also gave Skipper and Carpenter cookies when they brought Mason lunch and responded with small, luminous smiles to their conversation. They both agreed that Mason deserved someone as awesome as a Lilian Bradford in his life.

She'd been a useful source of information on Mason since the breakup with Terry, and what she had to say was troubling.

"Yes," she muttered grimly. "Hugh Goodman. Comes in every lunch, stares at Mr. Hayes with enormous cow eyes, and tries to make excruciatingly boring dates that Mason doesn't understand. It's like Mason isn't even trying!"

Skipper grimaced. "Well… you know… excruciatingly boring, right? Maybe he needs his dates to be exciting?"

Because whether he was squirrel bait or not, Terry Jefferson had fucked Mason's brains out his ears, and that hadn't been boring.

"But he's so *sad*," Mrs. Bradford complained. "He's… he's not like Mason at *all.* And he has a perfectly suitable young man in there, practically slobbering all over him, and Mason doesn't know he's alive!"

Clay risked another look at the closed door, where their meeting was probably wrapping up. He and Skip had brought Noodle House—they had that zucchini noodle thing going that fit right into Carpenter's diet. "Has he… you know… stuck his foot in it lately?"

The look on poor Mrs. Bradford's face broke his heart. "No! The man's name is Hugh—Hugh *Goodman.* I haven't heard even one *What's Up Doc* joke from Mason, not in two weeks!"

Skipper's eyes narrowed, and he looked at Carpenter for explanation.

"It's a Barbra Streisand movie," Clay said helpfully. "It's got a really great conversation about 'I am Hugh!' 'You are who?' We should watch it sometime."

Skipper brightened up—he did love new experiences—and then his entire demeanor fell. "Seems like it would be easy bait for Mason," he said sadly. "I mean, even I can do 'Are Hugh a Good Man'!"

"Right?" Mrs. Bradford nodded. "Do you know how he greeted the board during his first meeting?"

"No," Carpenter said, entranced. The more he could tell Dane about Mason, the less Dane worried, and right now, less was good. "Tell us!"

"Well, apparently he had some problems with chickens on his road—"

"They're all over the place," Carpenter confirmed. "I worry about hitting them all the time."

"Well, yes," Mrs. Bradford agreed. Fair Oaks was famous for them. A local shopping center had even made the dubious choice of erecting a six-foot stainless-steel rooster in honor of the local fauna. "Anyway, he walked into the boardroom, and as he was unpacking his briefcase he told the president of the company that he damned near—and I quote, 'Squashed a cock,' that morning, and he'd been so happy to see that thing 'popping up and bobbing down the road.'"

Carpenter had to sit down, and the only way Skipper could sustain his weight was by resting it on his hands as he leaned on Mrs. Bradford's desk.

"Oh my God!" Carpenter managed to say, trying to tone down his laughter and choking on it instead.

Skipper just shook his head and clapped his hand over his mouth.

"Do you see?" Mrs. Bradford was beside herself. "We really must have the old Mason back. The world needs that sort of man!"

Carpenter and Skipper both nodded, because they wholeheartedly agreed.

Mason's heartbreak over his squirrel-bait boyfriend was depressing everybody, including Dane, who was currently entertaining Carpenter's niece and nephew since their parents were gone for the summer. Yeah, sure, they had a nanny, and Gertrude on the weekends, but kids liked to have someone who would play volleyball-in-the-water-jungle or the-sun-is-lava with them.

Dane had cheerfully taken them on since Carpenter had to work and he was on summer break, and besides being grateful because Dane was doing his family a solid, Clay was also happy for the excuse to see Dane pretty much continuously when he wasn't working. It was especially convenient that Dane had agreed to take Mason's spot on the team, since making him play with Jefferson so soon after the breakup was just too cruel.

Playing goalie with Dane as a defender was like a reward for all the times Carpenter had tried out for sports in middle school and failed because he was too awkward. Dane thought the move, Carpenter mirrored the move, and together they kept the ball out of the goal. Carpenter was finally getting to a place where he could play an entire game while Singh subbed for the midfield, and as a whole, Skipper said they were actually winning on a regular basis. Everyone was giving him lavish praise.

Carpenter was not above taking it.

If Mason had felt comfortable enough to play, Clay would feel like, just this once, for a bright, shining moment, he had all the people he cared about in the same place and he could be happy.

Objectively he knew it was harder than that. Dane had another year of school to go, and Clay himself couldn't stay in the IT pool forever. Skipper had begun a grim and subtle campaign to get him off his ass and into a situation wherein he could use his degree at Tesko, but Clay wasn't ready.

Not yet.

Working with Skip had led to meeting Mason. Meeting Mason had led to falling in love with Dane. Carpenter was so very much in love with Dane—he wasn't ready to let go of the beginnings and move on to the rest of his life yet.

He'd never expected this sort of happiness. He needed to make sure it stuck, and it couldn't do that if Mason was breaking his fucking heart.

The door opened and Hugh Goodman stepped out. Shorter than Mason, tightly sculpted, he looked like the love child of a fitness guru and a CW television star. Carpenter actually had to swallow his tongue, and next to him he heard Skip's despondent, "Oh, Mason…."

Goodman nodded genially to Mrs. Bradford and gave Carpenter and Skip a social smile.

"I'll be back tomorrow during lunch," he said, biting his lip in a show of uncertainty that was probably uncharacteristic. "I…." He looked apologetically at Skip and Carpenter with their Noodle House takeout bags. "I mean, he doesn't have another appointment, right?"

"No, sir," Mrs. Bradford said crisply. "I shall pencil you in and let you know if that changes. Gentlemen? I do believe you can go in now."

Skipper and Carpenter met eyes grimly. Oh, they most certainly would.

"IT'S LIKE he doesn't even notice other people are there!" Clay complained to Dane later. "This guy was hot! I mean… hot! I'd fantasize about licking his abs—"

"You need to lick mine first, you know that, right?" They were lying in bed, because, per usual, Clay was staying the night. He'd started to wonder if Dane would be willing to put some of his prints up in the bedroom, and maybe move in a dresser or something. The couch they could leave by the side of the road—he'd already said his goodbyes.

"Of course, baby." Clay patted his head as Dane rested it on Clay's stomach and read. "Your abs are first in the licking. That's not my point here."

"Your point is that he's depressed and it's driving you crazy," Dane summarized. "Join the club. I mean, you can fantasize about rando-guy's abs all you want, *I'm* thinking about lithium blow darts. So who's more serious here?"

Carpenter's eyes widened. From Dane, that may or may not be hyperbole. "I just wish there was something we could do," he muttered. Then he brightened a little. "But we're having a formal little dinner party this Saturday. That'll be fun."

"A laugh riot," Dane deadpanned. "I'll be thrilled. By the way, the weekend afterward, me and Mason are taking my parents out for their anniversary." He let out a little grunt and rolled to his stomach, resting his chin on Carpenter's shoulder, which was a lot less comfortable than his head on Carpenter's abs.

"I'd bring you," he said pensively. "I mean, I want them to meet you. But I'm not sure—"

"This is private," Carpenter said, understanding. "You and me can go down later in the summer if you like—I'd love to meet them."

Dane grunted. "So, about *your* parents…." He gave Clay the puppy-dog eyes, and Clay dropped a kiss on his forehead.

"Don't worry. Next time I see them, I'll be all about my boyfriend, Dane, who's so very wonderful, which they already know since you've met them *half a dozen times* in the last six months."

Dane grunted again. "But not as your boyfriend."

Carpenter let out his own grunt. "Between my parents, my sister, and her husband, there's, like, six billion years of education in that house. Do you honestly think they haven't figured it out?"

"Clay—"

"All right! I swear! Next time I see them, I shall make all the things clear." He gave a little smile. "I'm really happy, you know."

"So am I." Dane sighed. "Or I would be…."

"If only your brother could get his shit together. I know."

It was worrisome. Clay was so preoccupied, in fact, that his meeting with his parents only dinged his radar on the edges. Maybe he should have thought more about it.

Their track record of listening to what he needed, as opposed to what they wanted, had never really been great, after all.

WHEN MASON and Dane left to visit their parents, Carpenter bid them goodbye early in the morning, grateful that there was no game that Saturday because the heat was already intense. Then he went to his apartment, which was getting dusty and starting to smell of disuse, to shower. He spent half an hour cleaning up, including taking the summer clothes he hadn't worn in the past month to the thrift store. If he hadn't liked it enough to schlep it to Dane's place and fold on top of his dresser, it wasn't a thing he particularly needed, was it?

He got to his parents' house around one in the afternoon, wearing swim trunks and a sunblock T-shirt. He didn't even bother to go inside, but instead went around to the back, where he could hear the kids in the pool.

"Clay!" Holly called from on top of the slide. "You came! Where's Uncle Dane!"

"He went to visit his folks," Clay called back as he went to sit by his mother. She was working desultorily on her laptop, facing the kids, and Gertrude, the nanny, was relaxing in the shade on the other side of the pool.

"Come play with us!" Jason begged plaintively. "Pleeeeeeze?"

"We'll have to see, guys. I may have to go home. Let me talk to your grandma first."

"Good afternoon, Clay," his mother said pleasantly. She lifted her cheek for a kiss, and Clay sat down in the shade kitty-corner to her so he could watch the kids play too. "So glad you could come help."

"Yeah, well, Dane's been doing a lot of the work. Sorry I've got the pesky day job, Mom."

She didn't roll her eyes, which was to her credit, but for some reason it was like he could hear that anyway.

"You know, there are so many things you can do with your degrees that don't involve putting people out of jobs, Clay. I wish you would—"

"Yeah, Dane's brother might have a line on something for me," Clay said reluctantly. He hadn't wanted to spill this, but he'd been talking to Mrs. Bradford and listening when Mason talked about work. It was a kind thing Mason was trying to do—create a position for Clay and Skipper to help employees who wanted upward mobility get more education so they could stay in the company and make more money.

"What does Dane's brother do?" his mother asked, and the unconscious snobbery in her voice made Clay wince. She didn't even know she was doing it. She just assumed Dane of the Jesus hair and sarcastic delivery and magical brain wouldn't know anybody who could help Clay out of his career funk.

"He's VP of mergers and acquisitions at Tesko," he told his mother, taking a little bit of joy out of watching her swallow her figurative gum.

"Oh," she said, blinking. "I… I didn't expect that. Dane's a joy, you know—having his help with the children in the last few weeks has been a real blessing. I just…. He's not a conventional young man."

Clay smiled softly. "Yeah, that's what I love about him."

He met his mother's eyes and hoped she'd hear the whole message. Her own eyes widened, and she looked momentarily startled, like a possum in the headlights, before she blinked and looked away.

"Be careful of how that sounds, Clay," she said softly. "You may give people the wrong impression."

"That I'm in love?" Clay prompted, just as softly. "Because it's true."

She swallowed. "You… you would have told your father and I about being… you know. Being gay before this. You had girlfriends. And this isn't funny."

"I wouldn't have told you about being bisexual," Clay said, trying not to be irritated. "Because why would I rock the boat unless I had to?"

"That's not fair!" she protested, looking at him finally. "Your father and I are very liberal—you should have known we'd be accepting!"

"Are you?" Clay demanded. "Because so far I haven't heard, 'Oh, Clay, that's wonderful! I'm so glad you're in a happy relationship!'"

"Well, I'm surprised, that's all! Seriously, is this what all the... the rebellion has been about? The weight? The refusing to get a decent job—"

"*I have a decent job*!" he snarled, surprised at the anger there. What right did he have to be angry? They'd fed him, clothed him, educated him, loved him—

But had they ever known him?

"Well, is this part of that?" she demanded. "Because you could do detrimental things to your life if you have a relationship out of spite, Clayton—"

"Mom, I'm in love. I've been in love with girls. I know how this feels. But it's not a girl this time. It's Dane. And he knows me for who I am. He knows I hate my degree, and that's okay with him. He knows why I eat, and he loves me whether I'm fat or fit. And I have seen him at his worst, and I would... I would drive fifty miles and put myself through an emotional blender just to see him smile on the other side. I know you try—you do. But you don't know me. I'm not perfect, and I don't want to try to be. I don't want to work in a cancer ward, but I think I've found a place where I can do some good that's *not* Sabrina's life. I don't want to be a Pac Sun medium—I don't care how tall I am. Sometimes, I want to sit on the couch and eat cookies, and sometimes I want to play soccer and eat celery. I want to not hate myself for the things that give me joy. And if that starts with not hating myself for upsetting your little applecart of whoever you think I should be, well, that's where it starts. I love Dane Christian Hayes. He's a goofy, snarky, bitchy mass of contradictions, and I wouldn't trade him in for six of my last girlfriend, and she was a great person. So you tell Dad, and you two can make your peace with me not being the son you planned on. And I hope you decide to love the son you have."

He took a deep breath and saw her expression transition from shock to irritation to hurt.

"Of course I love you—"

Clay shook his head. "You have to love the parts you don't like, Mom. That's part of the deal. I brought Skipper here during Thanksgiving because he's never had a mother, and he needed one. You guys were so kind to him.

You accepted him for all the great things he is. You did the same for Dane, in your own snobby way. Why can't you do the same for me?"

The hurt in her eyes deepened. "How do you know I don't?" she asked bitterly.

"Mom, do you remember when you came to my dorm room in my senior year, because you were worried? Do you remember the first thing you said?"

She shook her head.

"You said I'd gained weight. I was breaking my heart that year, and I was so confused. *So* confused. My girlfriend had moved to another school for an internship, and I had such a crush on my roommate, and I honestly contemplated dropping out and panhandling before taking one more goddamned science class. I hated what I was studying that much. And you and Dad got there and talked about how much weight I'd put on. And the rest of that shit froze up in my throat. Do you know how awful it is, to have love so close you can touch it, but so far away? To be afraid that just because you're not perfect, your entire support system might get yanked away?"

She held her hand to her throat for a moment. "I… I never meant for you to feel that way," she said brokenly. "I just… your father and I just… just wanted what was best for you, that's all."

Clay tried to keep the bitterness out of his smile. "Dane's what's best for me," he said, and then he stood. "Look, Mom. I just dumped a lot on your lap. If you want, I can go. I've got the keys to Mason and Dane's house. They said I could use the pool, invite Skip and Richie. I… I'll be honest. The way you're looking at me right now, I think we'd both be more comfortable if I take them up on that, okay?"

His mother nodded weakly, and he turned heavily to go. But before he took his first step, she said, "Clay, aren't you going to kiss me goodbye?"

He swallowed and dashed the back of his hand across his eyes, suddenly aware of how worried he'd been. For all his brave talk to Dane, he hadn't really known, had he? Which way this was going to go?

But then, maybe that was the point of the conversation—not just coming out with his sexuality, but coming out with himself. He'd never known, ever, which way being himself was going to go.

He turned back on his heel and kissed her wet cheek, taking her hand when she patted his on her shoulder.

"Clay?" she said, as he stepped back.

"Yeah, Mom?"

"I love you, honey. Your dad will still love you. You're right. It's going to take us some time. But I just… you know. Wanted you to know that before you left."

He smiled briefly. "Thanks, Mom. Call me when you're ready. Definitely let me know if you still want Dane to play with the kids, okay?"

She nodded, looking suddenly thoughtful. "Clay?"

"Yeah?"

"How long have you known? That you could like men too?"

"Since high school."

She let out a sigh. "That's a long time to eat a secret, son."

"It's not the only feeling I was eating, Mom. That much, I can tell you."

She nodded again, and it was time to go.

ALL CARPENTER had needed to do was text *I came out to my parents, want to come over?* to Skip before he drove to Mason's house, and Skip and Richie showed up with an ice chest full of flavored water and some sandwiches on wheat about a half an hour after he got there. They hit the pool for a little while, Carpenter included, because they were his friends and they wouldn't care. Then they took turns throwing the stick across the ravine for the dog. Finally, they moved in and watched movies, because they were good friends and weren't going to leave him alone.

About halfway through *What's Up Doc*, Dane texted, *Mason got hit on at dinner. He's like a man magnet—it's fucking weird. TTYL*

Carpenter laughed, and when Skip glanced at him, he showed the text.

"Fucking aces," Skip muttered. "God, I need him to be the guy that repels men again. This Mason is just so depressing."

"Terry's so sad, he's giving me hives," Richie muttered, pausing the TV. He looked at Carpenter. "You tell Dane about your folks?"

"Was gonna save it for a real convo," Carpenter admitted. "All sorts of shit to unpack, you know?"

"Yeah. But did they disown you?"

Clay thought about the kiss on his mother's tearstained cheek. "No. They're going to have to… digest, I guess. But I'm still part of their DNA. They're not gonna try to pop me off the face of the family."

"Like a zit?" Richie said, grinning. Well, he loved a gross metaphor as much as Dane.

"It's what I was afraid of," Clay admitted.

Richie's grin faded. "Yeah. My dad ain't talked to me since December. I'm glad you got a chance at keeping your family. That makes me happy. Right, Skip?"

Skipper nodded. "Yeah. I got a letter from my dad in March."

Carpenter stared at him. Skip's father had disappeared when he'd been in middle school, and his mother had hit the bottle after that. Hearing from family was a big deal for Skip, and for a moment, Carpenter wondered why Skip hadn't told him. "I did not know that." He grimaced. "God, fucking March."

"Yeah—you had some shit to take care of. Not your fault." And like that, Clay was forgiven. He thought he needed to take Skip to his parents' place more often, because he could give acceptance lessons just by breathing.

"So," Clay asked, "what did he say?"

"Something vague about being sorry he left and wanting to reconnect. I sent back a message that I was gay, and if he wanted to talk to me, he had to be okay with that. He didn't get back to me. I'm assuming it's not okay."

Skipper's voice was even and indifferent, but Clay knew him. Had heard him talk about his mother and how she drank herself to death. He'd seen Skip's face when he'd been worried about Richie. This hurt him—badly—but Skip wouldn't let that show.

Carpenter had the words for it, though.

"It should be," he said softly. "Skipper, you deserve the whole shebang—an entire family reunion behind you."

Skipper's full mouth curved up on one side. "Don't we all?" He wrapped his arm around Richie's shoulders—the kind of masculine PDA Carpenter had seen between the two of them, but not many other people had. "But this ain't bad."

It wasn't. Carpenter curled up on the couch while they sat on the floor, and they watched romantic comedies until the small hours, only breaking to walk the dog or refill on ice water.

It would be great if Carpenter's parents came around, and it would hurt if they didn't. But they still loved him, however awkwardly, and in the meantime, Carpenter had brothers who would go to the wall for him if he needed it.

He wondered when Dane would ask him to move in.

At Last

DANE HAD never watched two people make out in the middle of a soccer field. The experience would have been a lot more amusing if one of the guys hadn't been Mason and the other one hadn't been Terry Squirrel-Bait Jefferson.

Jesus, this was a long time in coming.

They'd seen the signs. Jefferson had shown up at a party the week before and spent the entire time looking longingly at Mason. Mason had been laughing quietly at texts during television time all week and had inadvertently propositioned one of the guys in the meat department of the grocery story by asking if the tri-tip was "cooked up hard, or did it stay limp and squishy and sad?"

Given that he'd also created entire new career paths for Skipper and Clay while he'd been in his funk, Dane's hero worship was still at full 1000-watt strength, but it was good to see him happy again.

This enthusiastic foray into each other's tonsils felt like icing on the Mason cake, and Dane was a fan.

The kiss broke off, and Dane and Mason moved back with Singh as defenders, and together they watched Carpenter's increasingly fit and lean ass as he guarded their goal.

"So," Dane said during a lull, as Jefferson took the ball to Skipper in what was looking to be a hard-fought play, "you want me and Clay to man the grill after the game today?"

Mason gave him a beatific smile. "We may have some things to talk about afterwards," he said with all the innocence of a puppy.

Dane waited until he was watching the game and then turned to Carpenter and made the time-honored blowjob face using his fist and his tongue in his cheek.

Carpenter lost his shit, laughing so hard he barely recovered when the ball got launched toward their end of the field.

MASON AND Terry showed up a little before the pool party petered out, and since Dane and Clay had done most of the hosting, Dane told them they were losers and were on for cleanup.

Mason looked so happy, he probably would have agreed to detail Dane's car *and* Carpenter's SUV at the same time, so Dane decided to go for the kill.

"Also," he said, "we're getting a cat this weekend. Maybe two. We're all on for cat box duty and vacuuming. Are we solid on that?" He had no idea if Jefferson was moving in or not—but he wanted a commitment, just in case.

"Sure!" Mason said, idiot grin still in place. God, he looked like he'd been fucked through the mattress, the floor, and the foundation of the apartment beneath Jefferson's. Dane was starting to wonder what else he could ask for—a new car? A porn subscription? A pony? The sky was the limit! "I'd love a cat! Wouldn't you like a cat, Terry?"

Terry's smile back at Mason was just as disgusting. "Oooh, I could pet a cat when I came over, right?"

"Yeah, Terry," Dane said, dripping sarcasm. "You can pet that pussy 'til it's sore."

Terry stuck out his tongue, and Dane laughed at his own bad joke. Clay grabbed his arm and pulled him away, murmuring, "Take the win, Dane. Take the win."

Clay dragged him past the pool, where stragglers were drying off and cleaning up, and out to the ravine, where Skip and Richie's dog was playing "chase the half-a-tree" with Richie. Richie looked over his shoulder as they approached and smiled tiredly. He and Skip had finally gotten to their tile floor in July—their kitchen looked like real live people from this century occupied it now, and Skipper had been cooking like a madman ever since they'd gotten the new stove installed. Game night had achieved new heights.

"What's up? Your brother ever get back?"

Dane smirked. "You mean get *some* back?"

Richie grinned. "Yeah, that's what I meant. So, did he finally get laid? Because I sure would like to worry about something else for a while."

"Like what?" Carpenter asked curiously.

Richie shrugged. "I don't know. Like how Skip's going to deal with his new job. How we're going to afford a new car. How I'm going to lie to Skip about the next thing he cooks, because, guys, I could sure use some plain old spaghetti with meat sauce about now."

Clay guffawed. "Oh my God. Tell you what. I'll buy a cookbook, and we'll see if we can't come up with some shit that doesn't make you want to hurl."

Dane eyed him irritably. "How about first you give up the lease on your apartment so you can stop pretending you live there?"

Carpenter turned mild eyes toward him. "How about you ask me to live with you? Maybe take me out to dinner? Wine me, dine me—make it classy. I like flowers. Don't you like flowers, Richie?"

Riche's chceks, always ruddy, escalated to almost purple. "Skipper brought me flowers last week," he mumbled. "I like flowers fine."

Clay and Dane both held their hands to their chests, the sweetness straining the snark from the moment. "That's adorable," Dane said. He couldn't find any irony at all.

"We should take lessons," Clay said.

Richie shrugged uncomfortably. "You can't take a good mate for granted, you know? I… I can't imagine a life without Skip. C'mon, Ponyboy. Let's go find Daddy."

They shambled off, and Dane took the opportunity to kiss the love of his life. "I won't," he said softly, after Carpenter's taste had saturated his senses.

"Won't what?"

"Won't take a good mate for granted. Move in with me. I know I still live with my brother—I don't care. Your parents are having us over for dinner next week. We can tell them then." Carpenter had been worried, but Dane hadn't been. He'd been watching the kids all summer, and Carpenter's parents had been kind to him the whole time. Maybe it was just with your own children that shit got awkward. "My education is up in the air, you start your new job on Monday—I'm over it. Life is never perfect. It's never settled. If it gets settled, I get bored, and you and me are never boring. Someday we're going to go for a car ride and come home married, and I'm fine with that. Are you fine with that?"

"I'd like to meet your parents first," Clay said softly. "Maybe they can come."

"My mother will love you. Just like I do."

Clay caught his breath softly, and Dane knew the rarity of the declaration hurt him. He would get better at saying it—it was more the truth with every heartbeat. "You love me?" he asked pitifully.

"More with every breath. She'll see that. First thing."

"You think?"

Dane couldn't even object to the insecurity, because they got to take turns doing this, needing the other one. It's how they worked. "You're the sanest person in the family. It'll be great."

Clay grinned at him through maybe a day's worth of scruff, looking almost lean after a very active summer. Dane didn't care. The first time he'd seen Clay Carpenter, he'd been a big guy—but the bigness had been like body code. It had just shown Dane the bigness of his soul and the impact he'd have on Dane's life. Now that Dane knew how big he was—in all the places that counted—it was fine that he lost a little physical weight. But even if he gained it back, he wasn't getting any smaller in Dane's heart.

"I love you," Clay said, with that way he'd always had of being honest to the bone.

"God, I love you. Through thick and thin."

"Through crazy and sane," Carpenter said, and Dane brushed careful fingertips along his jaw.

"Through you and through me," he said, liking the sound of it. "We'll be perfect."

Clay Carpenter laughed, because they wouldn't be. There was no perfect—perfect was the one thing they wouldn't be.

THAT NIGHT, after everybody had gone home, Dane waited until Clay was in the shower before pulling out the flower petals and the chocolate.

Yeah, he'd come prepared.

His brother's happy ending had pretty much announced itself, but it was more than that. Even if Mason had still been in his funk, Dane had concluded that he couldn't let his own happiness be dependent on Mason's.

That seemed like such a small thing—but it wasn't. It was huge.

He could be happy on his own. He'd made his own happiness. Well, Carpenter had made most of it, but Dane had chosen really, really well. And more than that.

It turned out that Mason needed him.

Not as dramatically as Dane needed Mason, but the last couple months of making sure Mason ate dinner, clowning around to cheer him up, shooing him to the movies once in a while—Dane had done that.

Dane and Carpenter and Skip and Richie had been Team Mason, all the way, and when Mason might have let his sadness overwhelm him, he had, instead, developed an entirely new department for Skip and Carpenter to work in.

Dane hadn't been an albatross around Mason's neck. He'd been a crewmember on board the ship that had seen Mason home. All of them were. Being part of that team, being *necessary*, not just to Mason but to Carpenter—that made him realize he could be that guy. Even helping Skip and Richie figure out IKEA instructions and tile their kitchen floor—that had made him important. He wasn't a brick, drowning the people he loved. He was a brick they could stand on so they could get their heads above water and take a breath.

When he'd left the Bay Area, he'd lost all his gaming friends, just like that. He and Carpenter could move to Timbuktu tomorrow, and not only would Mason help them find a house, but Skip and Richie would be on the gaming headphones next Friday and badgering them to find a soccer team.

Having people mattered. Having people made you a better person.

He figured this was probably a realization Mason had made a long time ago, but then, Mason was older. He'd had a couple of years without Dane at the beginning to get used to the idea.

But Dane was getting used to it now. If nothing else, the breakup with Terry had proved that Mason was not just more than human—he was vulnerable. He'd needed Dane these last two months, and Dane needed to take care of himself so he could be that guy too.

Part of being that guy too was taking care of Clay. Making him happy. Making him smile. Managing his illness had taught him that nothing was certain from one day to the next—not his reaction to medication, not his mood, not anything. This day he felt good and he was in love.

This day, he would do something special for the guy he loved.

So Dane sprinkled the sheets with rose petals and put the chocolate on the bed stand, loving it because it was corny and overdone and so full of schmoop, it almost gave him hives.

When Clay got out from his shower, Dane was naked, sprawled in the rose petals, hard cock in his hand in preparation. He was also grinning like a kid. Well, being naked had made him happy then too—and that was before he'd learned the real uses of naked!

Clay came out, toweling his hair, another towel wrapped firmly around his waist. "I had underwear on the back of the toilet," he said from under the towel. "But they're gone now. Do you have any idea where they—"

He pulled the towel off his head and looked at Dane in surprise.

"Went?"

Dane grinned gleefully. "What underwear? There are no underwear. Underwear are an illusion."

Clay laughed softly and dropped both towels on the ground. God, he looked good. Not a six-pack—but who needed a six-pack when they had that smile?

"An illusion?" He climbed into bed and reached for the light, and Dane stilled his hand.

"An illusion," Dane said softly, before kissing down Clay's body. Ah, nipples. They were such an enchanting shade of pink in the light. They even tasted pink. Carpenter let out a little sound of excitement before Dane released him. "So's the light. The light's an illusion."

"Why do we need the illusion of light?" Clay asked throatily, squirming and obviously thinking about reaching for the lamp again.

"Because I want to see you," Dane said. "Before, you know, I fuck you."

Clay pulled in a hard breath. "You, uh… I mean, uh—"

Dane had kissed down to his hip by now. "Did you wash all the places?" he asked playfully. He knew Clay had—he was meticulous about it. They'd had a lot of sex in the last few months—his asshole practically smelled like roses.

"Yeah—are we going to, uh… you know… *go* all the places?"

Dane gave his cock a teasing lick, noting that it was getting hard fast. "Salty," he said, licking again. "Sweet." He pulled it all the way into his mouth, bottoming out now, before it was fully erect, while he could.

"Nungh!" Clay's hands knotted in his hair, which had been trimmed recently and hung right below his ears. Dane sort of liked it like this—not nearly so many knots. "Dane!"

"What?"

"Are you uh… I mean I'm uh… but you're uh—"

"I was worried about hurting you," Dane said. He licked the underside again and plied the bell with his tongue, practically giggling as Carpenter moaned. God, he was fun in bed. Everything was exciting to him, even soft kisses on places like his shoulder.

Skipping straight to the goodies always made him hypersensitive too.

"And now?"

Dane grew quiet now, meeting Carpenter's eyes soberly. "I still might," he said softly. "Human bodies are an inexact science. It may hurt. It may not be as good for you as it is for me. But I want to try. I'll do my best. I'll stretch you out and make it sweet. We can only do our best." He breathed softly on all of Carpenter's vulnerable bits. "I want to do my best to make you come."

Carpenter let out a gasp that was probably part laugh and probably part arousal, because Dane had just taken a furry testicle very gently into his mouth.

He rolled it around there a little, letting spit trickle down between Clay's cheeks before letting it go with a lick.

"Hand me the lube," he said softly, and Clay's fingers shook a little with the hand-off. Dane set the bottle down and took a moment to lace their fingers together.

"Trust me?" he asked, semiseriously.

Clay bit his lip and nodded, wholly serious. "Yeah."

"It'll be great!" Dane promised, praying to the god of sex, whoever she might be. "Or, well, it'll be a learning experience. Either way, there's chocolate at the end."

Clay snorted, and Dane realized what he'd said and giggled.

"Well, hopefully the other end," he clarified. "You said you were squeaky clean."

"In all the places," Clay agreed, voice tight with arousal and probably embarrassment.

"Then this'll be fine. It'll be like I never said that." And with that, he clicked the bottle and drizzled a little bit of lubricant on his fingers, then probed gently.

Clay's head fell back against the pillows and his knees fell open and he made the most amazing sound. Mm… he was hot inside, tight and slick. But he'd relaxed enough for Dane's finger to slip in, and he stretched gently, listening to the sounds coming from Clay's throat.

They were mesmerizing.

His rim grew lax and wide, and Dane watched in awe as Clay's thigh muscles started to tremble and his hole grew to accept the invasion of another person.

"How we doing?" he whispered, entranced.

"Peachy," Clay rasped. "Don't stop."

"Really?" Oh, how wonderful. He added another finger, and Clay's moan went straight to his groin. He was doing this. He was making another person—*his* person—amazingly happy.

"Really!" Clay squeaked. He reached down to stroke his neglected cock, and Dane let him.

"Slow," he cautioned. "You come, your asshole gets all tight—it doesn't always end well for the top, okay?"

"Ended well for you!" Clay whined.

"Yes, but that's because my body worked that way. Let's make this good before we experiment."

"Oh my God! *Now* you want to be careful?" A thick pearl of precome leaked out of his almost purple cockhead, and Dane realized how close he was.

"Hey, hey…." Dane put a gentle hand on Clay's. "Here. You're ready. Are you ready? I think you're ready." He ground his own aching erection on the bed. "I'd sure like to see if you're ready."

Clay let out a rusty chuckle. "Baby, if you could, you know, hurry this thing along a little…."

"Yeah. Ready to roll over? It'll be easier on hands and knees at first."

Clay whimpered, but he trusted Dane and rolled over, his powerful arms and shoulders shaking with the promise of what was to come.

Dane got behind him, oiling his own cock, and appreciated the view. "You… you're all mine," he said happily. "All of you." Clay had definitely slimmed down in the last year, but that wasn't what was making Dane's heart tighten in his chest. It was… *all* of him. His heart, his willingness to try, the way he got Dane and had, right from the first.

"Yup," Clay said, voice as shaky as his body. "Including that part that I'd really love you to *fuck right now.*"

"Heh, heh, heh…." Dane placed himself carefully. "It's going to be uncomfortable until my head pops in—ready, right?"

"Yeah."

Dane went slow, in spite of his body's craving for release. He was in charge here—for once, someone was trusting *him* with the penetration, and God, he wanted to do it right. Slowly, slowly, slowly—he relished Clay pushing out, which made him open wider, to accept what Dane was giving.

The pop of his cockhead wasn't audible—but they both gave broken moans of relief.

"Better?" he asked, sweating. Oh wow. Look at him. He was *inside*. It was the sexiest thing he'd ever seen.

"Good," Clay said, voice thready. "Now move a little. Please. Like you can move, right? That would be great. If you could move. Yes. Like that. But… oh God. Like that but more. Don't stop!"

Dane gave his evil sex-god laugh again. "Not stopping," he promised, because the rush of topping was tingling in his *balls.* "Oh my God, not stopping."

He bottomed out, tightly sealed against Clay's backside, and Clay buried his face in the pillows and groaned, "Yes!"

So Dane pulled out slowly and did it again.

And again.

And faster.

Clay pulled a pillow in front of his mouth and screamed in pleasure, urging Dane on with every grunt and cry, and Dane—Dane was like a freight train. Nothing but orgasm was going to stop him now.

It happened in a rush. Clay spasmed hard around his cock, and not even the pillow could muffle his tearing groan of completion, and Dane had no choice. His hips rocketed forward, rutting madly, which was stupid because, oh my God, it was here, it was rushing everywhere, from his spine to behind his eyeballs, and yes! He was coming! Hard and fierce! Deep inside his lover's body where they could never be unmade!

He wasn't sure if he'd been shouting or not, but when he fell forward on top of Clay, he knew his throat was swollen.

Maybe it was the tears.

"Hey," Clay murmured, rolling a little to the side. He sounded floaty and out of it, and Dane smiled. He loved that feeling. He'd given that to Carpenter. His eyes burned more. "What's wrong?"

"It's really wonderful," he said softly. "I used to think…." How did he put this? "I used to think I'd never be so happy on meds. After that first kiss with you, I was so worried I'd never get that again, because the medication would fuzz it out. That my world would flatline—even touching the guy I cared about more than anything would just be… okay. That I'd be just okay my whole life. But right now, you're here. We just did that. It was awesome. You're going to move in, and our lives are going to be okay, and it's like I can touch the sky. But even if I do, I won't fall back down, I'll float."

"Mm." Clay closed his eyes and kissed him gently, his mouth opening for Dane's in a sort of languorous surrender. "Can I float down with you? I am feeling so high."

Dane laughed, but it was a gentle laugh. "Yeah, baby. We can float down together. Let me go get a washcloth."

"Not yet," Clay said dreamily. "Kiss me again first. I'm still excited that you're here at the end of the kiss."

"Always." Dane felt confidence promising that—a kind of confidence he'd never felt before. "I'll always be here at the end of the kiss."

"Good."

Their lips met, and Dane closed his eyes and sank into the afterglow.

The next morning, when they were changing the sheets and vacuuming rose petals, he realized that the chocolate he'd left on the bed stand had gone untouched. He didn't mention it to Clay, but it made him incredibly happy to know that Clay hadn't eaten a single feeling that night.

He'd given them all to Dane and had them returned a thousand times.

October

DANE WATCHED Carpenter's face carefully as he spoke to Skipper, hoping it was going well. He'd almost taken back his mother's invitation, the one for Mason, Terry, Dane, and Carpenter to go down to Redwood City and have Thanksgiving with her and his father, but he hadn't wanted to. The chance for his parents to meet Terry and Clay was just too wonderful to pass up.

But it was still going to bother Carpenter that he'd have to leave Skipper behind.

Skipper looked a little disappointed as they spoke, but not hurt, and Dane breathed a sigh of relief.

"Did he ask yet?" Mason asked anxiously, getting to the party a little late. He'd been by Terry's place doing God knows what—or, well, Dane had an idea, but they looked that happy all the time, so there was no telling if they'd actually had sex or if this was just residual afterglow from, like, every night they'd spent together since their reunion in August.

"Just now," Dane told him. "I think Skip's going to be okay."

"Okay is fine," Mason said. "Did he agree to watch your big needy whiny furballs while we're gone? Oh. Also, Terry's moving in. Now you know."

Dane blinked at him. "That's… new."

"No, it's not. I've wanted him to move in since March, but he wasn't ready. Now he's ready. There's going to be four of us in the damned house. Aren't you glad it's got four bedrooms?"

Actually, yes. Carpenter had given up his lease in September, and his transition from lover to roommate and lover had been pretty damned seamless. They'd converted one of the spare bedrooms to a gaming room so they could game while Mason and Terry watched television in the living room downstairs. It was as close as they could get to having two houses, right next door to each other, without paying California's outrageous cost of living.

"Very," Dane said dryly, and then he remembered that he was happy for Mason and Squirrel-Bait. He'd almost forgiven Terry for the breakup in the first place. "And congratulations. Now stop bagging on my cats. They love you best, you know."

Oh, they really did.

Dane had been so excited to find two Maine coon mixes to adopt, a brother and a sister. He'd discovered that brushing them was a form of tactile therapy—it literally raised his endorphins to the point where he felt a pleasant buzz. Sitting next to Clay while watching a movie and brushing the cats was one of his favorite ways to unwind now—and probably one of the reasons this school year felt so much less stressful than the last one.

Of course, part of that was Clay, and part of that was his friends. Another part was having Mason settled and happy, and the fact he'd chosen the slightly less stressful program, like his professor had suggested, and he refused to beat himself up over it.

He deserved to have cats. He deserved to have a boyfriend. And at the end of the year, he'd deserve to have a mildly decent paying job with health benefits and some stability.

Since Clay and Skipper had taken to their new positions like ducks to water and had been full of nothing but chatter about how exciting it was to help people transition into higher paying positions in the company, Dane had some hopes about that stability.

There were houses available in Mason's neighborhood, and it had occurred to Dane that not living with a member of his blood family didn't mean he was on his own. He didn't want to move *away* from Mason, but it would be great to live across the street from him, right? Clay had a job that paid him grown-up wages now, and soon Dane could help with the mortgage. It would be living independently, something he'd almost given up on. But Mason would still be within the first shout of help if he needed it.

And they could always meet on Saturdays and play soccer. And come to parties after the game, like this one.

Carpenter was looking at him and smiling, gesturing with his chin, so Dane took his courage into both hands and walked over.

"Sorry, Skipper," he said, and he meant it. "I didn't mean to steal him from you."

"Well, I'll miss him," Skip admitted. "But I guess we'll have your ginormous kittens to watch while you're gone. It'll be just like you're there!"

Clay snorted. "I mean, they're just as hairy," he said, indicating the scruff that he still didn't conquer most days.

"Speak for yourself," Dane said dryly. He'd been keeping his hair a little shorter, keeping his beard tightly trimmed. He didn't mind looking hip—but he was done looking wild-eyed and unkempt.

"Yeah, well, you guys have thumbs, so your grooming is on your own. Anyway, I get it. Meeting your folks sort of takes precedence."

Dane shrugged. "They keep claiming they're getting old. I think they want to see us happy."

What Skip said next made Dane's chest swell. "Well, this is going to be a good Thanksgiving for them. You guys are sort of revoltingly happy."

"But you and Richie aren't going to be alone, right?" Clay asked anxiously.

Skipper shrugged. "Naw—Thomas and Cooper will be over, at the very least." He glanced to where their two teammates stood, shoulder to shoulder, and Dane's radar started dinging fiercely.

"Uh… do you guys think they're—"

Skipper shook his head violently and held his fingers to his lips. "We're not going to say anything about that, okay? I think it's spreading."

"The gay thing?" Dane asked, enchanted. That was supposed to be a myth.

Skipper grinned. "Or the falling in love thing. Either way, the team is finally winning, and I don't want to jinx it." He sobered. "But me and Richie will be fine." His face softened, and he regarded Clay with the fondness of a brother. "I appreciate you asking, though. A whole lot sure has happened this last year, hasn't it?"

Clay nodded. "Yeah. Best year of my life."

Skip grinned. He was taking classes through Tesko now—but he liked his job mentoring new employees so much, Dane wasn't sure if he was going to move on to teaching high school. Either way, Dane remembered how Clay had looked at this man at the very beginning, and he realized he felt the same way.

"Mine too," Skip said, his eyes searching Richie out in the crowd. "I mean, I knew soccer was magic, but this last year has been sort of amazing."

"Yeah, Skipper," Carpenter said, that dry humor of his at the forefront. "That's what it was. The soccer."

Skipper grinned at him, and the talk turned to work while Dane's mind wandered.

That night as they pulled into the driveway, Clay paused before unlocking the SUV. The harvest moon was out, lighting the trees behind Mason's house in a perfect silhouette.

"What?" Dane asked anxiously.

"It has been, you know," Clay said, turning to him with luminous eyes.

"What?"

"A really good year. Best year of my life, actually."

Dane smiled, taking that as the biggest win ever. "Really?"

"You know how much I love you, right?"

"As much as I love you?" Dane asked, even though he knew the answer.

"More," Clay said, and they both grimaced.

"Really sappy," Dane said, but Clay just looked so delicious.

"Super sweet," Clay agreed.

"So true." Dane leaned into the kiss and felt it again. That buzz, that high end of the roller coaster, that thrill.

But he knew this ride—this right here, in Clay's arms, in the circle of his family and his friends—this was as safe as he'd ever been, as happy as he ever could be.

He'd take that win—he and Clay had earned it.

They'd be playing on this field forever and ever, until their last kiss and their last breath, because being together was the best game of their lives.

AMY LANE lives in a crumbling crapmansion with two teenagers, a passel of furbabies, and a bemused spouse. She's been a finalist in the RITAs™ twice, has won honorable mention for an Indiefab, and has a couple of Rainbow Awards to her name. She also has too damned much yarn, a penchant for action-adventure movies, and a need to know that somewhere in all the pain is a story of Wuv, Twu Wuv, which she continues to believe in to this day! She writes fantasy, urban fantasy, mystery/suspense, and contemporary romance—and if you accidentally make eye contact, she'll bore you to tears with literary theory. She'll also tell you that sacrifices, large and small, are worth the urge to write.

Website: www.greenshill.com
Blog: www.writerslane.blogspot.com
Email: amylane@greenshill.com
Facebook: www.facebook.com/amy.lane.167
Twitter: @amymaclane

Yellow

Amy Lane Lite
Light Contemporary Romance

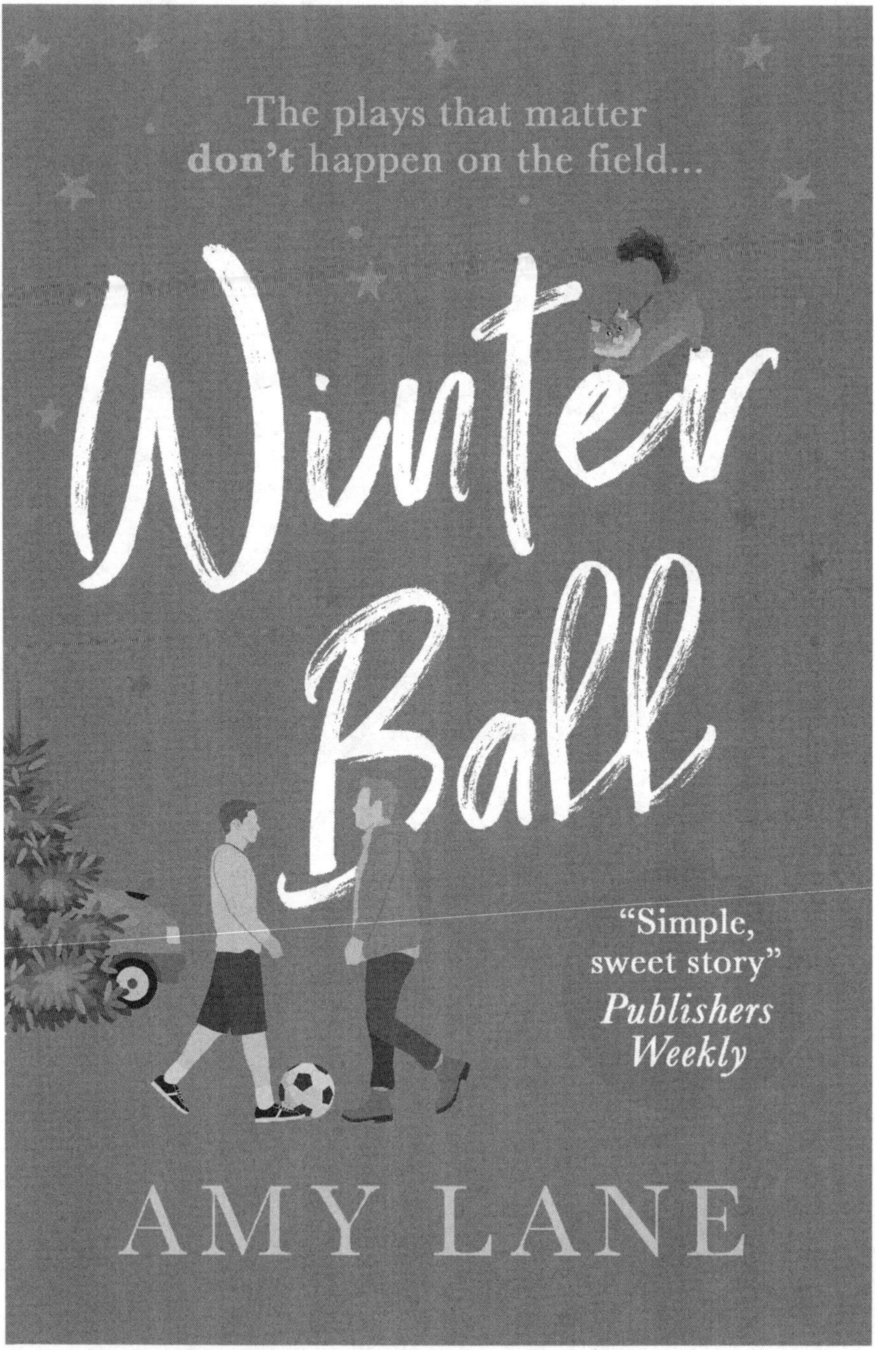

The plays that matter
don't happen on the field...

Winter Ball

"Simple, sweet story"
Publishers Weekly

AMY LANE

A Winter Ball Novel

Through a miserable adolescence and a lonely adulthood, Skipper Keith has dreamed of nothing but family. The closest he gets is the rec league soccer team he coaches after work—and his star player and best friend, Richie Scoggins.

One brisk night in late October, a postpractice convo in Richie's car turns into a sexual encounter neither of them expected—nor want to forget. Soon Skip and Richie are living for the weekends and their winter league soccer games—and the games they enjoy off the field. Through broken noses, holiday decorating, and the killer flu, they learn more about each other than they ever dreamed possible. Every new discovery takes them further beyond the boundaries of the soccer field and into the infinite possibilities of the best relationship of Skipper's life.

Skipper can't dream of a better family than Richie—but Richie's got real family entanglements he can't shake off. Skipper needs to convince Richie to stay with him beyond winter ball so the relationship they started on the field might become their happy future in real life!

www.dreamspinnerpress.com

The plays that matter
don't happen on the field...

Summer
Lessons

AMY LANE

A Winter Ball Novel

Mason Hayes's love life has a long history of losers who don't see that Mason's heart is as deep and tender as his mouth is awkward. He wants kindness, he wants love—and he wants someone who thinks sex is as fantastic as he does. When Terry Jefferson first asks him out, Mason thinks it's a fluke: Mason is too old, too boring, and too blurty to interest someone as young and hot as his friend's soccer teammate.

The truth is much more painful: Mason and Terry are perfectly compatible, and they totally get each other. But Terry is still living with his toxic, suffocating parent and Mason doesn't want to be a sugar daddy. Watching Terry struggle to find himself is a long lesson in patience, but Mason needs to trust that the end result will be worth it, because finally, he's found a man worth sharing his heart with.

www.dreamspinnerpress.com

FRECKLES
Amy Lane

Small dogs can make big changes… if you open your heart.

Carter Embree always hoped someone might rescue him from his productive, tragically boring, and (slightly) ethically compromised life. But when an urchin at a grocery store shoves a bundle of fluff into his hands, Carter goes from rescuee to rescuer—and he needs a little help.

Sandy Corrigan, the vet tech who eases Carter into the world of dog ownership, first assumes Carter is a crazy-pants client who just needs to relax. But as Sandy gets a glimpse of the funny, kind, sexy man under Carter's mild-mannered exterior, he sees that with a little care and feeding, Carter might be "Super Pet Owner"—and decent boyfriend material to boot.

But Carter needs to see himself as a hero first. As he says goodbye to his pristine house and hello to carpet treatments and dog walkers, he finds there really is more to himself than a researching drudge without a backbone. A Carter Embree can rate a Sandy Corrigan. He can be supportive. He can be a man who stands up for his principles!

He can be the owner of a small dog.

www.dreamspinnerpress.com